I0831371

DYNAMI'S WRATH

KELLY ST CLARE

Dynami's Wrath
by Kelly St. Clare

Edited by Melissa Scott and Robin Schroffel
Cover illustration and design by Amalia Chitulescu Digital Art

DYNAMI'S WRATH

Exosia

Kentro

Maltu

Pleo

Selkie's Cove

Syraness

Febribus

Portum

Charybdis

Neos

Zol

Caspian Sea

Dynami Sea
N
W
E
S
Exosian Realm

For A.J.

Who flies.
Free.
Forevermore.

ONE

Ebba was about to do something drastic. Something huge. Something . . . unprecedented.

Face propped up on her hands where she lay across Locks' bed, Ebba watched Verity dress for the celebration. Her eyes tracked the way the woman brushed her long, blonde hair, the way she braided it, and how the ex-soothsayer twisted the shining mass atop her head into a feminine knot.

Locks' one-and-only girlfriend usually wore plain dresses, occasionally trousers and a shirt, but tonight she'd selected a lavender dress that highlighted her periwinkle-blue eyes. The dress perched on the tips of her shoulders, the neckline plunging. The bodice was tight and flared out at the hips, ending just below her knees.

The simple fact there was a dress on Zol at all, let alone someone *wearing* it, was testament to how much Ebba's life had changed in the last three weeks. Their hidden sanctuary in the southern region of the Caspian Sea had never housed anything other than pirates—and the prince. Now it was filled with landlubbers and females. Females who didn't behave the way Ebba had seen her only other woman friends behave.

"Hey, Verity?" Ebba asked, licking her dry lips.

The woman grunted.

That's why Ebba liked her: she made normal sounds and didn't waste too much time with politeness. Verity was a survivor. She didn't take shite, she wasn't bothered by how people saw her, she was beautiful, and yet she was still willing to put on a dress to celebrate Ebba's eighteenth birthday.

She sat up, swinging her legs over the end of the bed to face the woman who'd single-handedly brought Locks to heel.

"Do ye think it'd be odd-like if I wore a dress tonight?" Ebba asked her.

Verity swished left and right, inspecting her appearance in a long, thin mirror. No one else had a mirror in their shack, but the hut she shared with Locks contained many new things that had simply *appeared*. Though no longer a soothsayer, Verity possessed what she referred to as 'simple healing magic,' which clearly included the ability to conjure whatever she wanted out of thin air.

"Of course not. You're a young woman," Verity answered without glancing back.

Asking her had been a test of how the others might react. Ebba released a breath, glad the healer hadn't laughed. "I'm not really a young woman, though," she pressed, studying Verity intently. "I be a pirate."

The healer shrugged. "You've already been harping on that you're a pirate and tribesperson. Why can't you be more than that? Just because you haven't wanted to wear a dress until now doesn't mean you can't change your mind. When you're fifty, you may decide you're a man."

"I do wear feathers in my hair sometimes now." She'd taken that away from her time with the Pleo tribe.

"Exactly, and no one thought that was strange."

Also true. Her fathers had commented on them, and Caspian, too, on the rare occasions he came out of his funk. She'd even caught Jagger's eyes on them a few times—though who knew what that really meant. He was probably planning to set them on fire as she slept.

Ebba sniffed and said casually, "I've been kind o' thinkin' about wearin' a dress tonight."

"What prompted the change?" Verity asked.

She toyed with a loose stitch on the bedspread. "Nothin'."

"Lie."

"It ain't—"

"Lie."

Ebba gritted her teeth and puffed a dread out of her face. "Fine."

She'd made the mistake of sitting down with the elder of Caspian's sisters, Princess Anya, last week. The *other* females, spawn of Barrels' sister Marigold, had flocked to join them like a hungry fish to fresh bait, and soon they'd started gibbering about kissing and fashion and all sorts of things that Ebba had never really thought about seriously. Or ever.

"I'm eighteen today, and. . . ." Her face flamed.

How to put her uncomfortable realization into words? Last week, all the women had talked about their first kiss. Ebba sat and listened as the younger princess, Sierra, just thirteen, had shared hers. The girl was five years younger than Ebba.

She swallowed. "Do ye think there be somethin' wrong with me that I haven't kissed a person my age?"

Verity snorted. "No, Ebba-Viva, I don't."

Ebba hadn't thought so either, but recently her priorities had shifted. Only months ago, her only urge was to fill her black dreads with beads, go on a quest, and become a fearsome pirate. That was before the crews of *Felicity* and *Malice* became embroiled in a war that turned into something much darker. Ebba's beads were gone now, and she'd set out on enough quests to last her until her thirties—when she probably wouldn't even want to do them anyway. Filling her dreads and embarking on dangerous quests weren't burning ambitions any longer, and Ebba had found her mind turning to other things. Things like not limiting herself by ignoring any possible femininity within herself. Things like Caspian's confession about holding a deeper regard for her.

He hadn't brought the subject up since—still coming to grips with his father's death. And she'd never given any response to his red-faced utterings, but like an itch she couldn't scratch, the blasted confession had burrowed into her skull. She had eyes in her head. She just hadn't been interested before. Now, Ebba was considering that she might be.

"You don't feel pressured into dressing a certain way because of the other young women, do you?" Verity had turned from the mirror and stood with her hands on her hips.

"No." Ebba drew the word out, frowning. "I don't know. I don't think so."

The healer gestured to her lavender frock. "I'm wearing this because I like to dress up every now and again."

"It be a pretty dress," she replied, scanning the lavender dress anew.

The ex-soothsayer was the exact opposite to her. Ebba had the dark skin of a tribesperson and moss-green eyes she'd inherited from her blood mother. Verity and she were both light-framed, she supposed, but the healer was a head taller. And where Verity's hair usually hung in a rippling curtain of gleaming gold down her back, Ebba's fell in thick, ebony dreads that hung to just below her armpits.

The bed dipped as Verity perched next to her. "What I'm saying is that you shouldn't wear clothing or change who you are for anyone but yourself. Do you *want* to wear a dress?"

She'd always liked accessories and clothing—though not the dresses that Sherry the brothel matron had put her in—the boning dug in something wicked. Recently on Exosia, Ebba mostly just pretended not to like the dress Marigold forced her into. Overall, Ebba wasn't mad-keen on how dresses restricted her movement and breathing, but for times like this, for a *celebration* when she didn't need to run for her life or dash up the rigging, she was beginning to think that maybe they were okay.

"Aye, I do want to wear one," Ebba confessed. "Just to see."

"Then wear one."

Ebba peeked up at the healer through her lashes. "Ye don't think anyone will notice or laugh?"

The healer's face smoothed. "I assure you they won't."

Was she really going to willingly wear a dress? Ebba grinned, saying, "Hey, Ver?"

"Don't call me that."

Ebba rolled her eyes. "Do ye have another dress?"

The healer arched a brow at her gleaming mirror. "I might be able to rustle up a little something. Did you have anything in mind?"

Ebba spent a portion of every day deciding what she'd wear. For the last week, she'd been thinking of exactly what kind of dress she'd wear *if* she ever wore one. "Ye could say that."

TWO

Ebba twirled inside her small shack, wishing she'd plundered Verity's mirror to ensure everything was properly in place. The dress gave her the sensation that her under-butt was on display, but frequent checks confirmed the feathers really did extend down to mid-thigh.

She twirled again in the tight space. Marigold had taken her larger shack, and Ebba couldn't really complain; her fathers had slept outside in hammocks for the last three weeks while they built shelters for the Exosian refugees. Yesterday, they completed the last shack, and Plank had furnished the beach hut to match the others. With their guests cared for, Ebba knew their departure for the Dynami Sea was nigh.

Not a second too soon, in her humble pirate opinion. And not *just* because Zol was overcrowded.

The pillars, six powerful immortals merged into one entity, regained their bodies a month ago after draining Verity of her soothsayer powers. In the space of a week, the evil force overthrew King Montcroix and seized control of Exosia. Soon, the pillars' dark taint would claim every soul in the realm—mortal and immortal. Caspian's subjects on the mainland probably fell victim to the pillars' method of feeding weeks ago. And once a person's eyes turned black, they were contagious; their taint could then transfer to anything living they came into contact with.

No one could outrun the darkness indefinitely, and Verity had described what would happen if the pillars succeeded in tainting the realm. Ebba's crew had to save as many people as they could by defeating the pillars. Something they could only do with a certain weapon, the root of magic.

Ebba glanced to where the *dynami* glittered, the rounded end of the tarnished silver tube sticking out from beneath her pillow. The *dynami* gave the bearer power. They also had the *purgium* that could heal anything, if you were willing to pay the unknown sacrifice. That tube was a similar size to the *dynami* but had two flat ends. It cured Ebba of the taint not so long ago and left her with three white dreads either side of her middle parting. They also had a third piece of the weapon now. The *veritas* was a sword that revealed the truth, though they weren't completely sure of the sword's parameters just yet.

If Verity was correct, three more parts were yet to be found.

Sally zipped into the room, tiny arms hugging a jar of pickled beetroot twice the size of her body. She dived under the blanket on the unmade bed.

The sprite peeked out, eyes wide, and pressed a finger to her lips.

"Where are ye, ye wee shite!" bellowed Peg-leg outside.

They listened as he stomped past, shouting.

"Ye know we have to leave food for the soft people while we be gone," Ebba chided the sprite.

Sally squeaked and emerged from the blanket, floating up to sit cross-legged as she opened her beetroot plunder. She popped a whole beetroot into her mouth. Purple juice squirted across the bed as she chewed, lips smacking together.

The sprite glanced up at Ebba and stopped chewing.

Her bulging mouth fell open and a few chunks of the beetroot tumbled out onto the bedspread. She squeaked and pointed.

"What?" Ebba scowled.

Sally's eyes moved over the linen and feather dress Ebba wore.

"What," Ebba said, her voice edged. When the sprite continued to gape, she added angrily, "I knew wearin' a dress were a bad idea." She reached for the bottom hem to rip the stupid thing off.

A tiny hand on her face stopped her.

Ebba glanced at the sprite who'd zipped over from the bed to float in front of her face.

Sally flew up and tucked the bristled end of one of Ebba's dreads underneath another dread. The three nubs left over from where the crew of *Malice* loped them off tended to stick up when Ebba's hair was pulled tight, as it was now. Verity had braided her dreads and the plait hung heavy down the middle of her back.

"Oh," Ebba said, smiling sheepishly. "Sorry, I thought ye were pokin' fun at my dress."

The sprite's face smoothed, and she shook her head, squeaking and swaying her hips.

". . . Thanks?" Ebba said, trying to decipher the display. "Do ye think I look all right?"

In a tight spot, Sally was half as likely to help as not, but Ebba loved her and often confided in the tiny sprite. Mostly because she couldn't talk to anyone here.

The sprite floated back and pursed her lips, scrutinizing Ebba's appearance from head to toe.

She hummed, flying in a slow circle around her. When she arrived back in front of Ebba's face, the sprite was nodding with one finger held aloft. Zipping over to a chest, she flung back the heavy wooden lid, displaying a strength that wasn't really in line with her pint-sized stature. From the chest, Sally drew out a black leather cord with an array of sea shells spaced out along its length. The sprite carried this behind Ebba and began to weave the leather cord through her thick plait, starting at the bottom and working up.

When the sprite finished, she patted Ebba's shoulder, holding up a thumb.

Ebba grinned. "Thanks, Sal. But ye don't think anyone else will notice I'm wearin' a dress, do ye?"

Sally snorted and shook her head. It could mean 'you're crazy, of course they will'. But Ebba chose to believe she meant 'I barely noticed myself'.

Ebba exhaled shakily, smoothing down the front of her tight dress again. "Good. Are they all there then?" It'd be better to just let everyone see at once, instead of one by one.

The sprite whirred softly in the back of her throat, which Ebba had learned meant yes.

She flew back to the beetroot jar which had overturned. The purple-red juice had poured all over the bed and was dripping into a puddle on the palm-leaf flooring. She grimaced, shooting Ebba a look.

"We're leavin' tomorrow anyway. I'll just sleep outside tonight." Ebba had bigger concerns. . .like if wearing this dress was a big, fat mistake. But Verity and Sally had both seen her, and Ebba would look like a coward if she didn't go through with it.

"Sal, I have an idea," Ebba said, fiddling with her gold hoop earring. "What if ye fly in with me and shine yer white glow really bright on the opposite side o' the fire pit? It'll draw everyone's attention away from me when I go in."

The sprite considered this and whirred, holding a tiny thumb in the air.

Ebba inhaled, cracking her neck. "All right then. Let's go."

She ducked out of her wooden shack at the end of the row and peered up and down the shadowed shore. She'd purposely waited for twilight so it'd be a bit harder to see her.

Palms sweating, she left the safety of the four walls and headed toward the fire pit where her crew, Verity, and all of their Exosian guests gathered for every meal. Jagger, too, if he deigned to grace them with his presence.

Their inlet was circular and lined by sheer white cliffs that prevented the small tribe on the island from attacking them. Turquoise water filled the majority of the space, bordered by a white-sandy beach mostly covered with coconut and palm trees. Previously, eight shacks had been erected in a row through small spaces they'd cleared among the trees. Now, there were sixteen. The only way to access their secret sanctuary was from a tunnel in the southern cliff that led to the ocean. This tunnel couldn't be navigated via rowboat, only by a ship with a removable mast—which only *Felicity* had.

Ebba pushed through the cooling white sand toward the fire pit, Sally perched on her shoulder. She tried to recall what Verity had said about being and doing what she wanted because she wanted it. The words made sense a few hours ago but didn't pack quite the same punch as her trepidation mounted.

Plank's laughter reached her through the coconut trees.

Ebba listened to the murmur of conversation of those gathered, trying to guess how many were there. She weaved between the last of the coconut trees and gulped as she saw the large logs around the fire pit were filled with Marigold's family members. They were laughing with the two princesses, kissing butt like usual because the two girls were royals. The Exosians were even worse around Caspian because he was the heir to the kingdom and all. No wonder he chose to disappear for hours at a time nowadays, though Ebba would be pretending if she didn't admit that was only one of the reasons for his absence.

Caspian lost his arm a while back, and just when he'd seemed to come to terms with that, his father was murdered. Any good was undone, and when they returned to Zol, Caspian fell into a funk worse than any before, isolating himself and shutting everyone out. On top of all *that*, Ebba knew he was wracked with guilt over abandoning his people to escape the pillars. Why did he feel so bad about that? Aye, he was a prince—or, actually, an exiled king. But if people weren't willing to take responsibility for their own survival, why should he feel obliged to help? If he was a pirate and not a mainlander, Caspian wouldn't be so burdened by it all.

She just had to figure out how to show him none of what happened was his fault.

Ebba watched as Peg-leg whipped around the fire, arranging a number of pots over the embers. The orange blaze of the licking flames drew the eye, and Ebba knew it would trick those on the logs around it into believing the early evening was darker than it actually was. Perfect cover for slipping in unnoticed. Ebba lurked in the tree line nevertheless.

Sally abandoned her shoulder, flying toward the fire.

"Remember our plan," Ebba hissed after her.

"What're ye doin'?" a cool voice asked.

Ebba inhaled sharply and spun away from her fire vigil.

Hard silver eyes stared back at her, shining in the twilight above a smirking mouth.

"Jagger, ye blighter, what're ye doin' sneakin' about?" she demanded, heart thumping in her chest.

He leaned against the coconut tree where she'd been . . . *pausing*.

Ebba tensed as Jagger lowered his head to hers. He towered over her, a couple of heads taller at least. *Oversized dolt*. She shifted her gaze from his face but flatly refused to step away. After four unsettling weeks in his company, Ebba was certain he only invaded her personal space to throw her off guard, and that riled her to no end.

"I asked ye first," he said eventually.

She shrugged. "I asked ye second."

"That doesn't make sense."

"Aye, it does. My question be closest to yer answer, so it should be answered first."

Jagger's smirk changed to a wide smile for an instant before it disappeared.

"Why aren't ye joinin' them?" he asked, watching her closely.

Too closely. Jagger made her feel like a fumbling, blushing moron sometimes. He wasn't particularly mean—not always, anyway. When he was, she could never be certain if the taint made him behave that way or whether the nastiness truly originated from him. Jagger's eyes weren't black anymore—so he wasn't contagious—but the taint still resided strong within him, just as it did in each of her fathers to a far lesser degree. He had to be struggling with it even if he'd somehow retained his will against the pillars for two years. Other than that, there was a list of reasons he infuriated her. He never pretended for starters, which she didn't appreciate. His silver eyes saw too much. And then there was the unsettling proximity thing that drove her to madness. *Something* about him made it incredibly hard for her to relax . . . especially when she'd elected to wear a dress for the first time and his lean, muscled body was too close and making her skin feel strange.

In a word? Jagger made her feel *wary*. Ebba was determined to hold him at arm's length until she trusted his character as much as Caspian's.

Her gaze had wandered up to his, but she tore it away to look forward to the fire pit. "I was just watchin' for a bit," she answered.

He hummed. "It be yer birthday though. *Why* are ye watchin'?"

"Why are ye askin' so many questions?" she shot back, cheeks heating.

"Are ye gettin' angry with me, Viva?"

Viva. He'd just started calling her that in the last few weeks, and it irritated her. Ebba was certain he had to have some secret mean reason behind it.

"Don't call me that," she said, mimicking Verity's stern tone.

"Make me, Viva."

She turned her head. "I thought ye were older than me, Jagger. Now I be wonderin' if that's the case." A pirate truth if she'd ever told one. Jagger was nineteen, like Caspian, but his self-sufficiency made him seem older. Ebba had seen him as a hostage, as a guide, as a pirate, as a tribesperson, and even as the king's prisoner, and he'd slipped into each role with a confidence that Ebba quietly envied. He was a pirate who told pirate truths, and he seemed to be good or bad depending on whether the outcome would affect his survival or the lives of his Neos tribe. Most of the time.

Ebba rubbed her forehead.

"Ye seem mightily at odds for a birthday pirate."

A pirate in a dress. "Aye. I've got a Jagger headache," she shot at him.

Ebba glanced out at the fire pit again, stomach twisting. Maybe she should change.

"I've never seen yer hair braided like that," the man beside her said suddenly.

She stilled, trying to appear nonchalant. "Verity did it. And Sal put in the shells."

"Looks nice."

Ebba looked at him and saw his gaze wasn't where it usually sat when her six fathers were around. Jagger's eyes trekked down, lingering on the dark skin of her bare legs.

She cleared her throat. "Why are ye starin' at my legs? Weren't ye complimentin' my hair?"

He jerked, and Ebba almost burst out laughing at his off-guard expression. Jagger liked her legs. She got it. Actually, she'd been guilty of looking at his thighs a few times, too. She'd have to be blind not to find him attractive. Didn't change a thing though when she couldn't trust the sod.

The flaxen-haired pirate inhaled and leaned away, taking a step back from her.

"Ye're not comin' in, I take?" she asked, then smiled. "It *is* my birthday, ye know."

He moved back another step. "Nay, Viva. There be too many mainlanders there for my liking."

She agreed, but her agreement was silent out of loyalty to Barrels. When Caspian first came to be on *Felicity*, there was only him to contend with. With a whole group of them together, it was like they encouraged each other to remain weak and a bit stupid. Ebba didn't envy Verity's job when their crew left. The healer would be the only person with survival smarts left on Zol.

"Well, have a nice evenin' then," Ebba told him.

Jagger turned to leave but paused, the long fingers of one hand splayed out on a coconut tree. He half-glanced over his shoulder.

"Ye should wear dresses more often-like."

From anyone else, that would be a compliment. From Jagger, she paused to wonder. Was he saying she wasn't a pirate? Setting her up to be ridiculed later? It was hard to tell, and Ebba wasn't brave enough to ask. He didn't give her a chance to anyway, flashing a smirk before disappearing amidst the trees.

She rubbed her temples again. Maybe Jagger headaches were a real thing.

Ebba dropped her hands to her sides.

Enough was enough. She'd navigated *Felicity* through Syraness; she'd survived the dark belly and taint of *Malice.* She'd brought down a stairwell on the heads of Pockmark and his cronies. Ebba-Viva Wobbles Fairisles was no coward.

She left the protection of the coconut tree and strode forward, edging between the gap of two logs in preparation to quietly sit down.

No one reacted. Everyone continued their conversations, and the knot within her began to loosen.

White light exploded above her head and Ebba flung her arms up to shield her eyes. Eyes watering, she glared between her arms at the wind sprite directly overhead. Sally was illuminating Ebba for all to see.

Flaming. Sod. She'd done that on purpose!

I'm going to pull your wings off, Ebba mouthed at her.

Sally's shite-eating grin widened, but after another few seconds, she dimmed her white glow and zipped away to join Pillage, the ship cat, on Barrels' lap.

"Ebba-Viva," Stubby breathed, his blue eyes wide.

Oh, no. Ebba lowered her arms, dread filling her.

Conversation had stopped. *Really* stopped—in an 'everyone can hear crickets' way. The fire crackled and popped; the gentle tripping rush of the waves remained too. All other sound? Gone.

"Ye look *beautiful*, lass," Locks said, pulling Verity in to his side.

Ebba looked accusingly at the healer, whose face was impassive. The expression gave her pause, however. Was she overreacting?

Maybe this situation wasn't that strange. Today was her birthday, after all. They were going to pay her more attention because of that.

"Our daughter." Peg-leg sniffed. "Wearin' a dress."

Nope, definitely the dress. The smile forming on her lips faded. She faltered under the gaze of sixteen adults and their ten offspring, who ranged from toddler age to young teen. The two princesses stared along with the rest.

At least their older brother wasn't here.

"Are those feathers, Ebba?" Grubby asked, venturing closer.

Ebba glanced down at her dress. The top half was black linen; the neckline curved at the same height as the jerkin she usually wore over her tunic. The bottom half, from her waist down to mid-thigh, was made of peacock feathers, like the ones she'd often seen on Maltu. The feathers were a myriad of browns, and vibrant blues and greens. She'd looped her longest necklace, a string of sparkling black pearls, around her neck and arranged the loops in layers. Along with the seashells in her hair, her white dreads, and bare feet, Ebba was happy with the outcome. She felt a bit pirate, a bit tribal, and—if truth be told—a bit female-like as well.

"Aye," she answered, standing straighter, though every part of her wanted to slink into a shadowed corner.

"Right pretty colors," Grubby said, beaming.

"I like the new look," Plank called over before continuing to hum his favorite daydreaming tune.

Her shoulders relaxed slightly. Ebba knew she could trust his opinion.

"You look absolutely gorgeous, my dear," Barrels said, petting Pillage absently.

Pillage didn't look that impressed. He disregarded her and began licking his paws.

Ebba blinked back at their Exosian guests and they back at her. Her fathers had all commented but still stared at her, unmoving and unspeaking.

"So," Ebba began, fidgeting awkwardly.

"Is something burning?" Verity asked Peg-leg.

"Are ye sayin' that after cookin' for my crew for near-on twenty years, I'm novice enough to let sumpin' burn?" Peg-leg scowled at her.

The healer sniffed the air. "Yes."

Ebba winced along with most in the clearing. Even the mainlanders knew about the cook's moods by now. Verity was the only one who didn't play along with pretending not to notice the charcoal coating the meat when Peg-leg was peeved. Luckily, Ebba was no novice at being a daughter.

She pushed through the sand to the fire pit where Peg-leg had started to shove pot lids back on with a clang, the usual warning sign of his state of mind.

"Did ye make all o' this for my birthday?" she asked, infusing her voice with awe.

Peg-leg stilled, glancing at her. "Aye, lass."

She gasped. "Ye must've been up at dawn. There's so much here. How ye're able to spread so little food so far, I'll never know."

"Well," he said, visibly softening, "not *dawn*, but that's only because I know what I be doin'."

Ebba leaned over and sniffed a pot. Blimey, that was definitely the burned one. "No one cooks so well as ye do."

His chest puffed out, and he gently nudged the pot lid into place before turning to her. He pressed a kiss to her forehead, his voice choked. "I can't believe ye be eighteen. Happy birthday, lass. I'm so glad ye're in our lives."

After *Malice*, Ebba understood just how much her fathers relied on her. Not anything she did as such; her mere presence kept them putting one foot after the other. Her fathers had sailed under Mutinous Cannon before stealing her. The pillars, when very weak, had abided within Cannon's body. He'd tainted the grog barrels with his blood, and slowly the taint seeped into his crew. The pillars began to feed off them, her fathers included, very gradually stealing their will. When the pillars became strong enough, they left Cannon's body to occupy *Malice*, the ship captained by his grandson.

"I'm glad to be in yer lives, too, father," she replied and rose up on tiptoes to kiss his ruddy cheek.

And she was. Whatever they'd been through in the last few months, she knew her fathers would die for her and she for them.

"Mistress Pirate," someone gasped. "Is that you?"

Ebba froze at the rich timbre of Caspian's voice and slowly spun to face him.

THREE

Ebba waved at the one-armed prince, the movement unaccountably awkward. Normally, she didn't hesitate to hug him to try to spread happiness into his dejected frame, but she was in a dress. The dress had made her more aware of her body, and how close her body would be to Caspian's if she hugged him.

Added to that, Caspian's whispered confessions from back on Exosia chose that moment to rear up again in her mind. Blasted things. . . . Except her curiosity about his confessions had been part of the reason she was wearing a dress in the first place.

Maybe that was it.

He stood in the middle of the pit area, russet hair disheveled, amber eyes dull but for a flicker of warmth, and mouth ajar as he took her in. His gaze swept up her legs, focusing on the feathers on the skirt of the dress before continuing up the dark skin of her bare arms to the capped sleeves. He scanned her face, lingering on her moss-green eyes before, lastly, looking at her braid.

"You look absolutely stunning," he announced, walking forward.

From his lips, the words sounded almost formal, but the declaration still made her cheeks warm. Caspian wasn't her fathers, and he wasn't a woman. How should she respond to the compliment?

Ebba fidgeted on the spot, burningly aware of the presence of her six fathers and the prince's sisters.

Caspian strode forward and bent over her hand, pressing his smooth lips to the back. Did kisses on Ebba's hand count as a first kiss? She thought it might have to be the lips. Honestly? If this was what it took to get a flicker of light in the prince's eyes, she'd wear dresses every day.

He dropped her hand, and Ebba cleared her throat, trying to ignore Peg-leg hovering directly behind. Caspian lifted his gaze above her shoulder and blanched slightly.

Ebba half-turned to glare at her father, and he returned her look with a bland, innocent expression, limping away to check another pot.

"Do ye like my dress then?" she asked the prince.

His cheeks were flushed, and Ebba clenched her jaw as someone giggled. His sisters, she presumed. Caspian had let his siblings know that the betrothal between himself and Ebba was a ruse, but the pair persisted in their giggling whenever he and Ebba were in close proximity. Not only that, they'd clearly clued in the elder three of Marigold's grandchildren.

"You look ravishing, Mistress Pirate. It exactly suits you. Did you make it?" he asked, blinking a few times.

There was definitely more light in his amber gaze. Was a dress all it took to lure him out of his funk?

"I thought it up, and Verity magicked it here." She walked over to a free space on a log, and Caspian trailed after her.

They sat together, and silence fell. Why was this awkward? Things were never stilted with Caspian. Even with him going through a tough time and staying silent about his troubles, the conversations they *did* have about superficial things were never stilted. He'd told her that he held a deeper regard for her, aye, but that hadn't cropped up again either.

Funny. Because right now, she couldn't think of anything else.

"How are ye doin', Caspian?" she blurted. "I haven't seen ye all day."

The murmur of conversation around them resumed. Finally.

Caspian's empty shirt sleeve was tucked into his belt. He, like all of the mainlanders, was dressed in pirate garb. Caspian appeared comfortable in the slop trousers, yellowed shirt, and black leather belt after several weeks of wearing it.

He smiled at her, a ghost of the smile he'd first sent her way on Maltu. "I don't want to talk of myself, Mistress Pirate. It's your birthday. I wish to talk of you."

"Me? Why? What's there to talk of?"

His smile grew, even briefly bringing a lost intensity to his focus on her. "For starters, how has your day been?"

She thought back. "I woke up and went swimmin' across the inlet to my sitting rock. Grubs was there, and he told me the octopus family be havin' more drama. One of the husbands made off with a younger man."

Caspian choked, but gestured for her to go on.

"Grubs was torn up about it, so I spoke to him for a bit." Ebba continued. "Then Stubby was frettin' about a scratch on his hobby ship, so I went and fetched him his tools. After that, I went to find Barrels to ask him sumpin' but came across Verity and . . . that be about it. Oh," she rushed to add, "Sally spilt beetroot juice all through my bed, so I have to sleep outside tonight."

The prince's shoulders shook, and he laughed, wiping at his eyes. A weight dropped in Ebba's gut at the sight because she knew the tears were only partly amusement. His sadness was so close to the surface that any strong emotion could make his eyes water. She'd seen Peg-leg do the same on occasion.

"*This* is why I ask to hear about your day," he said, shaking his head. "Mine wasn't half so eventful."

"Aye, but it ain't fair that I should always be tellin' ye a story and never gettin' one in return."

He peered at her. "Perhaps not. Are you hungry? The food looks ready."

Blatant deflection. Ebba scoffed, playing along. "I'm always hungry, ye dolt."

She stood and tried to be circumspect about pulling down the bottom hem of her dress. Damn thing rode up when she sat down. Slops didn't do that.

Despite the burned dish, Peg-leg really had outdone himself. He'd made all of Ebba's favorite dishes: fish with white sauce, fruit salad minus mangoes—Ebba went off them big time after her stint on *Malice*—battered calamari rings, shrimp salad, and potatoes he'd sliced thinly and laid flat on a grate to crisp. She inhaled the scents in the air and groaned. *Food.* And no coconut in sight. If she had to eat one more bloody coconut dish, she'd probably turn into one. Couldn't be good to eat so much of one thing.

She piled up a plate and returned to her seat. Marigold immediately sat down on her right, and the eldest of her sons took the place on the left. Sink her, Ebba had hoped to get through the night without having to talk to the mainlanders. Marigold wasn't all bad, really; Ebba liked Barrels' sister. Even so, she couldn't wait for Zol to just be pirates again.

"Happy birthday, my dear," Marigold said warmly.

Her peppered hair, so similar to Barrels', was neatly curled. When they'd left Exosia, Barrels had instructed his sister to bring the things necessary for survival, so naturally she'd packed her hair curlers. The older woman had a mostly white shirt on, tucked into a long skirt she'd brought with her. Gone were the dress hoops that lent volume to her garb and hid her frame; gone were the ruffles and lace and golden jewels. Marigold had taken a length of fabric and wrapped it around her neck, tucking the ends into the V neckline of her shirt to add a splash of dignity to her appearance. The sash looked pretty good, actually.

"Thank ye, Marigold." Ebba nodded at her.

The woman peered around the fire. "That I would one day celebrate a birthday with pirates never crossed my mind."

"That I would ever leave Exosia never crossed my mind," her son muttered on the other side.

"Would you rather be dead, Connor?" Marigold asked, a hint of steel entering her tone.

The middle-aged and rail-thin man sighed. "No, Mother."

He'd learned not to argue with her. Smarter than he looked.

"My family and I have a present for you. You're eighteen now; that's a big deal on Exosia." Marigold took Ebba's half-emptied plate and placed it beside hers on the sandy ground.

Ebba tracked her plate, still ravenous, and wondered if she should make an issue of it or not.

Connor whispered low. "Leave it. There's more food."

Aye, her thought exactly.

Barrels called from the far end of the log, "Did you say presents, sister?" He plonked Pillage and Sally on the ground before standing.

The sprite pulled herself up to sprawl over the cat's back as Pillage ambled closer to the fire to lay by the heat.

"I did, brother."

Barrels beamed at Marigold, and Ebba sucked in a full and content breath, knowing how much happier he'd been since reuniting with what remained of his family. Ebba had never thought of her smartest father as a sad or burdened person, but he was noticeably lighter now.

"I'll go get ours," Barrels announced, disappearing into the closest shack.

Marigold held up a leaf-wrapped parcel.

Ebba raised her brows at the older woman.

"We wrap gifts where I come from," she said in response.

What a useless thing to do.

Ebba took the gift and, ignoring the fact that everyone had stopped eating to watch her unwrap the present, she pulled on the loosest leaf. A bracelet sparkled in the middle. She picked it up, inspecting the gold circlet. Two thin bands lay parallel with an undulating wave moving between them, holding the two bands together.

"Thank ye, Marigold." Ebba lifted her head and peered around the logs. "And all o' yer family."

The sons and their wives smiled back at her, their ten younger spawn silent. For once.

"'Tis an arm band," Marigold said. "One I purchased for myself in my wild days but never wore for fear of angering my mother. I saw it in my jewelry box as I was packing to leave. You are exotic enough to pull such a thing off, my dear. The band will suit you far more than it ever suited me."

Marigold took her hand and slid the golden circlet up Ebba's arm until it was tight about the middle of her bicep.

"Huh," Ebba said, studying how the gold band contrasted with her brown skin. "I really like it. And the wigglin' line reminds me o' the ocean."

"It be lookin' right fierce, little nymph," Plank said from the opposite side of the pit.

She thought so as well. Who knew mainlanders had taste?

Caspian walked to her, his youngest sister Sierra on one side and Princess Anya on the other. He glanced at Sierra when they reached Ebba.

"Happy birthday." The princess held out a small glass tube, no larger than the size of Ebba's thumb.

Ebba took the corked tube. Inside, different colors of sand had been layered: white, pink, purple, deep blue, and then black.

"It's sand from this beach," Caspian said. "So you will always have a bit of Zol with you on our journey."

She dropped her gaze to the gift again, surprisingly touched by the thought behind it.

"Thank ye," Ebba said. "Ye dyed the sand di'ferent colors?"

"Anya's addition to the gift," Caspian said, smiling at his eldest sibling.

The *younger* princess was a devious, pirate kind of sort, but the eldest was definitely a mainlander. Still . . . though the different colors didn't seem significant in any way, Ebba appreciated the creativity behind it. "Very pretty. I thank ye."

Anya flushed and curtsied—in slops, which ruined the mannerly bob somewhat.

Her six fathers approached next, broad grins on their faces. An answering one spread across her own face. What in Davy Jones were they so proud of themselves for?

"For a long time," Plank began in his ominous and posh storytelling voice. The other five groaned, but he plowed on. "We didn't know if we'd be around for your eighteenth birthday. Ye know that you're the best thing that ever happened to us. The *best* thing."

"Aye," her other fathers muttered.

"Our gift to ye began as a way for us to never forget a moment," Plank continued. "We'd get Barrels to jot down the funny things you said and did, and all yer firsts. We kept them in a box in his office over the years, and in the last few weeks, we put them together."

He peered across at Stubby, who drew a large book from behind his back.

Ebba stood, her mouth drying as she neared the thick book. The cream pages were protected by a soft black leather covering that tied closed. Ebba took the book from Stubby's hands.

The book was huge. "All of these be memories?" she asked them quietly.

Undoing the tie, she turned the pages reverently, tracing the elegant swirling letters she knew to be Barrels' handwriting.

"Aye, lass." Locks squeezed her shoulder.

Peg-leg came up behind her and wrapped an arm around her shoulders. Grubby flashed her a toothy grin.

"What does this one say?" she asked Barrels, pointing to a short comment in the middle of a page.

Barrels craned to see, reading aloud, "Today Ebba ran away just as I'd taken off her diaper to wash her. She climbed the ladder quicker than lightning and proceeded to shite all over the deck—from Stubby."

Her fathers chuckled, and Ebba withheld a mortified groan, hearing snickering from some of the others.

As her father began recounting all the times she'd created a mess on the deck, Ebba continued flicking through the pages in silence. They eventually fell silent again, and a question she should have asked a long time ago rose to her lips.

"Barrels?" she asked. "Can ye teach me to read?" Ebba couldn't *not* learn when such a treasure had been gifted to her.

He took her hand in a gentle grip. "It would be my pleasure."

There didn't seem enough words to properly thank them. Ebba lifted her head and glanced around the circle of her fathers.

"I'll treasure it for the rest of my days. It means more to me than ye know." Ebba may've lost part of herself when she lost her beads, but she had this book now. Whenever she needed to remember good things, and whenever the memories of *Malice* weighed her down, she'd turn to this.

Ebba clasped the book to her chest.

Stubby passed a dirty handkerchief to a sobbing Locks, surreptitiously wiping a tear from the corner of his own eye.

"I have sumpin' for ye," a voice called from behind.

She nearly groaned aloud, recognizing Jagger's cool voice. He'd said there were too many mainlanders here for his liking. Why was he back? And he had something for her? He'd be as likely to gift her a manta ray or dried fish poop as something decent.

"What?" Ebba asked as she turned. She accompanied the word with a warning look.

Jagger lingered at the outskirts of the fire, one foot in the light and one in the shadows. In his hand was a woven leaf pouch, secured with yarn. He cast furtive looks at the gathering, who were already quiet from watching the present-giving.

"Sumpin'," he answered.

Oh good, that was exactly what she'd always wanted.

"What is it?" Ebba asked, wariness stirring her insides.

The flaxen-haired pirate strode toward her, silver eyes on her face with such determination that Ebba suddenly had the feeling Jagger might be nervous. And that made her *extra* nervous.

"What is it?" she asked in a louder voice, eyes searching his.

He stopped before her and held up the pouch made of woven palm leaves. "An apology," he grunted. "And a reminder. A rebellion, too, I s'pose."

Ebba took the bag tentatively. What did that even mean? "Can't ye just give a straight answer?"

"Never." He winked.

She studied him, certain that hadn't been a trick of the twilight and Jagger had genuinely winked. At her. Instead of smirking.

"Sumpin' in yer eye, lad?" Locks growled.

Verity snorted.

The best course was to pretend none of their conversation was happening.

She loosened the front flap of the woven pouch and peeked up at Jagger again before opening the gift. He was breathing too fast, his exhales harsh. There were many things she didn't trust about Jagger, but she'd always trusted that he was in control.

She didn't like that he wasn't. Not one bit.

Butterflies erupted in her gut as she reached into the bag. Her fingertips encountered smooth wood. A sensation she'd felt many, many times.

Ebba drew out a string of beads . . .

. . . That she'd last seen when the crew of *Malice*—Jagger included—cut them from her hair.

FOUR

An apology. A reminder. A rebellion.

Ebba perched out on the bowsprit of *Felicity* in the dark. Things hadn't gone 'well' after Jagger gifted her the beads. She'd stormed away from the fire pit without saying a word to him. Not because she was angry but because she'd been about to cry. Or maybe she'd been about to cry because she was angry at him. Two hours later, with night set in and everyone off to their beds, Ebba still wasn't sure which was correct.

. . . Was gifting back her own belongings even allowed as a birthday gift? *Cheap bugger.*

The first part of his explanation actually made sense. Jagger was the one to suggest that Pockmark take the beads to break her spirit. Had Jagger scrambled to collect them afterward? Not all of the beads were here; she distinctly recalled a couple disappearing out the ship's scuppers. All but four were accounted for, though.

Her beads that she'd never expected to see again.

"Yeeeoooow!"

Ebba glanced to the port bulwark where Pillage was watching

her. Clearly, the cat didn't trust her on *his* ship. "Go away, ye noisy bugger."

He hissed at her and maintained his watchful vigil.

She rolled her eyes, turning away again.

Jagger *had* made her angry with the gift, Ebba decided. Partly because she found it incredible that even then, after a month below deck in that dark, tainted room, he'd still possessed the willpower to collect the beads, intending to one day return them to her.

Was that what he'd meant by the third part? Was collecting the beads his rebellion? To do nice things even while aboard that ship? To fight back against the taint in such a small way. . . . Was that how the silver-eyed pirate had managed to hold on for two years against the taint?

The second part was giving her the most trouble and was the reason for her still being out here on the bowsprit three hours later. She might've thought his gift thoughtful, but if he'd given her the beads back to *remind* her of her time on *Malice*, she couldn't see that as anything other than a cruelty.

His 'gift' was a double-edged sword, as far as she was concerned, like everything else he did. And if she trusted him, she could trust his intentions, but Ebba didn't. What was Jagger up to?

"Mistress Pirate?"

Ebba straightened and then slouched again. "What do ye want, Caspian?"

"I thought you might want to talk."

"Like ye always do?" she snapped. "Maybe I'll just ask ye about yer day." Guilt stabbed her immediately. Blasted temper.

His reply was dry. "Fair enough."

Ebba glanced behind, spotting the prince at the base of the bowsprit. She didn't feel guilty enough to apologize for snapping yet. . . .

"If you don't come in, I'll have to come out," he informed her. "And I only have one arm."

"Ye're the only one who thinks that changes a thing," she countered.

"Yes, but Peg-leg said I should try and use it to garner sympathy and wealth when I can."

She snorted. That sounded just like something her father would say. And it was the first time the prince had mentioned his missing arm for weeks. "Oh, all right then. Come out if ye dare."

Caspian eyed the tapered and rounded beam jutting out from *Felicity*'s bow. Lips pressed together, he straddled the bowsprit, shuffling out.

Ebba's lips trembled. "Don't be fallin', Prince. I'm not inclined-like to get wet in my new dress."

His white teeth gleamed in the dark. "And I'm not inclined to *fall* in. I'm not even sure I can swim now."

She turned back around to wait for him to shuffle closer. The inlet was quiet and the full moon out and shining bright overhead. Zol was so peaceful when everyone was asleep.

A loud splash erupted below.

Ebba twisted to glance behind. *Shite!*

"Caspian," she called down. His head appeared below, bobbing above the surface, his sole arm flailing to keep him afloat.

She swung her leg over and pushed off to drop next to him. Warm water flooded around her, over her head, and Ebba immediately kicked for the surface.

The prince spluttered there, water dripping from his russet hair.

"Calm yer fish farm, Prince. Lay on yer back," she said, circling her legs underneath the water to keep her head above the surface.

He did as she bade, gasping for breath, and slowly relaxed in the position, obviously realizing he wasn't about to die.

"I fell off," he told her.

She checked her laughter, sensing Caspian was more than a little bitter about that fact. "Aye, I thought it had to be ye, or that a whale managed to reach the inlet."

He narrowed his eyes on her face, but then he laughed suddenly, harshly. "I can't even swim anymore."

After the *purgium* took the prince's limb, Peg-leg spent a great deal of time teaching Caspian how to live with one arm. It couldn't be easy, relearning every single thing from the start. "What are ye doin' now?" she asked.

Caspian sighed. "You know what I mean."

"Ye have to swim dif'erent now, but ye can still swim. There be another way ye could, too, like I'm doin'."

He craned his neck to watch.

"I'm treadin' water. Ye just sit upright in the water and circle yer legs underneath quick-like. With a bit of practice, ye can keep it up for ages."

The prince cast her a doubtful look but sat up and began circling his legs. "I'm not sure my hips are meant to bend that way," he said, puffing.

"Just softness," she explained, winking. "Ye'll soon be over that."

He kept treading water for a while longer before he floated on his back again. "That might work with practice, but we better go into shore before I drown."

Ebba splashed him and extended on her back next to him. "Aye, let's do that."

She stilled when the prince didn't move to follow.

"Are ye comin', matey?" she asked hesitantly.

He didn't answer, staring up at the shining moon.

Ebba sat again. "Caspian?"

He jerked and turned to look at her. "Sorry, Mistress Pirate. I . . . was distracted for a moment."

Ebba swallowed hard, hating the cold fear in her stomach. That was what she couldn't bear—those moments when he was unreachable, gone to wretchedness. When he was speaking, it was easier to ignore the deep-rooted worry within. And her deep and ugly suspicion that sometimes Caspian felt so burdened he wanted to escape somewhere she couldn't follow.

"We'll swim in, m'hearty?" she asked him gently.

"Yes, of course," he said with a quick smile.

They kicked for shore, and she listened to Caspian's quiet laughter whenever they went astray or bumped heads, wondering if she'd dreamed the despondent moment seconds ago. Yet he'd just mentioned his arm a couple of times, opening up again for the first time since his father's death. She should take that as a good sign.

When they reached the beach, Ebba squinted down at her dress and grimaced at the drenched and broken array of peacock feathers.

"Your dress," Caspian said, aghast. "I'm so sorry. I've ruined it."

"Just a dress." She walked up the beach a few steps before plonking down in the sand. A dress she'd planned to keep, but it was ruined now, so no point adding extra guilt to the prince's shoulders.

He lowered down next to her.

"Want to talk about the beads?" he asked.

The beads. She'd forgotten them for a moment. Bloody Jagger. "Nay, not really. Ye?"

"Nay," he mimicked her. "So what are we to speak of then?"

They could speak of what he'd told her back at the castle. But. . . .

Ebba's gaze dropped to the curve of his upper lip, tracing around the perimeter to his bottom lip. She'd felt his mouth on her hand several times and knew his lips were smooth and warm. Today, she'd turned eighteen, and tomorrow they'd all be leaving on a quest Ebba didn't know if they'd return from. Certainly, they wouldn't return the same.

If she'd known *Malice* would capture her, Ebba would've made sure to have her first kiss before then. While she was still . . . unchanged by the evilness surrounding them on all sides. It was too late for that now, but Ebba had no idea what the next stretch of time would involve, though if it was anything like their life in recent months, she could expect some hardship.

Maybe they didn't have to fill their time with speaking.

"Caspian?" Ebba asked, then froze. Sink her, she should've thought of how to phrase it before opening her gob.

The prince looked up at her, his russet hair still dripping, shirt plastered against his frame. "Mmm?"

"Uh," she stumbled. "Uh. . . ."

He frowned and took her hand. "Mistress Pirate, what is it?"

Ebba squeezed her eyes shut. "Look, don't be weird about this. But ye're my best friend." Her eyes flew open. "Don't tell Sally I said that."

The ghost of a smile crossed his lips. "I won't."

"Ye're my best friend," she repeated, watching as he grimaced. "And I would like ye to kiss me." She paused, adding, "Please."

Were Caspian's amber eyes usually so wide?

She waited patiently for him to talk.

The prince swallowed several times, darting a look around the coconut trees and into the shadows. "You want me to *kiss* you?"

"Have ye got water in yer ears? Aye," she said with a quick shrug. "That's what I said. Will ye oblige?"

"Oblige," he echoed. His amber eyes fell to her mouth, and she got the feeling the prince was doing exactly what she'd done and was tracing her lips. He didn't think they were too big, did he? She'd been called 'fish lips' more than once, and it hadn't been a compliment.

The quiet extended and Ebba shifted, plucking the wet top-half of her dress away from her skin. "I've made ye uneasy."

"Uneasy," he said with a short laugh. "No, not uneasy." His laughter faded. "Not entirely."

"I thought ye'd be okay with kissing me because o'. . . ."

"Because I told you that I have feelings for you?"

She blinked, tearing her gaze away. "Aye."

"It's not that *as such*," he said.

"Well, I just asked ye to kiss me, and yer takin' an awfully long time to decide," she reminded him, an edge to her voice. Should she ask if it was her lips that were the problem? He was still staring at them.

He lifted his chin and straightened. "I am, I apologize."

Enough talking already. This wasn't how kissing had worked in the brothel. Though, perhaps she shouldn't base all of life's lessons on what she'd seen there, given that everyone she'd met since behaved much differently.

"It's just. . . ." He trailed off, then exhaled. "I worry us doing that would mean something different to you than it means to me. I need to know what your reasons are so I don't read into the kiss in the wrong way."

Ebba nodded after a beat. "I didn't much think o' that, I'll admit."

"Why do you want me to kiss you?" the prince asked.

Ebba met his eyes. His molten orbs burned with the inner fire they'd lacked, and she inhaled, realizing just how lifeless his eyes had recently been in comparison. That was how he should look, how he used to look all the time. Riveted by everything, eager to learn and understand.

The prince was searching her face, and she felt her brows draw in slightly as the answer occurred to her.

"I don't want to die without being kissed," she said simply. "Maybe that's silly, but it's gotten into my skull. I trust ye in a way I don't trust others. Ye always make me feel safe, and ye'd never laugh at me. I want my first kiss to be with you."

His breath caught in his throat, and Caspian reached forward and pulled her wet braid over her shoulder, trailing his fingertips over the shells there.

"Then yes," the prince said, leaning closer. "I'll oblige."

Except now she was worried about him. "What will the kiss mean to ye?"

"It's just something I've dreamed of for months. No biggie," he said, quirking a brow.

His teasing tone made her stomach somersault. Caspian grinned at her, and after a few hesitant seconds, Ebba gave way to her fluttering stomach and returned it.

She brought her face to hover directly before his, excitement thrumming through her. The night was warm, but his breath was warmer. This close, she could count his individual eyelashes. Were they really about to kiss? The thought was foreign. *Enticing*. Like standing out on the bowsprit at deep sea.

Caspian touched his lips to hers.

Inhaling sharply, Ebba reared back, pressing a hand to her lips.

"What?" he asked, frozen with his hand hovering in the air where it had rested on her cheek.

She dropped her hand, heart thundering. "Sorry, ye gave me a fright. I thought ye'd announce it or sumpin'. But I'm ready now. Do it again."

Ebba moved back and, this time, was braced when the prince kissed her.

His lips *were* smooth, and Ebba thought softness might not be such a bad thing after all. His mouth moved against hers, and Ebba mimicked what he was doing, shuffling closer to seek better purchase.

Caspian brought his hand up and trailed his fingertips over her braid again, tugging gently on the end. Ebba smiled at the gesture and drew back.

They stared at each other in silence.

Caspian raised a brow. "Your thoughts?"

She struggled against her urge to grin and sat back, tilting her head to watch the moon. "Kissing makes me feel alive. I liked it. Thank ye."

He was watching her; his eyes boring into the side of her face in the way that used to make her uncomfortable. Now, she just wished his gaze would stay there always and that he wouldn't ever get lost in himself again.

The prince copied her pose and craned to see the moon. The full moon was a blazing silver, unhindered by cloud and so bright its light drowned out the stars.

"What did ye think o' it?" Ebba asked him, genuinely curious. The kiss felt great to her, and she'd really only thought of Caspian as a friend before. If Caspian had feelings for her, surely the kiss would be better.

He turned his head to her. "I think I'll keep those thoughts to myself, Mistress Pirate. I don't want to scare you off."

That meant he'd really liked it. Ebba hugged her knees to her chest, continuing to study him. "Ye know how ye have feelings?"

Laughter deepened his voice. "Which ones?"

"The ones ye have. For me."

"Oh, those."

She scowled at him in the dark. He was teasing her again. "Does it ever bother ye that I'm a pirate and ye're a king?"

The white of Caspian's teeth disappeared. He shook his head. "I've never once regarded it."

"Never? Why?"

". . . I guess that I believe a deep and true regard will surmount any obstacle in its path."

If it was meant to be, it was meant to be. An interesting thought.

Ebba turned away from him, peering back up at the moon. "Thank ye for obligin', Caspian."

"You're welcome, Mistress Pirate, but don't think you can die just because you've been kissed."

She tipped her head to rest on his shoulder that was minus an arm. "I won't be doing that. And don't think ye can be dyin' on me either."

FIVE

"You should pretend harder that you're sad to leave," Verity recommended in a way that sounded a lot like an order.

Ebba smirked. "But I ain't."

The healer shot her a warning look. "You'll hurt their feelings."

"Their fault for havin' them," Ebba said flippantly, sniggering when Verity threw her hands in the air and walked off.

Felicity was loaded. Everyone was aboard, aside from Locks, Caspian, and Barrels, who were dallying overmuch for her liking. The first rays of the sun were shining upon their inlet.

Soon, it would just be the pirates again.

The last three members of their crew finished their goodbyes and boarded the ship.

"Weigh anchor," Ebba shouted the second their feet left the wharf.

"*Goodbye*, Ebba-Viva," Verity called from the wharf. Pointedly.

Seriously? She'd already said goodbye.

"Bye, everyone. I'll miss ye." She wouldn't.

Or maybe Ebba was just eager to snap back to normalcy, except . . . normalcy wasn't normalcy anymore. She frowned. What lay ahead would be fraught with peril that she might not return from. In truth, she probably would miss the people, just not the unsettling mainlander nonsense they brought with them.

Marigold and her horde waved back, the children jumping up and down, and Ebba raised a hand to wave at them as *Felicity* drifted away from the wharf and toward the tunnel entrance.

Sod it, Ebba would miss them. Verity had thwarted her attempts to pretend otherwise.

She sniffed and shouted goodbye one last time, and then left her fathers to ready the ship as she disappeared down into the hold, blinking back tears.

Sally was already setting up her usual bed made of a sock stuffed with Barrels' cravats. Pillage was looking on, his tail swishing back and forth.

Ebba placed her hands on her hips. "I ain't sure ye should be bunked with the grog, Sal."

The wind sprite glared at her, squeaking and balling her tiny fists.

"I can't understand ye."

Sally zipped over in a blurry, glowing streak, head-butting Ebba in the gut. The wind left Ebba's lungs and she doubled over, reeling back a few steps. Of course, that was when Pillage decided to stick out his paw.

Ebba tripped backward, landing solidly on her butt. Her eyes watered as she coughed for air. "Why are ye attackin' me? I ain't the boozehead."

The sprite rubbed the top of her skull, shrugging.

Bloody eejit. Ebba narrowed her eyes at the ship cat, who was licking his paw, pretending nothing had happened. There would be payback.

She rubbed her stomach, saying, "Ye weren't in control around the grog, Sal, not by a long shot. Ye either left me and my fathers in the cages on Exosia because ye fancied the pink champagne fountain, or ye're really a traitorous sod. Which is it?"

Their gazes locked in a battle of wills, and Ebba was determined not to break it.

The sprite failing to come to their aid wasn't the worst thing that had happened to her—not even close—and maybe it wasn't Sal's job to rescue them. But discovering Sally hadn't been locked up while the crew of *Felicity* faced death *had* hurt. Sitting idly by didn't seem the kind of thing a friend would do, and Ebba believed them to be friends.

She *still* did. Ebba just wanted to understand why Sally hadn't helped them.

Scowling, the sprite glanced away and grabbed the open end of her bed. She swung the sock of cravats over her shoulder and floated down to sit astride Pillage.

"Come on then," Ebba said to her. "We'll fix ye a mini-hammock above mine."

She strode down the passage in front of the cat-riding sprite toward the sleeping quarters.

Eight hammocks were strung between posts, one high and one low. Except for her spot closest to the ladder because she had two trunks of clothing and knick-knacks to store. This didn't leave space for anyone else to move in with her. She guessed Caspian and Jagger would fight over the vacant hammock below Grubby.

Ebba threw open the lid of one of her trunks and rummaged through the mess of bangles, necklaces, bandanas, and sashes until she found two long leather cords she used to wrap around her ankle. Taking Sal's sock bed, she knotted the cord around either end. Ebba secured the sprite's new mini-bed directly above her hammock, stretching the cords and tiny sprite bed out between the two posts.

"There ye are," Ebba said, dusting off her hands.

Sally threw her a suspicious look and left Pillage's back to drift upward. She pushed down on the sprite-sized swinging bed to check if it would hold her weight.

Ignoring her, Ebba reached into her jerkin and drew out the flax pouch containing her beads. She stared at the pouch, her mind a buzzing mess, before heaving a sigh and tucking the pouch into the bottom of the trunk. There was a whole heap of thinking to be done about that, and she couldn't summon the energy or the courage just yet.

Reaching to the other side of her jerkin, she pulled out the arm bangle Marigold had given her. Surprisingly, the Exosian woman had given Ebba a gift she might've picked for herself. But the bangle also held sentimental value to the older woman, and while previously, Ebba would've taken that as a sign to always wear the jewelry, *now*—after the bead situation—she . . . well, she didn't trust that security any longer.

Important things were so easily lost. Better to keep both items here where they were safe in case she couldn't fight off her enemies.

Adding the glass tube of sand from the royal Exosians to her trunk, Ebba straightened and glanced at Pillage. Launching herself at the cat, she managed to scoop him up.

Running for the back of the sleeping quarters, she opened the first trunk she came to and deposited the cat inside.

"Ha, that'll learn ye," she said triumphantly, closing the lid and listening to him meowing within.

When Ebba reached her hammock again, the sprite was settled in her swinging bed and blinking innocently up at her.

Did Sal think she was born yesterday?

Setting off for the hold again, Ebba called back, "I'll be marking lines on Stubby's brandy bottles. Don't even be tryin' to drink any. And if I find ye've been in the grog overmuch, there'll be Davy Jones to pay, I assure ye."

In the hold, she made directly for Stubby's 'secret' brandy collection. There, Ebba etched lines into the bottles with the tip of her dagger.

The light in the hold, already scarce, darkened suddenly.

She cocked an ear to the deck. They must've just entered the tunnel out of Zol. Navigating the confines of the low passage to the outside ocean would take an hour at least.

"Ebba?" Barrels called through the bilge door. "I thought we could have our first reading lesson."

Sink her. They'd been sailing for *how* long and Barrels was already planning their first lesson? She'd known how eager he was to teach her, but she'd kind of anticipated monthly lessons at the most. Still, her urge to read was unchanged.

"Aye, comin'," Ebba called back. She moved back through the grog barrels and down the hall to the ladder.

She'd learn as quickly as possible, and then it would be over with. She'd be able to read her book of memories, and that'd be that.

"How is it ye don't know how to read?"

Ebba caught sight of Jagger lurking by her hammock. "Why is it ye always lurk in the dark?"

His teeth gleamed white in the dim light, but his fists were clenched tight. His silver eyes were darting around the room, never settling on one thing.

What was the matter with him?

She took his silence to mean he wouldn't answer. "Barrels tried to teach me, but I wasn't int'rested."

"Because ye're spoilt," he said, jaw clenched.

"I ain't spoilt," Ebba countered. She was. Wouldn't be pirate-like to turn away from the easy road.

Jagger scoffed. "Ye're not spoilt, and I ain't tainted. Is that how we'll be playin' it?" His chest rose and fell, and he continued scanning the hold.

"I didn't learn to read because I didn't want to. Now, I do," she said, stepping closer to her hammock and him. What was he doing there, anyway?

She eyed him. "Are ye okay, Jagger?"

"Fine," he snapped. He closed his eyes and then sighed. "I just came down to talk to Sally. I'm goin' now."

Jagger was absolutely, pull-out-her-dreads, *infuriating*. As he made to walk around her, Ebba stepped into his path, gazing up at him.

"Why did ye give me the beads?" she demanded.

He shrugged. "I told ye."

She rolled her eyes. "That wasn't tellin' me, ye cryptic shite."

"Not my fault I can't give ye the answer ye're wantin'."

The answer she *wanted*. . . .

In a bid to hide her shock at the pirate's words, Ebba turned to the bilge ladder.

Her beads had been her happy memories, a secret aspiration of what she could one day be, and something she'd held fast to for as long as she could recall. Those happy memories and aspirations shouldn't have disappeared when the beads were cut away, but somehow, they were gone too. Ebba wanted Jagger or her fathers or Caspian or Verity to tell her she was strong enough to wear them again. That losing them hadn't been her fault. That being restrained while the *Malice* pirates sawed the beads away didn't make her as weak as she'd felt. As she *still* felt sometimes.

Ebba needed someone she trusted to tell her that reaching for those happy memories and dreams again was okay. Except the only reason she had to be told was because Ebba didn't believe it herself. Which made her think that the only person who could give her permission *was* herself. Which didn't seem possible.

She placed her hands on the sides of the ladder, smooth from years of her sliding down.

"Will ye learn to read then? So ye can read that book from yer crew?" Jagger asked her.

He was closer. Ebba tensed. "Aye, that be the plan."

"Bet ye can't do it."

Ebba blew out a breath and whirled back. "That ain't goin' to work on me, ye weasel."

Jagger was directly behind her, and she blinked up at him, not liking how on edge he was. He was making *her* edgy.

He slowly lifted a hand, and Ebba watched him warily, ready to do a human-sized repeat of Sally's head-butt to the gut.

Jagger picked up her braid where she'd left in the decorative array of shells for a second day. She held her breath as he touched over the shells and tugged gently on the end of her dreads.

"Let go of my hair," she said, her voice not as fierce as she'd like.

Through the strands of his own flaxen hair, she saw his lips curve before he replied, "Are ye scared o' me then, Viva?"

Ebba tilted her chin. "Nay, Jagger. Yer tactics don't work on me. But ye can let go o' my hair all the same."

He glanced away from her hair. "Ye think I have tactics?"

In one word? Aye. "Let go," she ground out.

The pirate lowered his head, holding her gaze. "I'll oblige."

The words tickled her memory for some reason, but Ebba ignored the odd feeling to pull free. She climbed up the ladder, burningly aware of Jagger's regard from below as he climbed after her.

She pushed open the bilge door and then slammed it shut behind her. Hopefully in his face.

Barrels beckoned her from the step down into the helm. Half a dozen books lay scattered before him, as well as his quill and ink station and several scrolls of parchment. Letters. Words. She'd never had a use for them before, but she did now.

Ebba took a step in her father's direction and jerked to a halt. *I'll oblige.* Her eyes dragged back to the bilge door as it opened to admit Jagger.

He didn't immediately see her. Or rather, the pirate seemed preoccupied with sucking in great gulps of air and tilting his head to the sun.

The way he'd tugged on the end of her braid had been oddly familiar. *I'll oblige.* The same words Caspian said to her last night just before they kissed, just *after* he'd tugged her braid in the same way Jagger had just now.

Jagger lowered his head and smirked when he found her there.

"Ye saw us," she eventually said, certain acknowledging it aloud would steal some of his amusement.

Ebba wasn't embarrassed about the kiss itself—she'd enjoyed it and felt . . . excited to have kissed someone. But knowing Jagger had watched her kissing Caspian unsettled her in a big way. More than he usually did by just being in the vicinity. Had he laughed at them while watching her bumbling attempts? Had he secretly called her 'fish lips' in his mind? Was his cruel smile there because of the taint within him, because he enjoyed inflicting misery on occasion, or because of something else? The edge in his eyes under the gleam made her hesitant to assume his motivation for mentioning the kiss was so clear-cut.

"I saw ye," he replied tersely.

Her eyes narrowed. "Ye saw us *kissin'*." The word seemed forbidden. She glanced back to make sure Barrels hadn't heard her.

The pirate's smirk turned to a wide smile. "That wasn't a kiss, Viva. Not even close. Maybe I'll show ye sometime."

SIX

The strong wind was a welcome-home gift from the sea. So far, they'd made good time. All the better for it, in Ebba's humble pirate opinion. Every tainted pirate or otherwise—if there were any left with their will intact—would be fleecing the Caspian Sea for *Felicity* on the pillars' orders.

Tonight, they'd sail past Neos before sailing south of Febribus to enter the formidable waters of the Dynami Sea.

"My dear, if you do not concentrate, you'll always struggle," Barrels reprimanded from where he sat next to her on the single step that led into the helm.

His neck was flushed, and she could tell, despite his mild words, that he was irritated. During the first lesson, she'd been torn between watching Jagger sit far too close to Caspian and learning. Yesterday, between food and learning. Today, she was torn between boredom and learning. So much for one lesson each month.

"S'cuse me," she said, tearing her eyes from where Pillage lay beside her father. The cat hadn't started anything since one of her fathers freed him from the trunk, but she couldn't let down her guard. "What were ye sayin'?"

He reached over to set his stained quill in the inkwell on the deck. "We were running through the vowel sounds. Which are?"

Ebba already knew the twenty-six letters in the alphabet. Apparently, that wasn't all ye had to know. "Ah, eh, ee, oar, oo."

"Correct, and the rest of the alphabet are consonants."

Her face slackened as she stared up at him. He looked back at her.

"Yer teachin' her wrong," Jagger called from the opposite bulwark. He held loosely to the rigging, swaying with the lurch and pitch of the ship.

"Excuse me?" Barrels sputtered.

Ebba didn't turn to look at the flaxen-haired pirate, but called back, "He be teachin' me just fine-like."

The red flush creeping up her father's neck rose to his jaw. Barrels wasn't as happy-mannered as Grubby, but he wasn't prone to bouts of temper like some of her other fathers. He considered such outbursts an embarrassment.

Jagger might've touched on the one subject guaranteed to rile her bookish father.

The pirate ambled over the deck to where they sat, standing over her. "Viva's a person who learns by the feel o' a thing, and from a likeness to objects that make sense to her."

Barrels voice could have frozen the entire ocean. "And I suppose you are about to inform me what 'makes sense' to my daughter."

"Survival," Caspian said, approaching from the bilge door behind.

Was *everyone* listening to her lesson?

Ebba glanced at the prince and smiled anyway. He beamed back.

She was glad he wasn't acting strange after their kiss on Zol. Actually, with a closer look, Ebba noted the healthy flush in his cheeks and the sharpness of his gaze. Her smile widened, and his did too. Perhaps being back at sea was all the prince had needed to make him happy. Ebba hoped so.

Nothing had changed on *her* end after the kiss—she'd half

wondered if it would. He was still Caspian, though, and there clearly wasn't any tension on his end. Ebba just knew what his lips felt like now. Which . . . was making her think of them. She dropped her gaze to his lips.

"Survival, you say?" Barrels said, scratching his chin and leaving a black smudge.

Ebba jerked out of her stupor.

The red flush on Barrels' neck had receded, and she threw the prince a grateful look for intervening. Her fathers considered Caspian a part of their crew. They'd saved his life, and he'd saved theirs. Somewhere during the discovery of the taint and everything that had gone with it, he'd been unofficially welcomed into their tightknit family.

Jagger had not.

Barrels would take comments from one man that he wouldn't take from the other.

"Put the learnin' in terms she understands." Jagger spoke again, standing over them.

Barrels appeared to drag his eyes back up to the pirate. "I'm all ears."

Ebba refrained from remarking that Barrels didn't sound like he was all ears—more like he was all daggers.

Jagger gestured to the lattice of rope squares overhead. He crouched before the inkwell and drew out a sheet of parchment from where they were pinned underneath the ornate wooden and brass block. Taking up a quill and dipping the tip in ink, Jagger scratched out a word.

Ebba peered over his shoulder, reciting the individual letters in her head. *R-I-G-G-I-N-G*.

"How many vowels in the word 'rigging'?" Jagger asked her.

That was how you spelled 'rigging'? Huh, it looked different to how she thought it would. "Two," she said, half in question, half in answer. "The two I's."

Jagger nodded. "The rest are consonants."

"Always?" she asked. "Everything but the vowels?"

"The letter Y can be both," he replied. "Kind of like how the foresail is useful for extra speed and stability. The Y has two jobs."

That made a heck of a lot of sense, but Jagger's ego was big enough as it was. She grunted.

Jagger folded up the paper, concealing the word etched there. "How do ye spell 'rigging'?"

"R-I-G-G-I-N," she recited.

"That be riggin', not rigging," he countered. "You missed the G."

Ebba shrugged though her mistake hadn't been purposeful. "That's how I normally say it. Seems okay-like to me."

Barrels grasped her hand. "You spelled 'rigging'."

But the happiness didn't reach his eyes. "We'll resume the lesson tomorrow," her father said softly, gathering his books and quill station.

He hurried to the bilge door and disappeared below deck.

Ebba shoved Jagger. "Good one, ye dolt. Ye hurt Barrels' feelings." She wiped her hand on her slops after, just in case some of his taint had gotten on her skin. His eyes weren't black, but she really didn't want to be tainted again. Part of her was glad the pirate was sleeping above deck for that very reason. There weren't enough hammocks in the hold with him *and* Caspian here anyway, but Jagger had almost leaped at the chance to sleep above deck, saying he'd rather sleep there than next to a murderer's son. Thinking back on it threatened to unbalance her temper all over again, but with Jagger above deck, it was easier to sleep at night, knowing he was out of killing distance of Caspian.

"Ye were goin' around in bloody circles," Jagger shot back, standing again. "It was doin' my skull in."

"Then ye could've gone away somewhere else." Ebba stood as well, tilting her head to scowl at him. "He's been waitin' forever to teach me to read."

His jaw was clenching. "A thank ye would be nice."

Ebba was going to attack him. Either that or pull her dreads out.

"Oi," Peg-leg hollered as he approached them from the box. "I'm thinkin' we should double check the d'rection quick-like afore we go too much farther. Just in case the next part o' the weapon has moved. I ain't enterin' the Dynami if I don't have to."

She didn't break off her glaring match with Jagger.

Caspian stepped forward and gripped her arm. "Perhaps we should do it now while we're all assembled?"

Not wanting to alert the pillars to their location, the three of them hadn't repeated what they'd accidentally discovered when she tried to stop Jagger from killing Caspian back on Exosia. Peg-leg was right though. Ebba didn't want to unnecessarily enter the Dynami Sea either—the angry, black sea that pirates never entered because no pirate ever came out again.

Ebba threw a final scowl at Jagger, turning away. "I have the *dynami*," she said, gesturing unnecessarily to the tarnished silver tube tucked in her belt.

"I have the *purgium*," Caspian said. "The sword is down by my trunk."

Jagger was already moving to the bilge door. "I'll get it."

Ebba watched him disappear below deck. "That was awfully helpful o' him."

"I agree," Caspian replied after a lengthy pause.

Veritas was the royal family's sword, but Jagger's father—general of King Montcroix's army before he was murdered by the king himself—had carried it for many years. Is that why the pirate was so eager to hold the blade?

She could understand that.

Jagger emerged, one hand holding the sparkling hilt of the truth sword.

Drawing in a breath, Ebba prepared herself for what happened next.

Unlike when two of the objects were held by one person, what they were about to do didn't hurt. But the phenomenon caused when the three of them touched did weird her out some, simply because they had no idea *why* it happened. Ebba wasn't immortal, and yet magic could shoot out of her body? That didn't sit right with her.

Jagger stood in front of Caspian, staring flatly at him. Rolling her eyes, Ebba quickly placed herself between the two men. She placed one palm on Jagger's chest and the other on Caspian's.

Just like the first time, torrents of white light blazed outward, an inferno aura that lit the sky in all directions, casting their skin in an unnatural, otherworldly glow. The gentle heat crept up Ebba's arms, spreading across her chest and bathing her in bronze. Her dreads hovered about her shoulders as though lifted by a breeze. Jagger was awash with a silver hue that made his eyes appear otherworldly while Caspian was lit with an ethereal gold glow.

More important was the thin yet unbreakable beam of light shooting from their trio into the distance. As their ship continued on its current path, the angle of the beam's trajectory grew sharper. Like the last time they'd touched, the distal end of the beam was fixed on a point out of sight.

To the next part of the weapon—or so Verity had theorized.

The beam was pointing firmly east and slightly north of their current location, straight into the Dynami Sea.

Ebba lowered her hands, feeling a twinge of loss as she broke the connection between herself, Caspian, and Jagger. By comparison to the glowing explosion of a moment before, the world now appeared almost dull.

The three of them stood still in the wake.

Caspian was frowning. "It happened just like the first time. I'd almost convinced myself that it never happened."

"Still in the Dynami." Jagger stared in the direction the beam had pointed.

"I'd really like to know why and how that be happenin'," Ebba said shakily, glancing up at the men either side of her.

Peg-leg hobbled over. "Pass me the majiggy, lass."

She sucked in her gut and slid the *dynami* free of her belt, handing the tube to her father.

He tucked the cylinder into his own belt and limped forward, clutching Jagger and Caspian in what appeared to be a grip bordering on painful.

The prince grimaced, dropping his shoulder in a failed attempt to dislodge her father. Jagger stood still, though Ebba smirked as a wince flickered across his high-boned features.

"No light," Stubby said, watching the trio. "Give it to Grubs. He be the youngest."

Peg-leg wiped the hand that had touched Jagger on his slops. Seemed like all of them were taking the same precautions against the taint.

Locks snorted, the tiny scars on his face stretching. "Ye're thinkin' the magic has an age limit?"

Stubby ignored Locks and nudged Grubby to take hold of the *dynami*. None of her fathers would touch the *purgium*. They had no way to predict what sacrifice would be demanded if they should touch the thing while still carrying the taint from Mutinous Cannon. What if the healing needed was so great the *purgium* demanded death in exchange as it had with Ladon?

Then there was the *veritas*, which no pirate in their right mind would want to touch.

She'd touched the truth sword once, and the experience still gave her the willies. What if the blade showed her something terrible? Or forced her to admit something she was pretending? Of course, a small amount of truth was necessary for survival. Complete ignorance could quickly get you killed and hurt others' feelings. But to know everything? Surely that wasn't good for any person. King Montcroix had stopped touching the sword—preferring to let his general hold it. Honestly, Ebba couldn't blame him.

Grubby slid the *dynami* behind his ear. The tube was too large to be placed there and forced his ear out at an unnatural angle, but he didn't seem bothered as he took Caspian's hand and then Jagger's.

Plank threw Ebba a look, and they both turned away from the trio to hide their smiles. It would never occur to Grubby that holding hands might be overstepping the mark with the two younger men. The prince was smiling kindly, however, while Jagger's face was almost soft as he watched her father.

No glow blasted off into the distance.

Grubby stepped back, grimacing at the hand he'd used to touch Jagger. Her father quickly wiped his hand off on his dirty tunic.

Stubby scratched his chin, glancing at Plank. "Just Ebba, Caspian, and Jagger, it seems."

"Aye," chorused her other fathers, except for Barrels, who still sulked below deck.

Ebba took the *dynami* back from Grubby. "But why? We didn't know each other until recently. It was just chance that I met Caspian. And chance that Jagger was the guide needed for Neos. And chance that I got taken by *Malice*." She trailed off. That was a lot of chances, now Ebba thought about it.

"Jagger's and Caspian's parents knew each other," Plank pointed out. "Maybe that be part o' it."

The change in Jagger was like lightning in the air a moment before it strikes the ground. Everyone turned to watched as he whipped the sword up, resting the blade against the prince's throat. Jagger's expression was pure menace. Caspian's amber gaze more resigned than intrigued.

Ebba choked on a scream, frozen to the spot.

Caspian sighed heavily. "Are you going to kill me then, Jagger? If so, just get on with it. I'm sick of the threats."

If Jagger did, she would use the *dynami* to drown him and then throw him all the way to the oblivion.

The pirate smiled, his expression marred by the narrowing of his gunmetal eyes. "Ye know the deal, *heir*. I'll only kill ye when ye wish to live. Maybe that'll be next week, mayhaps next month. Or maybe when ye feel the touch o' the woman ye love." His eyes darkened as they shifted to Ebba, who blushed at the blatant jab. "But I wanted ye to feel this blade against yer neck while ye were still alive, to feel what my parents did when yer father slaughtered them."

Locks grunted in the following quiet. "That be a serious resen'-ment, lad."

"Aye," Stubby said, lips pursed. "I wonder if yer parents would be wantin' ye to harbor such hatred."

"I don't know, do I?" Jagger said, jaw clenched. The hand holding the blade against Caspian's neck trembled. "They were taken from me."

Ebba stepped closer, ready to intervene. He was tainted. Who knew if he was currently in control or not. Though he wasn't edgy as he'd been below deck a few days earlier.

"I don't know why my father did the things he did," Caspian said, swallowing hard against the gleaming sword at his throat. "I am trying to figure it out with the *veritas* though. I need answers just as much as you."

Is that what the prince had been doing alone all this time? Trying to use the truth sword to understand his father?

Plank circled behind Jagger. "Caspian's father was killed by pirates. Can't that be enough for ye?"

"Mayhaps ye could be sorrowful for what he be goin' through?" Locks suggested.

Jagger scowled. "Montcroix got what he deserved."

The prince flinched and turned his head away. He took several harsh breaths before answering the pirate in a whisper. "I'm not sure that he didn't."

Ebba whistled silently. Caspian thought his father deserved being killed? That was . . . unexpected. And spoke for the dark place he was currently in.

Stubby rested a hand on his shoulder. "He was yer father, lad. Even if he made mistakes, many mistakes, ye can still love him. Ye can even dislike him at the same time. And ye can certa'nly miss him every day as much as ye need. Sorting through all that will take a bit. Ain't no rush."

Dull amber eyes perused Stubby, unresponsive. Blasted Jagger. Just when she'd thought Caspian was getting better. Her temper rose to a simmer and she struggled to hold onto the frayed edges, catching sight of Grubby trying to twist his hands off in agitation. Tension rested over *Felicity*'s deck like a thick blanket.

Casting her mind frantically about, Ebba peered at the blackening sky. "Who be on night shift?"

She casually walked to the prince and dragged him several paces away from the blade, continuing to peer at the sky.

"Ye need somethin' a smidgen stronger to distract from a death threat, lass," Peg-leg said. "Try a fire or cutting the sheets next time."

Ebba pursed her lips. "What about seeing somethin' in the water?"

"Might work," he answered after a beat. "But only if ye really sell it. Remember, ye need to put yer whole body into the motion, not just a surprised voice."

"I'd swing the boom at one o' yer other fathers' heads," Locks added, then frowned. "Perhaps not Grubs. Not sure he can do with another hit."

The others scowled at him.

"Come on, lad," Peg-leg said to Caspian. "Let's get ye somethin' to eat down in the hold." Throwing an arm around the prince's shoulders, the cook led him away.

Grubby stepped forward. "I'll do the night shift."

She smiled at her youngest father. "That was just a ploy to get Caspian away from—"

"Okay," Stubby blurted.

In the time it took her to spin in a full circle, the others were gone, leaving her with Grubby and Jagger.

Ebba shouted at their backs, "Ye ain't allowed to take adv'ntage, ye spineless codfishes!"

No answer. She could guarantee it wasn't Grubby's turn, judging by Stubby's hasty agreement.

"*I'll* do the night shift," she declared, walking over to squeeze her father's hand.

He smiled his token toothless grin. "Nay, Ebba-Viva. I'll do it just like I said. Don't ye be worryin' about it."

She heard the strain beneath his words. He'd be anxious about annoying her other fathers.

"Okay," she answered, trying to keep the irritation at the rest of the crew from her voice. "But I'll be takin' yer next shift, no discu'sion about it."

Caspian wasn't dead. Grubby wasn't anxious. The next part of the weapon was definitely in the Dynami Sea. That only left one mess made by Jagger that she had to clean up.

As she strode away to find Barrels and soothe his hurt feelings over their reading lesson, the flaxen sod fell into step beside her.

"Can ye trust the halfwit not to lead us astray?" he asked as they neared the bilge door.

Her simmering temper exploded into a full boil. Ebba saw crimson. Whipping the dagger out of her sash, she rushed the taller man, surprising him enough that he stumbled back at her attack. Ebba extended her arm high, the dagger just under the pirate's throat as *veritas* had been against Caspian's.

Jagger swallowed, the lump in his throat rising and falling, but she didn't release the digging pressure.

Ebba breathed hard through her scalding fury. "Call my father 'halfwit' again, and I'll kill ye. I swear I will. Ye be on our ship, Jagger. Mind yer tongue if ye wish to stay alive."

The smirk spreading across his face wasn't as satisfactory of a reply as she would wish.

"And don't kill Caspian," she hissed, digging the dagger in harder. "The sea be makin' him better; don't get in the way."

"Ye think the sea be makin' him better?"

She stalled at the amusement in his gaze. "What?"

"It ain't the sea," he gasped against the jagged blade. "It's ye. And the hope for more."

It . . . it was? But she and Caspian were very clear about the terms of their kiss. Or were the pirate's words just the start of another Jagger headache?

"Shut yer gob," she snarled at him, the furious fire in her words faded. "Just leave him be."

Jagger arched a brow, too calm, as though he didn't have a sharpened blade at his throat. "Should I kiss him instead?"

Ebba was just angry enough to shove down her mortification and return his smirk in full measure. "Nay, Jagger. For he'll be busy kissin' me."

The pirate blinked slowly, and she pulled away the dagger, shoving him back against the bilge door.

Jagger watched her with a hooded gaze, stepping clear as she made to wrench the door open and hit him with it.

Ebba held her head high as she leaped onto the rungs of the ladder and gripped the sides to slide to the bottom. Glancing back up, she caught sight of Jagger peering down after her.

Holding his gaze, she very deliberately wiped her hands off on her slops.

SEVEN

Stretching, her jaw cracking with the whale of all yawns, Ebba called through the sleeping quarters, "Mornin'."

She smiled as Barrels' wheezing snore halted for a second before resuming.

Ebba tilted her head back and squinted up at the mini-hammock swinging over her head. Empty. Where was Sal?

Groaning, she swung and leaped from her hammock, landing on soft feet. If the sprite was in the grog, Ebba would tie her to the hammock at night. She grabbed her brown leather jerkin from the day before—and the day before that—and slid it over her frayed linen shirt. Fishing in her trunk, she pulled out the first piece of material her fingers encountered, grimacing as they also brushed the flax pouch containing the beads.

Ebba squinted at the material as she yanked it out. A green sash to match her eyes. She didn't often wear sashes to hold her hair back, usually opting for a bandana instead. The ends of the longer material flying across her face in the wind irked her, but today felt and sounded calm enough.

She fastened the green sash around her hairline, half over her forehead and half over her dreads, knotting the sash at the base of her skull to one side. She let the ends trail over her shoulder.

Her hands fell to her sides, and she halted.

The sea was *oddly* tranquil today.

The southern seas were generally rough. The closer they sailed to the Dynami Sea, the bigger the swells would become. So why was the sea so still?

Ebba smelled fish stew.

Leaving her slumbering fathers, she hustled up the ladder and flung the bilge door open, looking out over the starboard side. The sea was too light, dark blue where it should be blue-black.

Ebba shut the bilge door and turned to look port side.

Her jaw dropped. "Shite."

She lost no time wrenching open the door again. "Show a leg, lads," she shouted.

Ebba shook her head and glanced over the bulwark a final time to make sure she wasn't hallucinating.

"What be amiss, lass?" Locks croaked from below.

She sighed. "We're at Neos."

That got them moving. She left the bilge door open and started searching the ship for Grubby who'd been on night watch.

"Flamin' eejit," Stubby seethed, appearing from below deck. "He went for a damn swim instead of watchin' where we were headed."

Ebba pressed a finger to her lips as her mind worked. "Nay, Stubs. We be anchored."

"Over here," Plank called from the helm.

They raced to the helm where Grubby was tied to the wheel.

"Mornin'," he said cheerfully.

Her eyes narrowed, and Ebba gritted her teeth as the answer came to her. "Where be Jagger?" He wasn't just insulting Grubby last night—or at all. He'd been testing the damn waters.

Her fathers lifted their heads, exchanging looks.

"Shite," Locks howled at the sky. "He's gone to look for his bloody tribe again."

"I knew he was offerin' up the hammock to Caspian too easy-like. We shouldn't've left him on deck," Peg-leg said, the hand that often gripped his cooking machete tightening.

"He knows Ladon and his snakes have taken over the island. Why has he gone there?" Ebba stared at Neos mountain, just visible in the distance.

Stubby lifted a shoulder. "If ye were on there, nothin' could keep me away. Canny bugger, keepin' us off the scent of his plan by playin' up against Caspian yesterday."

If that was what he'd been doing, Ebba had fallen for it hook, line, and sinker.

"It's gone," Caspian said from behind. He stood at the top of the bilge door, russet hair disheveled from sleep. "He took the *purgium*."

"But he can't touch it," Plank said. "He's tainted like the rest o' us."

"I can't find it anywhere," Caspian said, running a hand through his hair. "It was on me, in my hand as I fell asleep last night. I'm so sorry. I—"

Barrels lifted a hand. "It's hardly your fault. Don't be so hard on yourself. We were all tricked."

"The *veritas* is still here." Caspian's quiet voice interrupted her musing.

Well, Jagger could hardly hold two. But Plank was right, Jagger *couldn't* touch the *purgium*. He'd die—or risk dying at least. Though he'd traipsed off to Neos, so clearly he was willing to risk his life anyway. However, the much likelier answer was—

"Sally," she said through gritted teeth. "Sally be gone. She took the *purgium* from ye and went with Jagger."

Barrels glanced at her. "She's not passed out in a grog barrel?"

It was possible. . . .

"I'll go and check," Peg-leg said.

Plank sighed as Peg-leg hobbled away with the customary *tap-tap-tap* of his wooden limb. "At least he anchored us far enough away from Neos that Ladon's snakes can't reach us."

"Ladon is surely more powerful-like by now," Locks countered. "Jagger can't've known how far away we were last time. He took a mighty risk by placin' us here without us knowin'. The snakes could've overrun us as we slept."

Her fathers' faces settled into grim lines.

"He's clearly where he wants to be," said Ebba. "Let's leave him." Though even as she said the words, an odd pang twanged in her gut.

She'd never been good at leaving people behind, but her surprise couldn't be stronger to find that included Jagger too.

Barrels exhaled loudly. "No, my dear. Not only does Jagger have Sally, he has the *purgium* and, as we found yesterday, we need Jagger's help to find the next part. I'm afraid he's got us trapped."

Ebba thumped her closed fist atop the bulwark. "Ye're right."

She glared at the Neos shore, only a thin strip of gray from where they were anchored. "How long will he be? We're grazin' seahorses."

Locks hummed in agreement. "Aye, I don't be liking the exp'sure with the most powerful and darkest magical power o' all time after us."

"Nay," they all muttered.

A terrible, ground-cracking rumble rent the air. Ebba stilled alongside her fathers, staring at Neos.

She whispered, "Do ye hear—"

The movement under the ship changed abruptly, and Ebba hastened to peer over the bulwark. Curved rivulets had appeared in the previously tranquil waters. The rivulets grew to small waves moving *away* from the island, slapping against *Felicity*'s sides in their haste to escape. The ship pitched as the waves grew larger, and she widened her stance.

Peg-leg reappeared from the hold as the waves smoothed out again. "What was that?"

Ebba focused on the island before them, which now appeared hazy. "Was it an earthshake, Barrels?"

"I'm not sure, my dear. It didn't last very long, if so."

Plank came to stand beside her, squinting at Neos. "Wait, look at the mountaintop. Can ye see anythin' strange?"

She shifted her gaze to the center of the island where, she knew from horrible experience, the mountain sat. Though. . . . "Where be the mountain?"

"Aye, little nymph. That be my point."

Ebba blurted, "Ye don't think Jagger and Sally did that, do ye?" She backtracked. "Ye think the noise was the mountain tumblin' down?"

Surely even Sally's glowing magic wasn't that strong. And neither Jagger or the *purgium* could have caused such damage.

"Nay," Plank said, tilting his head, "I be thinkin' the rumble we heard was Ladon himself. Maybe he brought down the mountain."

Ebba gawked at Neos, her gut twinging.

Grubby's voice broke the stupor that had settled over the ship and all its occupants. "Could someone untie me? I'm hungry."

"Sorry, Grubs," Locks said hastily.

He unraveled the rope and Ebba's part-selkie father stood, coming to stand on her other side.

"Grubby, do ye remember what happened?" Ebba asked. She shot a cursory glance at her other fathers and saw her sheepishness reflected on their faces. They'd forgotten Grubby was actually on deck at the time.

"Oh, aye, Ebba-Viva. Jagger said he was goin' to defeat Ladon to save his people, and would I be so good as to let him tie me to the wheel for a time. I said, 'Aye, of course, I hope ever'thin' be goin' well for ye.'"

Stubby closed his eyes, expression pained.

Jagger specifically went to defeat Ladon? But he'd seen how strong Ladon was during their riddle encounter with the lizard beast. And that was back when Ladon had only just returned and was weak. Who in their right mind would willingly fight him now?

Jagger. He definitely wasn't in his right mind.

"Do you think if we kill Jagger when he gets back that we can still use his body to show us the way with the beam o' light?" Plank asked.

Her crew paused to contemplate this.

"Irreversible if we kill him and it don't work, methinks," Locks said.

Ebba didn't remove her eyes from the shore. If the mountain of Neos had crumbled to the ground and Jagger was on top with Ladon, how could the pirate possibly have survived? Not only had he put the entire crew and ship in danger. He'd put himself in danger too. The odd pang twisted her stomach again.

"I say that if Jagger is ever comin' back, we have a punishment ready that requires him to be alive," she whispered, fists clenching.

Evil smirks spread across the faces around her, Caspian's being the only exception.

"Aye, little nymph," Plank gripped his cutlass, "a good plan."

EIGHT

Jagger returned at low tide. His back was to them as he heaved on both oars to return their rowboat to where it belonged. Sally was perched on his shoulder, clutching the *purgium* in her arms.

All eight of the remaining crew lined the port side of the ship, arms folded, expressions impassive.

As though Jagger felt their burning scrutiny, the pirate glanced back and up at them. His profile didn't show fear, or shock, or defiance—just calm acceptance that, aye, he'd stolen the *purgium*, taken their rowboat, and put them in danger on several accounts. And was a bastard in general.

The rowboat came alongside *Felicity*.

"Here," Plank called to Jagger in a silken voice, "let me help you with that."

Her father began to lower the rope ladder over the side, and Jagger tensed, as well he should.

Ebba set murderous eyes on her pet sprite.

Betrayed *again*, and for the last time as far as Ebba was concerned. She could accept that Sally had her own mind and motives, but those motives had clashed with her own agenda too many times now. If the sprite was going to actively put her fathers in danger, that was where Ebba drew the very solid line.

Sally avoided her eyes and floated over to Caspian, passing him the *purgium*. He accepted it without a word, and she zoomed back to disappear beneath Jagger's flaxen hair. The same place she liked to occupy on Ebba.

"*Ye really did switch sides,*" she muttered under her breath.

Stubby and Locks helped to winch the rowboat up and secure it.

"Did ye save yer people?" Grubby asked Jagger.

He scanned the rest of them. "Don't know. If they be in hidin', they won't come out until they're knowin' it be safe."

Caspian stared at the *purgium* in his hand, a wrinkle between his brows. "And Ladon?"

Ebba hadn't uncrossed her arms, but she reluctantly listened for the pirate's answer, half an eye on the prince.

Jagger smiled; a smile that actually reached his eyes for once. "Gone."

"Dead gone?" she pressed, catching herself before asking how he'd done it.

"Dead gone," he answered shortly.

Caspian lifted his focus from the cylinder, his amber eyes dull. "You healed him, didn't you? You healed Ladon."

Jagger didn't reply, but Plank's interest had been stirred enough to abandon his silken voice.

"The witch stole the good of Ladon's soul," he said slowly. "It was why he so zealously guarded the apple for mille'nia, so that he could be askin' for the good of himself back over and over. His soul was broken." Plank cut off and regarded Jagger.

Ebba's eyes rounded as she caught up. Before actually meeting Ladon, she'd felt sorry for the immortal beast left forever seeking the lightness in his soul. Jagger had healed his soul?

No one spoke, and Jagger eventually raised a shoulder.

"Aye," he said. "I healed Ladon. And the price was death."

She watched the silent pirate closely, hesitant to trust a single word out of his mouth after the latest stunt. "Ye just went up and said, 'Here, matey, touch this'?"

Jagger's silver eyes raked her face. "I offered him what he'd been searchin' for. He begged for freedom in the end."

"And you saved your tribe?" Caspian whispered. "If they still live, that is. You saved them all, and any of the villagers who still live?"

"Aye, *heir*. I do not leave my family and friends to die."

Caspian flinched violently before he turned away, knuckles white where he still clutched the *purgium*.

"He didn't only have one immortal creature to heal," Ebba snapped. "Ladon be a blip compared to the pillars, and ye know it."

"It's okay, Mistress Pirate," the prince said, though he didn't turn back. "It's nothing I don't think of myself. I shouldn't have run with you that night. I shouldn't—" He broke off and cleared his throat before stating, "I shouldn't have done so many things."

Ebba stared at the dejected set of his shoulders, at a loss of what to say.

But he continued, voice twisted with bitterness. "I shouldn't have told the navy ship to deter from the usual route. I should have returned to Exosia the first time we anchored in Kentro. I should have told my father what was happening straightaway. I should have been by my father's side when Pockmark's crew killed him. I should have fought them and fought for my people. I know all of this. And I can handle it."

His shoulders shook.

Caspian wasn't fooling anyone. He couldn't handle what had happened one bit.

Before Ebba could reach him, Caspian was striding for the bilge.

As soon as the door closed, she rounded on Jagger, hands clenched into fists. "How can ye be so cruel when ye know how he's hurtin' inside? Does it make ye feel better to say such things? Dunkin' someone when they already be sinkin', ye gutless swine?"

A tiny flicker in Jagger's eyes made her feel he *might* regret his words. He looked after Caspian and back at her. Then the flicker was gone, a dark coldness in its place.

"Why are ye even back, Jagger?" Peg-leg growled. "Seems odd-like to me that ye ain't searching for yer family after killin' Ladon."

Jagger stilled. "I freed them from one danger. I am yet to save them."

Ebba supposed if the pillars were allowed to take over the realm, Jagger was right. His tribe was out of immediate danger but by no means safe. Still, his words didn't quite ring true.

The pirate was here for something else too.

"Hmm," Peg-leg said, limping closer, "so ye say. Regardless-like, I ain't sure returnin' was the smartest thing ye ever did."

Jagger lifted his head as her fathers closed in around him, not bothering to move.

"Get him," Stubby ordered.

⧗

EBBA DIDN'T TAKE a full breath until they passed south of Febribus without incident.

She wasn't sure when she'd come to be partially afraid of the Caspian Sea, and of what the waters held, but Ebba couldn't rest easy among the islands therein anymore. Every passing second, the pillars' power grew, their taint spreading unchecked. She knew the horror of their power firsthand and would move Davy Jones' itself to never lose her soul and will to the pillars again. And that went for everyone she knew and loved. Even her enemies didn't deserve that fate.

What scared her the most though?

The thought that she'd only experienced the very tip of the iceberg; that the terrors she'd been through were nothing compared to what the pillars were really capable of. Verity had told them the pillars' taint would spread across the realm, overpowering the will of all creatures, mortal and immortal. What would the realm be when only shells of beings remained, and when their only drive was to enact the will of the six pillars?

Ebba ignored the soft moan overhead, and a louder thud as the upside-down Jagger swinging overhead from the second boom smacked into the mast. With his arms latched to his sides, there really wasn't a way to protect himself when the lurch of the ship catapulted him against the solid wood. His face had to be really sore right about now.

She stole a peek up, and her eyes widened at the purple tinge to Jagger's face. Looked as though his head was about to pop right off. And if that didn't happen, Pillage would probably attack him. The ship cat appeared constantly hypnotized by Jagger's rhythmic swinging. He'd barely taken his eyes off the pirate since he was strung up there.

"Do ye think we should get him down?" she asked Barrels.

Barrels sniffed, pausing in the act of writing a word on parchment for her. "No, I don't."

Her father *might* still be harboring a small grudge over Jagger's interruption to his lesson the other day—although he had taken on the new approach.

"What does that say then?" she asked him, leaning forward to read the parchment. There were four letters: M-A-S-T.

"Sound it out," he replied. Using a smaller square of parchment, he covered the last three letters.

Ebba pressed her lips together. "Mmm."

He revealed the A.

"Mmm-aah."

Barrels beamed, revealing the third.

"Mmm-aah-sss." She was one step ahead of him, adding a sharp 'tih' sound. Ebba squeezed her eyes shut. "Mmm-ahh-sss-tih."

Ebba opened her eyes and blinked at the revealed word. M-A-S-T. "Mast," she exclaimed, shooting to her feet. "Mast."

"Yes, my dear," Barrels said, reaching forward to squeeze her hand. "That was fantastic."

She grinned at him and sat back down, ignoring more overhead moans. "Do another one then."

"My pleasure."

Barrels scratched another word down, and Caspian walked over to join them.

The prince glanced up at Jagger, displaying the dark shadows beneath his eyes. "Is skin meant to be that color?"

Since his outburst yesterday, Caspian hadn't spoken a word. Had he been up all night with his guilt and regrets? She expected so. His sense of responsibility was going to drown him one day.

Ebba craned to see Jagger again. "Nay, I don't s'pose so. We best be gettin' him down soon."

"I'm not sure. He doesn't exactly seem sorry," the prince remarked.

Seemed like everyone was harboring some type of grudge against Jagger.

She had to agree with him though. Just like the first time they'd taken Jagger hostage, he hadn't made a single peep at their treatment of him, except the moaning in the last few hours. No pleas, no shouted apologies, no sobbing or screams. His strength was probably admirable to some people but seemed stupid to her. He could've been free a lot sooner if he'd just faked a few whimpers. Not that she could talk. Pretty sure she'd kneed Pockmark.

"What does this say?" Barrels asked.

Ebba glanced down. S-A-I-L. She sounded it out, saying, "Say-eel?" That didn't sound like anything she knew of.

"Sail," Barrels corrected her.

Ah. Sail. Ebba glanced around the ship. She now knew rigging, mast, and sail. "How long will it take me to learn all o' the ship parts?"

"At this rate, my dear, not long at all. And once you've done that, perhaps we can move on to putting words together or reading some of my books."

Ebba grimaced. "How about my present from all o' ye?" That was the only book she was interested in reading.

He dipped his head. "We can do that."

Barrels collected his teaching supplies, and Caspian sat in his vacated spot. The prince was frowning at the empty space where his arm used to be.

"Feeling yer limb again?" she asked.

He glanced up at her. "Yes. It's never faded, and I thought it would. But I can feel my arm there, my elbow and hand and each of my fingers as though my arm were never taken." A slight breeze played with the curls around his ears. "I can feel the wind touching my skin," he continued in a darker voice, "and I swear I thought I'd trapped it in the bilge door the other day. I felt physical pain."

"That'd be mighty irritatin'."

"It is," he admitted. "More that it's hard to accept something is gone when everything you feel says otherwise."

Did he refer to his arm or to his father?

Ebba surveyed the rest of him. His right arm was much larger than it used to be, probably because he only had one limb to do everything now. His chest was larger on that side also, and the right side of his neck. "Ye've finally hardened up, methinks."

He attempted a smile. "Have I? At last?"

An aching ball pained in her chest. She couldn't take it anymore, watching a person try so hard to keep up appearances. Biting her lip, she shifted closer. "Caspian, ye had no choice but to leave yer people. Ye had to get yer sisters safe. Goin' off to save the courtesans that *Malice* took to the mines were a fool's quest. Ye would've surely died. Then what help would ye have been to anyone?"

The prince's eyes faded, and he stared ahead to where they drew nearer to the Dynami Sea.

"The more I go on," he replied as the wind swirled around them, "the more I understand there are far worse things than death. Guilt and regret are more powerful than my fear of the end. I should've listened to my instincts that night. I should've tried to help them instead of running away with my tail between my legs."

"The odds were impo'sible, Caspian," Ebba said, her chest tightening. Why couldn't he see that? There was responsibility, and then there was stupidity.

She had to redirect the current flowing through his mind somehow.

"The odds were impo'sible for Jagger too." His words were twisted with bitterness. "Yet look at what he has done. He willingly went as your hostage to Neos in the beginning so that he might check on his people; he bargained with your crew on Febribus for his chance to return again. He hijacked *Felicity* and defeated a beast that killed the tribespeople, or at the very least drove them away, and who wreaked havoc in the Neos village. He did all that without encouragement, when the world told him no, and knowing he would likely die—*and* did it while controlled by the taint. He made it possible. And I should have done the same. My father would have."

Ebba thought Caspian's views of his father weren't accurate and certainly didn't mesh with the criticisms he'd voiced in the past. But if he wanted to put King Montcroix on a pedestal, Ebba wasn't going to destroy the illusion.

By the sound of it, the prince envied Jagger a great deal.

Ebba could follow his reasoning, but she couldn't see how the situations were the same. "He didn't fight Ladon. He offered to heal his soul, and the *purgium* did the rest. You would've had to fight hundreds of mindless pirates and the six pillars. And without this root o' magic we be searchin' for, ye would've lost. Ye're tryin' to compare a ship to a fish. Jagger's battle weren't the same. It's just the sadness in ye that won't allow ye to admit it."

He stared off into the darkening ocean and made no answer.

She'd been wrong; being at sea wasn't enough to fix the prince. And after what Jagger let slip, Ebba had an inkling she'd viewed the return of Caspian's energy and interest entirely wrong. But if he was acting like himself again because of his feelings for her, she wasn't about to lead him on. That fell on the immoral side of her pirate morals. Except nothing that had happened recently was enough to offset the demons in his head.

Red crept up her neck and into her face. She took his hand in both of hers, trying to swallow back her temper. Maybe a direct approach was best. "I'm sick of ye mopin' about. I want ye to be happy."

Caspian pulled his hand free. "I don't do it to annoy you."

"But it does, if only because I can't understand why." She took his hand again and resisted his efforts to yank it back.

Ebba stared into his dull and shadowed eyes. "Yer *alive*, Caspian, alive when many others ain't. The villagers o' Neos, the tribespeople o' Pleo, the pirates who be lost to the taint and, aye, no doubt some of yer people, too. But ye're *not*—"

Ebba's mouth dried as the answer occurred to her.

He was overwhelmed by everything he hadn't done, all his regrets. And she knew that nothing trumped his sense of responsibility, so *that* was the answer. That was how she could redirect the current.

She tightened her grip on his hand, excitement grabbing her. "Ye do them a disservice by not avengin' their memory. *Fight*, Caspian. If ye have regret and guilt, fight so that ye may absolve yerself. Only the weapon we seek can destroy the pillars, so throw yerself into findin' the remainin' pieces. Put things to right alongside the rest o' us. And then, when we meet the pillars again, ye won't have to run because ye be ill-equipped to battle them. Ye can still save yer people, don't ye see, Caspian? This ain't over. The pillars just landed the first punch."

The prince slowly blinked. He straightened next, his amber eyes glinting in the moonlight.

She whispered low and fast. "Don't look back anymore. Look forward to what ye can do. The past has set sail, matey, but ye can be navigatin' the rest. Yer people are waitin' for ye."

He swallowed hard, and *Felicity* rose and fell, continuing her journey, untroubled by their conversation.

"You're right," he said hoarsely.

Ebba didn't dare make a noise and interrupt the whirring of his mind.

Caspian nodded, and his drawn face was determined when he turned to her again. "There is still time to do the right thing and fix this. We must get this weapon and save my people. Even if their souls are already lost to the pillars' taint, I'll figure out a way to free them. I won't let them down again."

He stood without warning.

"Where do ye think ye're goin'?" she asked.

"I'm certain I saw an old map of the Dynami Sea amidst Barrels' collection of papers."

"I don't think any map will be accurate-like, matey," she said, pursing her lips. "No one's made it out o' that place afore."

"Then how does everyone know not to go there?" he countered, lifting both brows.

Ebba wrinkled her nose. "What do ye mean? If seven ships go in and none come out, no one has to be doin' any tellin'."

Caspian laughed, and it was so similar to the person she'd first known that her heart leaped into her mouth. She'd done it. Or at least started him on the right route.

She just had to keep him there.

Ebba leaned back on her elbows as the prince disappeared below deck to rummage through what, in her opinion, were the only boring possessions aboard the ship. She tipped her head back and froze as she encountered Jagger's gaze.

"What're ye lookin' at?" she snapped, covering her fright. She'd bloody-well forgotten he was there.

His eyes were bloodshot and swollen. Jagger *really* didn't look too well. Ebba was going to get him down.

"He thinks he'll beat the pillars?" The pirate hacked out a semblance of a laugh.

She rolled her eyes. "Ye think *ye'll* beat the pillars?"

"Aye."

Of course he did. "Ye'd do anythin' for yer people; Caspian'd do anythin' for his. Ye think ye'll beat the pillars, and so does he. Seems like ye ain't so different from each other."

"As dif'rent as night and day."

"So ye say," she scoffed. "Even night and day meet twice a day, ye dolt."

The pirate closed his eyes. "Never said I wouldn't be meetin' him."

When it came to revenge, Ebba could only serve hers hot, but Jagger served his icy, icy cold. For her, the longer she spent around someone she hated, the less likely she'd be to kill them. Ebba couldn't forget that Jagger didn't work the same way.

The pirate opened his eyes again.

"Sounds to me like the princeling don't want to die anymore," he uttered, a pained edge to his words.

Shite.

Double shite.

Ebba sat bolt upright, breaking off the stare with the swinging pirate. What idiocy compelled her to have such a conversation with the prince in this very spot? Though she couldn't recollect Jagger moaning or making a single peep during the earlier talk. He'd surely stayed so quiet so he could listen in.

Stubby approached her from the helm, eyeing Jagger askance. "His color ain't lookin' great. Let's get him down."

Jagger would kill Caspian over her dead body.

She said to her father, "Nay, Stubs. Let's not get him down just yet."

NINE

"What's the sword tellin' ye?" Ebba asked Caspian as he stared at the *veritas*. She'd barely left his side since Jagger's veiled threat two days prior—though the pirate had holed up in the crow's nest to recover.

His back against the bow's bulwark, the prince presented the blade to her. Ebba whipped both hands behind her.

"Nay thanks," she blurted. "Gives me the willies just thinkin' o' it."

Caspian lowered *veritas*. "It's really not that bad."

Ebba eyed the sword. "Aye, but too much truth ain't good for a pirate."

He grinned, and she returned it.

"So what does it do?" she pressed him again.

"As far as I can tell, you just hold the sword and think of what you want to know. But it doesn't always work. That's what I'm trying to figure out."

"Is that what ye were doin' on Zol, all alone?"

He lifted a shoulder. "Part of it, I suppose. If I tell you it was that and not wallowing, would you believe me?"

"Nay."

The prince laughed.

She was a head lower than him in their sitting positions and he looked down at her, his eyes full of that burning intensity. Ebba quirked a brow in question, and the smile faded from his face.

His mouth bobbed open a few times.

When he didn't speak, she asked, "What about the future? Can it see that?"

Ebba shivered for a reason that had nothing to do with the waves breaking over the figurehead and showering them regularly with cold spray. Imagine knowing every single truth? A person wasn't meant to have such power. She shivered again.

"Ah, *that* I have tried," he answered. "The sword didn't show me a thing."

The silver sword gleamed in the beating sun of midday, and Ebba studied the weapon. "I wonder how it decides what to show ye."

"I'm not completely sure. . . . But what it shows is definitely related to what I'm thinking. Sometimes though, it takes me to moments I haven't personally witnessed—and some of those moments are in the past, from what I can tell."

She hummed. "That's confusin'."

"I'll figure it out," Caspian said, shuffling closer.

"Aye, ye will," she said with a soft smile. "Ye're a right smart bugger."

He shot her an amused look. "You know, in the stories my father used to tell me, he said the sword could force others to speak the truth."

She whistled. "Now *that* could come in handy-like. Have ye recalled anythin' else?"

Caspian shook his head. "I keep thinking about how shocked he looked when he last touched the sword. What do you think the sword showed him?"

Ebba thought for a minute, remembering the king's expression just before he'd tossed the sword at her and closed the door that ensured his death. "I don't think we'll ever know, matey. But the sword let him see through the charmed necklace I was wearin'. He called me pirate."

"You believe *veritas* lets us see through magical illusion?"

"Could do. Unless the charm had already worn off."

The prince's voice strained. "Is there anything you remember?"

She thought back to the moment she'd been blasted into the treasury by holding two parts of the weapon at once. The king had picked *veritas* up and— "He looked at peace, content-like, afore he threw the sword to me. Like he'd accepted sumpin'. Whatever the sword showed him, I be thinkin' it was what he needed to see afore the end."

"Do you think so?" the prince asked urgently, reaching for her hand. "Do you think he died without regret?"

His urgency startled her, but Ebba kept her face smooth. Truthfully, to her way of seeing, Montcroix had died years before she met him. He'd mentioned his queen in Ebba's hearing and, real or not, she'd chalked up the king's reluctance to touch the sword to the events surrounding her death.

Yet through his cynicism and bitterness, something true had remained. "He loved his children. Ye and yer sisters. In that, he had no regrets at all. And if he did, I'll eat my hat."

Caspian swallowed, releasing her hand to draw a sleeve over his wet face. "He loved my sisters. I'm afraid I tested his patience with my daydreaming."

He accompanied the comment with a harsh laugh, but Ebba wasn't fooled by it. She picked her words with care—for what could be the first time in her life. "He was proud o' ye. I saw that with my own eyes."

The little she'd seen of Montcroix had shown her the man was hard as nails. He'd barely shown affection when inches from his death. That had to be confusing for Caspian. A father who couldn't show affection, and a father who placed duty over family was no father at all.

"I'm sure as day is day that he loved ye," she told him firmly.

The prince's lashes were wet when he faced her. She took his hand again, and his gaze dropped to their clasped fingers. He lifted his head, staring at her lips.

Was he thinking of their kiss? Well now *she* was. Ebba eyes sought his mouth. How did that always happen? As soon as she thought back to the kiss, she wanted to do it all over again. The excitement reared up within her and the unexplored ground between she and Caspian beckoned her. Perhaps the mainlander women were right. Kissing was . . . enticing.

Felicity lurched, jolting Ebba out of her stupor.

Seeing Caspian watching her intently, she blurted. "So, how does *veritas* make a person tell the truth?" If the grog level got low and Sally didn't fess up, she'd be using the blade on the sprite.

"I only know what my father told me," the prince said, staring at the shining sword. "I have to lay the blade on the person's skin."

Ebba held up a finger. "The sword won't show me the truth, aye? Just make me tell it?"

"I believe so," he said, nodding.

Rolling up her slops, Ebba stuck out her leg.

The prince glanced at her limb warily. "What are you doing?"

"Test it on me," she said, grinning impishly.

Locks ambled over from the bilge door. "What're ye doin'?"

"We be seein' if *veritas* can force someone to speak truth," she told him.

Plank called from the mast. "Ye don't say? That could come in handy-like."

"You don't want to see the truth, but you're okay with telling the truth?" the prince asked her, mouth trembling.

"I am now," she told him honestly. Perhaps there was a time when she had trouble admitting the truth, but that was mostly behind her. Mostly.

Locks crossed his arms. "I ain't sure I'd do either."

"I'm thinkin' I'd maybe do it," Plank said after a beat. "Tell it that is."

Caspian pressed his trembling lips together. "Right. Let's try it then. What shall I ask you?" He rested the flat of the *veritas* on her shin and Ebba held tensed, half expecting to be shown something she didn't wish to know. Like if they'd fail and the realm would go to shite.

Plank folded his arms. "Ask her if she was the one who locked Pillage in my trunk. He pissed on my second to last good tunic."

The prince turned to her, awaiting permission.

"I didn't do it," Ebba replied haughtily. "Ask if ye will."

Caspian cleared his throat. "Did you lock Pillage in Plank's trunk?"

The sword flared white, eliciting a jump from all of them.

"Aye, in revenge," Ebba blurted against her will. "Pillage tripped me on purpose."

Caspian lifted the sword and her mouth fell ajar.

The *veritas* actually worked.

She grimaced, glancing up at Plank. "That sword makes ye lie!"

"Good try. Ye owe me one of yer tunics."

Ebba jerked her head at the prince as the rest of the crew joined them. "Rest it on Plank then." She knew for a *fact* he had one of her necklaces.

"Now, now," Plank said, hands raised.

"Ye ain't got nothin' to hide, do ye?" she asked sweetly.

His eye twitched. "All right. But I won't see truth, aye? I'll just have to tell it."

Her father appeared as creeped out by that possibility as Ebba was. She answered, "Nay, I didn't see anythin' untoward. I just couldn't. . . uh."

Locks sniggered as she trailed off.

Her father neared Caspian, who rested the blade on Plank's hand.

"Ask him if he makes up his stories," Stubby immediately said.

Peg-leg snorted. "Aye, ask him if they be a whole heap o' shite."

Plank scowled at the other fathers.

"Do you make up your stories?" the prince asked.

The sword flared white. Those who weren't present before jumped, gasping.

"Nay," her father answered.

The others booed his reply. Her fathers were full of it. By now they all knew Plank's stories held some element of truth. But the question was interesting. How *did* Plank know so much about magic when immortals were locked away hundreds of years ago?

"Really?" Caspian asked him. The word wasn't dubious, like Ebba's reaction, but full of excitement. There was so much they didn't know about immortals. How many there were, where they resided, and what powers they possessed.

The prince kept the blade on Plank's palm. "How do you know so many stories about magic?"

The *veritas* glowed again.

"I was told them by another. She got them from her mother, who got them from her mother and so on." His expression darkened.

Who was 'she'? Ebba could see the question on the prince's lips, but Plank jerked his hand away and, eyes narrowing, walked to stand behind the rest of her fathers.

Caspian said quietly to her, "I didn't mean to pry."

"It ain't a biggie." Ebba had a feeling the *she* might be Plank's murdered wife that he'd never spoken of.

Before the awkward moment could drag on, Barrels weaved between Locks and Peg-leg and knelt down with a groan. "Well, I have some exciting news. Caspian was right—I had an old map of the Dynami Sea in my collection. No idea when I happened to pick that up, but it might just help us now."

A map? Boring.

"It's of the Dynami Sea then?" Caspian asked, shuffling to crouch closer as Barrels unfurled the map.

"Indeed it is." A pleased smile sat on Barrels' lips.

Ebba reluctantly dragged her butt to look as the others gathered around Barrels and Caspian. Getting to her feet, she glanced over the prince's shoulder at the crumbling map.

"We'll enter here, I assume?" Caspian asked, an excited edge to his voice.

Ebba stood on tiptoes to see the spot where he was pointing. Happiness filled her at the energy in his voice. Their conversation had definitely sparked something. *This* Caspian sounded like the Caspian of old. Of course, with the prince's change of heart, a new problem had arisen—namely, Jagger's promise to kill Caspian as soon as he wanted to live.

She lifted her chin and saw that Jagger was on the opposite side of the map. He stood just behind Grubby, watching the prince like a hawk on the hunt.

So he'd finally come down from the nest.

Her eyes ran over the array of yellow bruising on his face from where he'd repeatedly hit the mast while swinging upside down. A twinge of remorse echoed in her gut and she winced at the bloody streaks in his silver eyes. Jagger glanced her way, and Ebba extinguished any pity she felt. Scowling darkly at him, she toyed with the hilt of her dagger.

His reaction was displeasing. But the amusement in his features was most likely there because he was scared.

Jagger might be playing it cool, but she knew he wouldn't draw attention to his plan until he struck—just like with Neos. Ebba didn't trust him around Caspian as far as she could spit. Or maybe a lot less than that because she could spit pretty far. The pirate was holding a grudge against the wrong person, and he wasn't allowed to hurt her friend when the prince had been through so much. Killing Caspian because King Montcroix apparently murdered Jagger's parents was like killing *her* because of the misdeeds of her fathers. It just didn't make pirate sense.

Jagger winked one swollen eye her way and returned his attention to the map. Why did he keep winking at her? Was this his latest trick to unsettle her?

She glared at him a few seconds longer and then did the same, scanning the old map rolled out on the deck.

The realm consisted of the Caspian Sea and the islands within that sea. The Dynami Sea lay beyond the islands bordering the realm on the east, Febribus and Maltu. This map showed the Dynami Sea as being larger than the Caspian. Whether the map was any good was anyone's guess, but Ebba *was* certain *Felicity* would soon enter new water—if the darkness of the swell and rising winds were anything to go by.

Ebba would kill for a sighting of an albino dolphin right now. Or some other small pirate-lore assurance that everything would be all right.

"What does that there say?" Locks asked. He pointed at a mark on the map in the waters before them.

"Ebba?" Barrels asked, holding his breath.

T-H-U-N-D-E-R-B-I-R-D.

The word was too long. Jagger would laugh at her. "Nay, too long."

Her father almost appeared to pout at that. "It says 'thunderbird'."

"Ahh, the thunderbird," Plank repeated in his ominous story-telling voice.

Stubby groaned, grimacing at Barrels. "Why did ye have to set him off?"

Ebba spoke over her fathers. They were just roasting Plank, but seeing as the thunderbird label sat in their immediate path, she wanted answers. "Is the thunderbird magic?"

Caspian, who'd crouched by the map, turned to listen with riveted attention. Jagger ambled to lean against the bulwark, farther away from the prince, and Ebba relaxed a smidgen.

"Long ago," Plank said, scanning them all, "in an age far removed—"

"Can't ye bloody fast-forward to the imp'rtant part?" Peg-leg asked, rubbing his face.

Plank waited, jaw clenched.

Peg-leg rolled his eyes. "Oh hurry up then."

"—there lived the god of souls, a creature with a curved beak as large as our ship."

"*It's the lack of plaus'bility that always gets me*," Locks whispered to Stubby.

Plank only spoke louder. "His wingspan was so great that if he had the inkling—and he often did—the god of souls would beat his wings and create powerful storms to crush all who displeased him. They called this god—"

Ebba shot her hand up. "Thunderbird."

"Is this your story?" Plank demanded. "Is it?"

She jumped, staring at him. "Sorry."

Her father regained his composure after several deep breaths, saying, "They called this god 'thunderbird.' He was a power of the oblivion, in charge of guiding those souls that were more good than bad to rest within birds so that they could soar through the ages as reward for the lives they'd lived."

Every pirate knew that birds contained the souls of those passed, but she hadn't known there was a winged thing in charge of the process.

Ebba leaned forward. "Where does the god live?"

Plank faltered. "Uh. I think—"

"He don't know," Peg-leg said flatly. "Fraud."

"*—he lived in the sky with all the other birds*," Plank said through clenched teeth.

Peg-leg grunted.

Barrels had returned his attention to the map a while ago, but he glanced up. "I don't suppose you know the frequency, duration, and average swell height of the storms he creates? We'd be foolish to disregard his presence after seeing so many magical creatures, but solid facts would do us greater benefit than . . . your story."

Plank sucked in a breath, crimson flushing his face.

Ebba cast a look at Grubby's stricken face and quickly asked, "Do ye know what displeases him, Plank? If we can be avoidin' that, we might be able to get through."

"Aye," he answered haughtily. "I do. The thunderbird will use his storms to kill anyone who has sought war on his souls."

She wasn't alone in looking at him blankly.

"Anyone who has killed a bird," he said, sighing.

Ebba sagged. "Phew, well, I ain't done that."

Her fathers added their nays to hers. Everyone knew killing birds was a dreadful sin. No pirate worth their salt would do it.

Caspian's brow was wrinkled. "You know, I don't believe I have. I've hunted pig and deer but I can't recollect having slain a bird."

They all turned to Jagger.

He returned their scrutiny, blank faced. "I've lost count of the birds I've killed."

Ebba groaned with the others. "Of course ye have."

"We eat fowl in the tribes. Our customs are different from your own."

"I've got a woman waitin' for me. If ye kill us, laddy, I'll be comin' back as a taloned eagle to claw yer face to shreds." Locks promised, emerald eye blazing.

Stubby snorted, clapping him on the back. "Ye ain't comin' back as a bird, matey. That's just for the good people."

Locks paused. "Aye," he admitted with a grin.

Her other fathers laughed.

"I could be goin' for a swim to see if I can talk to my selkie kin," Grubby said hesitantly. "They may be knowin' some stuff. And Jerry said he'd keep in touch about what's happenin' on Zol."

Jerry was one of his octopus friends. "Huh," Ebba mused. "That'll be handy-like."

"See? Even Grubs thinks yer stories are shite. He's offerin' to go get *facts*." Peg-leg nudged Plank, who turned stiffly and stormed off, disappearing through the bilge door.

Barrels waited until he was gone before sidling closer to Grubby. "My dear fellow, going for a swim is a grand idea. . ."

Ebba wasn't sure how she felt about anyone going in the water as they neared the Dynami Sea. Who knew what lurked under the surface.

She pursed her lips, glancing at the thunderbird label directly before them. "This map can't be ac'urate, can it? Odds are we won't even see the god o' souls."

No one replied, and she couldn't blame them.

Even *she* couldn't pretend that well.

⌛

SHE'D SAILED through bad waters in her time. The tropical climate of the free seas, where they'd always roamed, brought all the drawbacks of humidity with it—cyclones, sudden and violent storms, torrential rain that could last days without breaking.

But this.

Somewhere in the early evening of the previous day, she'd felt a ripple run over her skin, an awareness that something had changed, a warning from her body that all was not right, even if her mind couldn't fathom a literal change. At first glance, the black seas before them were no different from the turquoise waters they'd left behind. On closer inspection, a creeping feeling settled upon her, lingering in her ears like a vicious whisper. This sea was no more barren to the naked eye than her home sea, yet it seemed exponentially so: void and bleak, empty of life.

The wind didn't groan; it whistled high in a breathless scream. The sun was far overhead, but the rays of light brushing the backs of her hands felt strangled of heat. Normally, in the middle of the day, rivulets of sweat would be running down her neck and back, yet she was barely perspiring.

The sea spray was like shards of ice as the ocean waves slapped against *Felicity*'s bow.

They'd entered the Dynami Sea.

Peg-leg eyed the ocean ahead, shuddering. "We need to be walkin' on tiptoes here, lass."

She nodded absently. If they could sneak in and out of the Dynami with the next piece, all the better. "Aye, it makes me want to have my pistol out and cocked. Like somethin' be ready to jump out at us. Or like *Felicity* is bein' watched by things deep underwater."

"I hear ye," her father said. "Ye know better than to cock a pistol ye ain't sure to use, though."

Ebba shot him a look. "I was just sayin'."

"Aye, aye, I know. But while we're talkin' of such things, I've been meanin' to say that the next time ye hold a dagger to a man's throat who be fair taller than ye, hold a second dagger to his inner thigh. There be a fat artery there, as ye know, and the two daggers'll deter him compl'tely where the one dagger might not."

Ebba glanced at the cook who was rubbing his knee. "Ye think Jagger could've gotten free yest'rday?"

"Aye, I do. He's a freakish tall fellow."

That he was. No wonder he slept on deck—he'd need to dangle his legs over the side of the hammocks, anyway. But Ebba wondered if that was the only reason Jagger had opted to caulk up here. Down in the sleeping quarters the other day, he'd been so cagey. And long ago, he'd once told her that fresh air and staying above deck helped him evade the taint.

Was Jagger coping with the taint still within him? He seemed outwardly okay. And even if he wasn't, Jagger didn't strike her as the kind of person who'd want to sit down and chat about his dark feelings.

More importantly, she wasn't impressed by the notion that he might have humored her yesterday by not turning the tables and extinguishing her attempt to put him in his place. Peg-leg was right. Next time—because she had zero doubts there would be a next time with that pirate—she'd use the second dagger. If he moved, she'd open up his artery and let all his grog spill out.

She cackled aloud, drawing Peg-leg's curious gaze.

Water burst upward and, despite knowing Grubby had gone for a swim, Ebba had to force a squeal down as he flopped on deck, soaking wet and clothed in just his slops. This sea had her sails pulled too tight.

"Find anything?" Plank shouted from the mast.

Her selkie father always took a minute to stand after a swim. Ebba thought it might be his skull reminding his body it was human and not seal—even though he didn't have enough selkie in him to transform.

When he stood, Grubby's face was ashen.

She rushed to him alongside Plank and Peg-leg. Her fathers gripped each of his arms, steadying her selkie parent.

"What happened, matey?" Ebba bit her lip, insides twisting. "What did yer selkie kin say?"

"Th-they said to turn around."

Peg-leg huffed. "Did ye tell 'em we had to go in? They already knew that we were goin' to the Dynami Sea."

Grubby's face screwed up even as his teeth chattered. "N-nay, they didn't," he said. "Forgot to mention it afore we left."

Plank ambled over from the opposite bulwark, carrying Grubby's discarded tunic from before the swim. "They say why we can't go in?"

"Nay, I could only just hear 'em," Grubby said, accepting the tunic from Plank. "They were sayin' not to go in and then cut out."

"Was Jerry there?" Peg-leg asked.

Grubby shook his head, teeth chattering. "Nay, he'll take a bit to catch up. Said he might turn followin' us into a family trip—smooth things over with his wife after the affair with Roger."

They took a moment to absorb that.

Plank raised his brows. "What else did ye see down there, Grubs? What has ye so shaken?"

Her selkie father paled all over again. "Uh . . . uh. . . ."

"Spit it out," Peg-leg pressed.

"Red eyes," he blurted, trembling.

. . . Red eyes. Ebba shared a glance with the others.

Grubby's lip trembled. "Tentacles."

"Like yer octopus friends?" she asked. The smile faded as her father frantically shook his head.

"Giant tentacles," he clarified.

That . . . didn't sound great.

Plank wrapped an arm around Grubby, throwing them a worried look over his head. "Come on then, matey. Let's get ye dry and put some grog in ye."

When Grubby got like this, it was best to give him time to settle.

"Did I help?" her selkie father asked, glancing at them.

"I can't be the only one who sees how much yer selkie blood helps us survive, m'hearty," Peg-leg answered drily.

He beamed and walked off to the hold with Plank.

Ebba whacked Peg-leg's gut once they were gone. "His selkie blood has helped us, ye know—to get out of Selkie Cove *and* to help me get away from *Malice*."

The cook shrugged. "Aye, I know. Be nice to know more about what we were headed into is all. I don't like puttin' ye in danger."

"And I don't like puttin' any of *ye* in danger. But we've been in danger and always pulled through." Not that they'd ever been in the Dynami Sea. And not that any pirate had ever come out. But she kept silent on those counts.

He smiled, ruddy cheeks pushing up as he did so.

"Do ye want me to get the turmeric salve?" Ebba asked Peg-leg as he grimaced and rubbed his knees again.

Peg-leg sighed, extending his leg with a heartfelt groan. "Nay, lass. I'll be fine. Ye know the limb don't do well in the humidity, but it does worse in the cold." He glanced up at the seemingly blazing sun, a wrinkle between his brows as he continued rubbing.

Ebba glanced around the deck.

Caspian, Barrels, and Stubby were absent, down in the office studying the map further. Jagger was up in the crow's nest, healing his face and making sinister plans. Plank and Grubby were in the hold, and Locks was hammering away down at the helm, fixing something that likely didn't require fixing to keep Stubby off his back. And better for Locks to be kept busy—or he'd break into one of his ballads about how much he missed Verity and the curves of her body and drinking copious amounts of tea.

She wrinkled her nose.

"I lost my leg in a sea battle against the navy while on *Eternal*," Peg-leg said suddenly.

Ebba turned back to him, eyes rounding.

Peg-leg smiled at her surprise, saying, "I be thinkin' it's about my turn to be tellin' ye my past, nay?"

Did she want to know? Aye. Though her reasons had changed. Before, Ebba demanded her fathers come clean because they'd broken her trust—or so she'd thought at the time. Now, after *Malice* and everything since, Ebba understood, *really* understood, why they couldn't tell her the whole of their time sailing with Mutinous Cannon. The taint was still within them, dealing out all its dark whisperings of self-hatred and doubt.

"Ye can, if that's what ye feel like. But ye don't have to," she answered, watching him for any sign of real reluctance. She wouldn't put it past her other fathers to be blackmailing Peg-leg into talking.

"It be time," he said, taking a deep breath. "As I was sayin', ye know a cannon shard caught me below the left knee. The Battle for the Seas had been goin' on for twenty years by that point, and King Montcroix was slowly winning. But where most other pirates had fallen or were scamperin' inland to wait for a change in tide, Mutinous refused. He'd never lost a fight, and this was no different. We lost many lives that day, though sink me if I even gave a single thought to them at the time, so gone to the blackness I was—"

"It was the taint," Ebba reminded him firmly.

He lifted his gaze to her. "Aye, lass. I know."

Ebba interpreted the tone to mean his mind knew, but not his heart and not his soul.

"My leg was about fifty-fifty as to whether it'd heal or need chopped off," Peg-leg continued. "But when I was wounded, the pain knocked me clean out. I'd been operatin' a cannon, and when I blacked out, it left a gap in our defenses. Those we lost were lost because of that, including the captain's first mate."

Ebba had a feeling what happened next was going to be about as sickening as Locks' and Barrels' stories.

"Aye, the odds were fifty-fifty, but Mutinous took matters into his own hands and ordered my leg amputated."

She gasped, covering her mouth.

"He made Locks do it, and thank the oblivion he did, lass, for there were others onboard who wouldn't have cared half so much about the job they did."

Her mouth hung ajar, and she could only stare at Peg-leg at that startling piece of information. *Locks* had taken his leg off? "How is it ye don't hate him for that?"

Peg-leg paused in rubbing his knees to stare at the enlarged and worn left joint that bore his weight through the wooden peg strapped in place under his slops.

"I wouldn't have put it past the other men in the crew to take off much more o' my leg than was needed," he said. "They might've even missed and murdered me on the sickbed. Nay, if I was black against Locks it was for a short while only. Maybe only one or two years."

Ebba snorted and Peg-leg winked at her.

"Then what happened?" she urged, leaning forward to prop her elbows on her knees.

Peg-leg thought a moment. "Well, then Stubby was promoted to first mate. And another pirate became second mate, a position I was bein' vetted for afore."

"Is that why the two o' ye are so comp'titive?" Her eyes narrowed.

He lifted a shoulder. "We were always buttin' heads, lass. It don't mean he ain't my crew. And compared to how we were on *Eternal,* the odd spat we have now ain't nothin'. Truth be told, I wouldn't've been a lot of use in those first months after my leg was takin'. Mutinous thought I'd died, and I likely have Locks to thank for that too. When I limped out onto deck for the first time, Cannon's ire was quick-like to recall what I'd done."

Ebba gritted her teeth. "Ye didn't do anything but black out because ye were wounded."

"Aye, but ye can't be reasonin' with a madman. My pos'tion on the ship went from one o' his top crewmates to bottom o' the barrel. He made it known I was the low of the low and any job the other mates didn't want to be doin' could be mine. I was lost to the taint long afore that moment; my mind all a haze, like I was always drunk and stumblin' about, my head ringin' so hard I couldn't recall what was good or bad, just that I should keep breathin'. But whatever I'd done afore that moment—and there was a lot o' bad—I'd never lost pride in myself and what I could do. After losin' my leg, and when Cannon began humiliatin' me, my pride was taken, lass. I couldn't climb the riggin' anymore, which didn't help, but a pirate can only take so much brutality afore they crack-like." He broke off to swallow, blinking several times.

He hung his head. "I cracked, and the whole crew were witness to it. I cried. I'd be cleanin' out the poop at the back of the ship or scrubbin' the deck or throwin' dead bodies over the side of the ship, some o' them so decayed they fell apart in my hands, and I'd cry and cry and cry. My body would shake; great sobs that built in my chest and came out as wailing sounds. The crew thought it were right funny. They'd laugh and jeer, Mutinous joinin' in when he liked, and for the life o' me, lass, I could never fight back or think o' a word to hurl at their heads."

Ebba reached out her hands to grip his trembling ones. She could barely look at her father's hurt straight on, but he was talking, and she would listen. Her fathers had carried their burdens for far too long, and Ebba was determined to relieve them of all the sadness she could. They'd never forget, but she'd settle for their memories fading. If something happened to her, her crew couldn't fall apart. She wanted to know they were okay enough within themselves to continue being a family in her absence. Who knew what awaited them in the Dynami.

He wiped at his eyes. "When Ladon said Mutinous broke my

pride, he was right. It was broken long ago, and try as I might, I can never be rid o' the doubt I'll ever get it back."

"That be the taint talkin'," she replied. "Ye said no person could take endless brutality. I would've cracked as surely as ye did; so would any o' our crew, or any pirate. Ye put too much shame on yerself for yer reaction to their cruelty. When I cry, my tongue gets tangled up, too. And so what if ye cried and shook? I can't be thinkin' ye care what any o' that crew, barrin' those who left with ye, thought."

Peg-leg held her hand and her gaze. He appeared faintly bemused. "Aye, I guess I don't. They be dead and gone anyway. Though in the early days, it was hard that my co-parents had seen me at my lowest."

"If it were yer lowest, then there only be one direction to go," Ebba quipped, smiling at him. Another idea came to her. "What about Mutinous?" she asked. "Did ye care what he thought?"

He stilled, his grip tightening on her hands. She glanced up and saw the downward turn of his mouth.

"Mutinous was . . . a terrible, cruel man. A man filled with a dark power, as we now know was the taint. But I'd be lyin' if I didn't admit I always envied his ambition, his fearlessness, his det'rmination. I s'pose because those were the things I lost when my leg was taken from me. How much I wish I could look Cannon in the eye one last time, defiant, or after bestin' him in some way. And I wish I could say with cert'inty that I was capable o' that but," he said with a frown, "there be a doubt within me, even with him dead these last sixteen years or more. I still don't know if I'd be strong enough."

Ebba felt nothing but relief that Mutinous eventually became fish fodder. *One* Pockmark—if he was still alive after she'd brought a stairwell down on his head—was bad enough. To meet an older version of him would be terrifying.

"Thank ye, Peg-leg. I'm glad ye told me."

"Aye, Ebba-Viva," he said quietly, the lines around his eyes never appearing deeper than now. "And I'm glad to have done so."

The thin strands of Locks' voice reached them from the helm.

She groaned, recognizing the ditty and Locks' droning, long-winded rendition of it.

Her golden hair of woven sunlight
Her skin of pearls and clouds
Her eyes of life, forever young
Her voice, hope in fog's shroud.

Her body be silken happiness
Her toes a pirate's dream
Her smile, a beam of truth and will
Her anger makes lesser men scream.

"Should've left him behind." Peg-leg grimaced, standing with a moan.

"Bad songs and all, he be part o' the crew," Ebba replied. She'd never liked when her fathers were separated from each other, and it was no different now. In fact, the notion of six of them entering the Dynami and the seventh remaining behind made her feel faintly sick.

She jerked violently as a ball of white light bolted from the bilge door straight for her face. Sally. Clutching her chest, Ebba watched the squeaking sprite. They hadn't spoken yet after the whole 'help Jagger destroy Ladon' thing—not that they'd ever spoken, really.

The wind sprite was windmilling her arms, eyes wide as her wings flapped frantically at her back.

Peg-leg spoke to her. "Aye, Sal, I don't be likin' Locks' singin' either, but better that than speakin' to him about Verity. The songs are only ten minutes long, the convers'tions at least an hour."

Sally slapped her forehead. Placing her hands on her hips, the sprite observed them.

Ebba waited, pushing back an errant dread as it whipped across her face. She slid her red bandana of the day backward from her forehead and wrapped it three times around the middle of her hair to confine her dreads in the swelling wind.

The sprite's expression brightened, which was saying something when she was a glowing creature to begin with. Sally placed one hand in front of her mouth, moving her hand in a talking motion, and the other arm she extended out to one side to flap.

Peg-leg leaned over, whispering, "Ye hid the brandy, didn't ye, lass?"

Ebba hummed. "Just marked lines on the bottles."

Sally moved around in circles, making wave motions. As the sprite pretended to die, Ebba said to her father, "When should we tell Sally we know she means the thunderbird?"

The sprite, hovering in thin air on her back, sat bolt upright, glaring at them.

Ebba snorted with Peg-leg.

But a thud from behind cut their chuckling short. She spun as Jagger unfolded to his full height after jumping off the rigging.

"Giant bird," he said mildly. "Up ahead."

TEN

"Do ye have the magic with ye?" Locks asked Ebba.

The shout had gone up. Everyone was on deck now as they sailed closer to where Jagger saw the thunderbird a few minutes before.

She placed a hand over the *dynami*. "Aye."

Glancing behind, she saw Caspian and Jagger both had theirs. The *dynami* seemed like the only part of the weapon that might be helpful for what lay ahead, but maybe the others would be useful—the *purgium* had with Ladon, after all. Or maybe the thunderbird desperately wanted to know a secret and would let them pass with a short hold of the *veritas*.

Sally floated over to her, and Ebba narrowed her eyes. *Nuh-uh.* Jagger had faced his punishment, and the crew had reverted back to treating him as they always had—with wariness bordering on rudeness. However, Sally hadn't been punished. Ebba wasn't yet ready to forgive the sprite, even if the realm was free of Ladon.

Shoulders dropping, the sprite flew to Jagger instead, and perched on his shoulder.

Traitor.

Felicity lurched forward, and their crew spread themselves out on the deck before the mast, her fathers in a row before her.

Ebba peeked over their shoulders and gasped at her first sight of the creature descending from the dark clouds in the distance.

The thunderbird's sheer size stuck her tongue to the roof of her mouth. He demanded attention even from a thousand feet away. And as they sailed closer in the ship, his wingspan blocked out everything behind him.

The massive bird continued to lower until it hovered just over the water. The thunderbird's feathers had the same pearly sheen as the one beneath the surface of the tubes, a sight Ebba had learned to attribute to the presence of magic.

But that wasn't the weirdest thing. . . .

"How is he hovering above the water without beating his wings?" Caspian breathed.

"No notion," she whispered back. "But we should be glad he ain't flappin', if the story o' his storms be true." Though the bird wouldn't need to create a storm to finish them—he could simply bite *Felicity* in half by the looks. The god of souls' beak was hooked with a wicked and sharp appearance.

Her head tilted farther and farther until *Felicity* bumped against the creature's feathered stomach. No one uttered a word as the thunderbird's enormous height cast the deck in thick shadow.

Ebba's head was almost fully craned, her hand on the hilt of her cutlass.

As if they stood any chance against this creature.

"Mortals," the god of souls spoke, tucking his wings tight against his sides.

Her heart jumped into her mouth at the sound of the creature's voice. Though not a particularly beautiful sound, the timbre of it shot like an arrow directly under her ribs. She gasped, pressing a hand over her heart.

Lifting her head, Ebba saw the rest of the crew were in a worse state. Some of them hunched or doubled over.

The thunderbird's eyes flicked to where Sally sat upon Jagger's shoulder. The gigantic bird inclined his head to the sprite in a nod and then blinked, directing a narrowed stare through the ship deck for a lengthy moment.

"Mortem," the thunderbird hissed.

Uh . . . what?

"You carry a feline aboard your ship?" the god of souls continued.

Barrels shared a look with them. "Yes, thunderbird. We do. He is our ship cat."

"We can give him to ye if ye're inclined to let us pass," Stubby blurted, ignoring Barrels' gasp of horror.

The god of souls lifted his gaze to them once more, tilting his head all the way to the right. "You seek entry into immortal waters."

Immortal waters?

"We seek entry into the Dynami Sea," Stubby puffed, half doubled over from the effect of the god's voice.

The thunderbird blinked, but Barrels was quick to intercede.

"In this age, the waters of the Exosian realm are named the Caspian Sea and the east side is the Dynami Sea. We did not know these were immortal waters."

"Both mortals and immortals were and are free to reside where they like. The Dynami Sea is harsh, and mortals gravitated to the easier climate on the west side of this world, leaving the east waters free for marine immortals to live."

The god of souls hadn't attacked them and was offering information freely. That felt like a good sign.

"Are there a lot o' marine immortals here at the moment?" Plank asked, a pained edge to his voice.

"Those who wish to be, yes. Magic has only recently returned to this world. Most are yet to trust this development, preferring to wait. Only the courageous or the foolish—or those drawn to mortals—have chosen to come here."

Ebba wasn't so sure she like that last part.

The creature preened its great wings with a small shake. A gust surged from the god in a wall. With a cry, Ebba was lifted off her feet and flung backward.

Her palms hit the deck with a stinging slap before she entered into a bruising roll across the wood. Her frenzied tumble was halted when she bowled into someone already jammed against the hull.

She coughed and scrambled to extract her limbs from Jagger's, shoving his warm hands from her waist as he tried to help her up.

Her fathers groaned, pushing back to their feet. She hurried over to help Barrels up, marveling at the immortal's strength; a single shake of the thunderbird's feathers sent them *sprawling*. No wonder the bird didn't flap its wings to stay above the surface.

Fear tingled under Ebba's ribs, and a newfound—and *healthy*—respect swept through her. The kind of monstrous storm the god of souls was capable of creating was not one she wanted to be caught in.

"The test is simple, mortals, but you must be sure you wish to take it?" the thunderbird said, tilting his head to the side to peer at them once more.

Ebba shifted her feet wide and braced herself to avoid hitting the deck a second time. But the movement of the creature's head didn't send her flying. The storm-making quality seemed confined to the bird's wings.

She didn't want to anger him but dared to ask, "If anyone can live where they like, why do ye need to test mortals afore they enter?"

"I test anyone who passes this point, be it west or east, mortal or immortal. I test because there must be consequences for those who disrupt the peaceful afterlife of a deserving soul."

Beside her, Plank froze. "Yer vessels? Souls from this realm, ye say? They go on?"

Ebba shot him a look. Why was he asking stupid questions? They already knew that.

The thunderbird inclined his head. "This world and others. If none aboard your ship have killed the vessel of a light soul, then you may pass."

Ebba threw a glare at Jagger, who appeared uncommonly serious as he gripped the hilt of the sword. Was the *veritas* telling him he was about to die?

Most likely.

Plank and Peg-leg exchanged a look.

"All right, thunderbird," Locks said with a low bow. "We would like to pass. How will ye test us?"

"Oh," the bird said, slanted eyes glinting. "That is the easy part. But are you certain you will not turn back? Can you speak for *all* onboard?"

Stubby raised a hand. "Just to be clear-like, will we have the option to throw a person overboard if it be just one or two o' us that fail?"

The thunderbird contemplated this, tilting his head to bird-like angles again. He spoke, and Ebba winced anew at the jolt to the space under her ribs. Was that her soul reacting to the god? She had no idea, but it didn't feel good—which might mean she should re-evaluate her life choices.

The god surveyed them, the thin light reflecting off his pearly feathers. "If the number of you who pass the test is greater than the number who fail, I will allow you to be rid of those to save your own lives."

Ebba frowned. "But won't that make our soul rot? I don't want to pass now, only to fail when I'm sorted into the good or bad pile in the oblivion later."

The god's slanted eyes shot to her, making her regret speaking. Suddenly, Ebba was far less sure of whether she'd killed a bird in the past.

"Killing a person does not determine your soul, brown child."

Brown child! Her jaw dropped.

"It is how you kill, why you kill, what you do after you kill, and your remorse for misdeeds that are weighed. And as long as there are consequences to those who kill my vessels, I care not in which form it takes."

He was mighty protective of these vessels. More so than he cared for mortals, anyway. Ebba smelled a double-standard, but she had a feeling mentioning that might leave them with a one-way ticket to oblivion. And seeing as she wasn't one for too much remorse, Ebba supposed she'd be going to Davy Jones' locker anyway. Better not anger the big bird and get there sooner.

"Enough." The thunderbird snapped its beak and pulled back its wings.

Felicity pitched at the tiny movement, her bow fully lifting off the ocean with the resultant drag forward. Ebba crouched to steady herself with a hand on the deck seconds before the ship landed with a slapping explosion of water.

She still landed on her butt—as did everyone else by the sounds of her fathers' groans, louder this time.

Ebba got to her feet a second time, ignoring Jagger's grunt as she removed her elbow from his gut.

"Will you turn back, or will you be tested?" the creature asked, his eyes sliding over *Felicity* and their crew.

Stubby rubbed his butt, wincing. "If we turn around, can we enter the Dynami Sea from somewhere farther north?"

The god's eyes flared. "I am found in the heartline of this realm, no matter where a being crosses."

Ebba's heart thundered in her ears as she, alongside the others, stared into the immortal's great orbs, now filled with a rainbow of different hues.

"Yer eyes remind me o' the Earth Mother," she mumbled, standing utterly entranced by the swirling midst of the thunderbird's eyes.

"The Earth Mother," the god repeated coolly. "Do not insult me, infant."

Ebba couldn't be certain if she preferred 'infant' or 'brown child' more. "But ain't she a power o' the oblivion too? Just like ye?"

"*I* care for the light souls and banish the dark souls to the corner where they belong. What *I* do rewards those who have earned peace and exacts darkness on those who have caused chaos. *I* maintain balance in the abyss. The Earth Mother merely creates on a whim and thwarts my efforts to punish her original people for killing *my* vessels. If she put a bit more effort in and didn't stand in the way, maybe there wouldn't be so many twisted souls filling the abyss. More and more of them." The god cut off, eyes sparking.

Ebba was inclined to think she'd stumbled on a sore spot for the thunderbird. "Do ye think more bad souls be comin' to ye because o' the six pillars?"

The thunderbird stilled. "How come you to know of the pillars of six?"

She lifted a shoulder. "They're takin' over the seas and land west o' here as we speak. The Earth Mother said all sorts about how they'd been evil and why me and my fathers had to stop them." At the time, Ebba hadn't cared one jot about destiny although the foretelling painting of her in the sacred caves on Pleo had always stayed with her. Now, Ebba very much wanted to know just why her crew was entangled in this mess.

"You're the ship of mortals destined to meet the pillars?" The creature seemed doubtful. "Papatuanuku has told me of you."

And likely not in a favorable light. Perhaps they'd botched saving the realm so far, so she could blame the two powers for their doubt. Their crew had just lacked . . . commitment. "Can ye tell us why we were chosen?"

"You were chosen. The root of magic has always been in control of such things. The Earth Mother can see what is possible, but the root of magic selects the path that is *apparently* best for it."

Ebba glanced at the *dynami*. She wasn't sure it hadn't been the other way around. They were the ones who'd embarked on the quest in the first place. The root of magic hadn't chosen them. Or it didn't seem that way.

Jagger stepped forward. "Ye said *you* were chosen. Did ye mean Ebba or the whole crew?"

The thunderbird frowned. "The brown child was selected by her two counterparts, clearly. Such a mortal always comes with a . . . crew. Is that what you called it?"

And with the way the beam of light shot out of her, Jagger, and Caspian, Ebba could wager a guess who the two other counterparts were. Again, Ebba really didn't see that as true. She and Caspian had met by chance. And Jagger was only here because they took him hostage for a different reason months ago.

But something else occurred to her. "I don't suppose ye'd be lettin' us pass, seeing as we're tryin' to save the realm and all from the pillars?"

She caught Peg-leg's approving look but kept her face impassive.

"No," the creature answered, deflating her hopes immediately. "Do not seek to thwart the rules. I do not care who you are. There *must* be consequences for those who kill my vessels. Your crew had chosen not to turn back. And now you shall face my test."

Ebba took a breath.

"I demand that all here look into my eyes," the immortal said softly. "Do not look away, for that I shall consider a failure also."

She shared a long glance with her fathers and Caspian. As one, they faced the thunderbird again.

Ebba clenched her hands before peering straight into the bird's left eye.

The rainbow swirling in his eyes was moving faster, *faster*. Ebba wavered on her feet as the sight of the rapid circling threatened to unbalance her. A pain stabbed in the area under her ribs, but the needling sensation spread out across her chest, across her torso, and up her neck to fill her skull.

Her eyes watered, and she struggled to maintain her stare into the thunderbird's eyes.

Just as a scream hovered on the edge of her lips, the pain stopped.

Ebba staggered forward, still not daring to break her stare with the god of souls. She dragged in a long, hitched breath.

The swirling in the creature's eyes slowed until eventually they were once more lazy currents of rainbow hues. "Pass," the thunderbird said to her.

The immortal worked down the row of her fathers, dropping each pirate to their knees during the test. But he announced a pass for each of them.

"Pass," he said to the prince next, who hadn't uttered a single word nor shown much pain during the test. Guess all landlubbers were 'deserving souls'.

A glance at the prince showed his amber eyes were huge and fixed on the god of souls. Unlike the rest of *Felicity*'s crew, he hadn't glimpsed a more fearsome magical creature than a selkie or sprite yet. Ebba probably looked like that when she first saw Ladon.

The thunderbird peered at Sally afterward, and his eyes softened. "Pass," he announced in a ringing voice.

"Should probably check her again," Ebba muttered under her breath, shooting the sprite a glare.

Sally scowled at her.

The god of souls focused lastly on Jagger, and the bird's eyes flared as he spoke a single word.

"Fail."

ELEVEN

Ebba covered her ears as the thunderbird's roared screech speared through her. The god reared back to his full height. And then she was flying through the air again.

In a ball, she smacked against the bulwark and, this time, she stayed down.

"You have killed many of my vessels, mortal. I could glean but little from your soul, but the pieces I saw were riddled with the hunting of my flock," the bird said, and the sound echoed like thunder.

Lightning flashed in the distance.

Jagger had landed away from her this time. He spoke from closer to her feet. "It is customary for my tribe to eat birds."

"Good one, eejit," she whispered to him. *Tell the ginormous bird that you eat his family.*

Did that mean all tribespeople went to Davy Jones? Seemed harsh. Ebba had never killed a bird, but she'd sure eaten them when they brought fowl from the markets.

"To kill my vessels is a grave offense, even if the Earth Mother deigns to protect her 'original people,'" the god declared in a terrible voice. This time the thunder was closer.

Jagger was one of the original people? Ebba's mouth rounded in an 'O' as she connected that 'original people' meant tribespeople.

Three bolts of lightning struck the water around the ship, bursting on impact into millions of white currents that flittered out across the water. Ebba couldn't say much for the fish in the water, but unless the bolts hit the actual ship, the crew would be fine.

Still flat on her back, Ebba scanned the gathering black clouds above that had blotted out the afternoon sun. Her stomach clenched with foreboding.

"Fail," the thunderbird bellowed again.

"Ye said we could throw him overboard," Stubby said hastily.

From where he was kneeling close to the hull between three of her sprawled fathers, Caspian hissed at them, "He has to live. We need him to find the next part."

Shite, they did need him. But that was her second thought.

The *first* thought was panic at the thought of Jagger leaving the ship. And that . . . surprised her. A lot.

Ebba wasn't sure if the mean way he sometimes acted was due to the taint or because he was *actually* cruel. Yet she wanted to be sure his meanness wasn't from the pillars' power before any overboard-throwing went on. Was that why panic had surged within her at Stubby's comment?

Sally zipped from the hull to the bow and rose higher and higher until she hovered before the god of souls.

"What is she doing?" Barrels asked from where he was hunched by Ebba's head.

"Dancin'?" Grubby offered, the only one on his feet again.

He wasn't that far off.

Sally's arms waved in the air, and Ebba felt safe assuming the sprite would be squeaking up a storm. Except the thunderbird was nodding and shaking his feathered head at intervals like the dance made complete sense to him.

She sat up against the bulwark.

"He understands her," Jagger said, shuffling closer to Ebba.

"Get away from me," she replied out the corner of her mouth. "He's about to kill ye."

Sally descended back to the ship where she perched once more on Jagger's shoulder. The sprite peeked at the pirate through her lashes and Ebba noticed a pink tinge spreading across her cheeks.

Why was Sal blushing at Jagger?

Ebba narrowed her eyes on the pair. The sprite couldn't . . . Sally couldn't fancy Jagger, could she? She sniggered under her breath, waving off Jagger's inquiring glance.

The thunderbird spat, "The queen of the wind sprites assures me that the *Jagger* is not what he seems."

Hold on a salty second. *Queen?* "What did ye just call Sally?" Ebba demanded.

The god of souls cast her a baffled look, cutting off whatever he was saying.

"That sprite right there?" Ebba jerked a thumb at Sally. "*Queen* of the wind sprites? Yer skull be half emptied o' rum, matey. She ain't nothin' but a boozin' midget with wings."

Ebba turned to glance at Sally, half expecting to be bitten or kicked for the remark. Instead, Sally sat straight, arms folded and chin tilted high. Almost regally.

This had to be a joke. Sally. The queen of the wind sprites.

Plank, on Jagger's other side, was the next to break the stunned silence, aside from the hiss and slap of the waves. "We never realized," he said.

"Then she did not wish you to know," the god of souls answered, still glaring at Jagger.

"No kiddin'," Ebba muttered. The pink tinge on Sally's cheeks deepened.

The thunderbird surveyed them dispassionately. "The queen has informed me that you already possess three pieces of the root, and that the slayer of souls aboard your ship is needed to help guide you to the rest of the parts."

Jagger asked, "Will ye let me pass then?"

The god ignored him. "That is not what interests me, evil infant of the original people."

Ha! She wasn't the only infant.

"The queen has also spoken of your past. Of the ship you sailed upon and *resisted*. Tell me, mortal. How long were you aboard the pillars' ship?"

"One year, eleven months, and twenty-one days."

That was specific. Ebba guessed when each day was horrible, a person would end up counting them. She glanced at Jagger who tensed but otherwise didn't acknowledge her inquiring look.

The thunderbird's rainbow eyes swirled, their light brighter than his brilliant feathers. "And yet, here you stand with your will intact. You also show great resistance to my powers. It is almost unprecedented. Almost."

Jagger didn't reply, and the thunderbird didn't seem to expect one.

"Immune," the god of souls breathed, his feathered head flattening to rest against his chest as though an instinctive reaction to his intrigue.

Ebba straightened. What did that mean?

"What is an immune?" Barrels asked, shifting to sit straighter. "We've never heard the term."

The creature didn't answer, his gaze not erring from where it fixed on the pirate at Ebba's side. Sweat broke out on Jagger's forehead, and he panted under the immortal's intense regard. A pained puff left his lips as the thunderbird continued to pin him with his swirling rainbow eyes.

Ebba was glad Jagger was showing some kind of pain. There wasn't any way Jagger was a nicer person than her.

The god of souls ruffled his feathers, and Ebba was glad she hadn't stood.

Grubby managed to brace himself as the gust shoved across the deck. Caspian thudded to the deck again with a muted *oof*.

"What to do with you," the thunderbird mused, tilting its head once more. "You have killed my vessels. Torn the very souls from them so that they will always be lost in the abyss, dead and gone in truth."

"I did not know that was what I was doing," Jagger said hoarsely.

"You speak truth, yet did you not pause to hear the rich warble of forest birds or stop to smile as they took flight? You beheld the colors under their wings and wondered at their beauty. Still, you sought to kill the thing that brought you gladness."

Jagger bowed his head. "I did."

"Yet you are an immune. *The* immune, and much rests on your fate. There must be consequences, but . . . I find myself uncertain for the first time in eons." He muttered lower, "The Earth Mother would never let me hear the end of it."

Ebba knew the big bird had a serious hang up about his vessels being slaughtered. That was kind of understandable, but she wasn't going to die because he was in a pissing contest with the Earth Mother.

Caspian staggered to his feet, clutching his side, and gasped. "Have you encountered many twisted souls of late?"

"Yes," the creature said, shifting his focus to the prince. "Too much darkness. The place I hold the devoid is only so large. As light souls fly free, the space where I contain twisted souls expands so there is more space to contain them and maintain balance. There must always be balance. If I cannot fill the skies with lightness through my birds, room will run out to hold the others."

"What will happen then?" Grubby asked from the prince's side, his Monmouth cap gripped tight in both hands.

"Then darkness roams free again," the god said with a snap of his beak.

Caspian was deep in thought, a furrow between his brows.

"The taint is spreading unchecked through the realm as we

speak," the prince said, glancing up. "More and more dark souls will come to you, and eventually, no good souls at all. We are on a quest to rid the world of the taint. Perhaps, God of Souls, our interests are aligned more than either of us suspected. We are also working to restore balance of a sort."

She shot a look at Stubby on the starboard side. He lifted a finger to his lips.

Aye, Caspian sounded like he was on to something.

"If we are successful in removing the taint, then your balance of light and dark will also be restored," the prince continued. "If you will not let Jagger continue with us because he is the immune," Caspian stumbled over the term, "please allow him to continue for that reason. As the queen said, we need Jagger to succeed."

"Well of course you do. He's the immune," the god said impatiently, tilting his giant head again. "You forget I know the path your ship is destined to take. Yet the root brought you here, knowing of the judgment I have always dealt to those who killed my vessels. *That* is my dilemma. I do not wish to err and go against the root of magic's design. I could adversely affect the fate of this realm myself."

"Ye know," Peg-leg spoke, "If this be about what other immortals would think, then if we ever came across the Earth Mother, we wouldn't be mentionin' a thing about what happened today. It'd stay secret-like."

"I am not concerned with what *she* thinks."

Sounded like he was. In fact, it sounded like he held this in higher regard than saving the realm. Ebba held her breath, sensing their fate was in his hands. Or his wings.

"However, I shall allow you passage into immortal waters," the god of souls decreed.

The sigh of relief from the crew was audible. Ebba shot Caspian a triumphant look, and he smiled in return, straightening his shoulders.

"Immortal waters, ye say?" Stubby asked.

The thunderbird tilted its head. "Marine immortals have long preferred the quieter and more rugged sea floor of the Dynami. Many have returned here since the wall crumbled. Is that no longer known?"

Another immortal out of touch with the current state of the realm after being locked away. How surprising.

"Nay," she answered. "Sailin' into these parts be considered bad luck by our kind."

"*Bad* luck," the thunderbird repeated, blinking twice. "In times gone by, mortals passed my checkpoint without fear."

Well, she could assume that was a lie. No human who saw the sheer size of the Thunderbird could remain calm.

Locks cleared his throat. "If it be all right with ye, we'll just be on our way then. Out o' yer. . .uh, feathers."

"I was not finished," the thunderbird boomed, "I grant your passage. But on behalf of the Jagger, you will all answer the call of justice. *That* is the condition of your passage."

They all turned to glare at the flaxen-haired pirate, who shrugged a shoulder.

"Three days and three nights of storm," the god of souls said, eyes swirling faster. "Survive *that*, and you may enter the Dynami whenever you should choose. Make haste to set sail, pirates, for soon I shall start the beating of my wings, and you will not wish to be near this place when that happens."

Her fathers didn't need further encouragement. They leaped into action, racing to their stations aboard deck to ready the ship for a magical storm unlike any they'd seen.

Too soon as it turned out.

The thunderbird swept back his right wing, and the sudden motion dragged the ship forward with a violent lurch. Her fathers were thrown to the deck once more as *Felicity* was dragged forward by the pull of the immortal's movement.

The shadows covering the ship gradually receded as the ship floated farther away.

She stood, Caspian and Jagger not far behind, and Ebba didn't pause in running to the helm to peer back at the gigantic god of souls.

"Kill another bird, Immune," the god of souls called after them, his feathered back to *Felicity*, "and I do not care who you are or what you are meant for. Next time, your soul is mine."

TWELVE

Ebba held steady to the bulwark, blinking rain out of her eyes as Locks hurried to the port side and emptied the contents of his stomach.

Dashing away the water on her face again, she returned her attention to the dark and monstrous swell.

The thunderbird hadn't been wrong. They were one day into the storm, and it still grew. She'd never experienced anything of the like. Though no one spoke of drowning or dying before the storm relented, the constant groaning and shrieking of the ship reminded them how much duress the elements were piling upon them. The torrent of rain pounding the deck was barely managing to flood out through the scuppers.

Felicity lurched over the side of another crest and plummeted down into the trough, barely leveling out before the next swell was upon them. The waves towered high over her mast and were becoming steadily higher. There wasn't much point worrying whether the waves would eventually become so high they'd flip *Felicity* back on herself, but that didn't stop Ebba eyeing the constant black wall of water in front of them with an apprehensive lurch in her stomach.

The barrels and buckets on deck were latched down or had been tossed into the hold, Pillage included. The sheets were down and the sails furled. Stubby and Locks were on the wheel, trying to direct the ship straight into the swell.

On the whole, they were at the utter mercy of the thunderbird's storm, adrift to wherever the swell pushed them. Which hopefully wasn't into a nice pile of rocks.

"Time for us to rest, Wobbles," Peg-leg called to Ebba, limping over, one hand clutching the bulwark. "Can ye wake the others when ye go down?"

They were taking the three-day storm in rotations; the rest of her fathers and Caspian already slept below.

"Aye," she said.

Ebba looked up in the direction of the crow's nest where she knew Jagger to be. No pirate enjoyed climbing the shrouds in a storm, let alone a magical bird storm, but Jagger had leaped at the chance. Yet again. . . .

She jumped as lightning struck in the distance and thunder clapped its massive hands overhead. The charcoal clouds churned and swirled, the wind howled and whistled, and the water sucked and shoved in never-ending repetition.

Ebba planted her feet either side of the bilge door. Her legs worked overtime to steady herself as she wrung what water she could from her dreadlocks and clothing.

Sopping wet, with two days to go, but no good would come from whining about it.

She clambered in a water-logged mess down the ladder instead of her usual graceful slide.

Moving to Grubby first, she gently shook his shoulder and then Plank's and Barrels', smirking as she dislodged Pillage from where he was napping on her eldest father.

"Time for yer shift, mateys," she said.

As her fathers climbed up the ladder to the deck, Ebba picked her way to Caspian's hammock. She stopped, scanning the prince's peaceful face. He'd never been in much of a storm. Rain and high wind, but not a fierce storm whose only intention was to send you as a shattered mess to Davy Jones'. Should she wake him?

"Aren't you going to wake me?"

Ebba dragged her eyes to his amber gaze which was fixed on her. She'd been staring at him like a bloody nufty. Had he been awake the entire time? The shadows beneath his eyes and the red streak within them said aye. And even in the soft light of the sleeping quarters, illuminated by the sole lantern fixed in the midst of the hammocks, a green tinge was visible on his skin.

"Ye feel sick?" she asked. "I've lost my stomach twice today. Damn sea got into my boots."

His expression didn't shift. "Ebba, were you going to wake me?"

She blew out a breath. "Aye, I was. If ye'd given me half a minute." Caspian needed to be woken for more reasons than he'd needed to remain asleep. She was worried about his safety on deck now that his balance was going through a rough patch. Yet Ebba didn't want him to feel inadequate or feel that any of the crew felt that way.

Caspian sat, avoiding her eyes. "I gave you half a minute. I gave you two. I won't get in the way. I'll help."

"I know."

He shoved his feet into his boots, tucking in the ends of his tunic single-handedly in short jabbing motions designed not to accidentally push his slops to the deck.

"Good," he said, finally looking at her. "Then I guess you were just staring at me because you find me handsome?"

Caspian half-grinned at her.

Ebba quirked her brows. "Is it flattery ye're after then?"

"You are well aware what I'm after, Mistress Pirate." He stepped closer.

She was. And wasn't. That Caspian held something for her had been established. That he smiled more since they'd kissed also seemed fairly certain. That she thought of his lips too much these days was in that mix as well. The prince teased her right now in a flirty way, not in the way a person teased their friend. The thing was, Ebba might not be opposed to exploring the new waters between them. She was a pirate after all. Except Caspian already felt something for her and had for a while. Even if she wanted to, Ebba wasn't willing to explore the waters and get his hopes up only to maybe decide no and leave him hurting.

The silence extended between them, hardening into a thrumming tension.

She licked her lips, tilting her head back. "I'd like ye to wear a rope out there."

Caspian's face closed down. "Because I have one arm."

Ebba groaned. "No, because ye're harder, but ye're still a flamin' landlubber, Caspian. I don't wish to lose ye over the side."

"Is anyone else wearing a rope?"

"Any o' the pirates? Nay."

"Jagger isn't a pirate. He's tribe."

Being a pirate wasn't so much about where a person was from, it was about their instincts and their movement, and about understanding the sea. Some people got it quick, some slow, and some never. Some people were just royal landlubbers.

"*Please*, Caspian," she said, holding his gaze.

His amber eyes burned. "No, I won't do that. I don't need to."

She threw her hands in the air. "Then ye're a fool."

"That's really what you think of me?" he said, frowning.

"Nay, o' course it ain't." Ebba stomped to her hammock and ignored the prince as he drew alongside her space.

He sighed. "Goodnight."

"Night," Ebba grunted back.

He quietly left, and she shucked her wet outer layers and, lacking any dry ones, wrapped a blanket around herself before falling into the hammock face first.

Sally whirred in question, glancing up to the ceiling.

"Still bad out there, your *majesty*," Ebba said sarcastically.

The thunderbird had to have that wrong. Royalty didn't behave like her pet sprite. She'd met a king and a selkie leader, plus two powers of oblivion, *and* she knew a prince-turned-king. There just wasn't *any* way.

Sally remained silent, swinging in her mini-hammock over Ebba's head. Surprisingly, though the sprite harbored a flame for Jagger, she hadn't set up her hammock above deck to be near him. Maybe, being a queen, Sally was used to certain comforts—such as being out of the elements and close to entire barrels of spiced grog, jars of pickled mangoes. And champagne fountains.

"Why did ye never tell me, Sal?" she asked, safe in knowing Locks, Stubby, and Peg-leg were yet to come down. "After the last month, I feel I don't know ye at all. Do you even like me? Or have ye just laughed behind my back the whole time, turning on me when you liked?"

Sally floated from her hammock to sit cross-legged on Ebba's chest.

She began whirring and squeaking, waving her arms.

"I can't understand ye," Ebba said in frustration. "But I know ye can get a point across when ye wish. How hard is it to mime a crown or sumpin'?"

The sprite looked down at her hands and lifted them to hide her face.

"The thunderbird was right. Ye really didn't wish us to know." Ebba shook her head. "Queen or not, it weren't decent to lead us on. Then again, ye've been doin' a whole heap o' things that ain't decent lately."

Sally's shoulders slumped, but when Ebba didn't relent in the heaviness of her disapproving gaze, the sprite drifted up and hugged her face, delivering the realm's tiniest kiss on her cheek. She lifted back and pointed at her eye, then her heart, and then to Ebba.

I love you.

Ebba sniffed. Damn, that was really, really cute, but she hardened herself against the gesture.

Ebba wanted to give her friend the benefit of the doubt again. In some ways, the sprite was her only confidant, especially now that Caspian was frothing over her. That was why Sally's fickle loyalty hurt so much, perhaps. When Ebba loved a person, she loved them completely and for all time. For whatever reason, Sally didn't have the same standards. Or she didn't love Ebba in the same way.

If the sprite turned tail again, Ebba didn't want to be hurt again.

She didn't return Sally's message, just gazed at her in silence.

The sprite whirred sadly and flew back to her mini-hammock.

Ebba closed her eyes, bitterness singeing her insides. Caspian was angry at her; Sally was disappointed in her. She heaved onto her side and stared at the bottom of the ladder, willing blessed sleep to come.

It was going to be a long night.

⧗

EBBA JOLTED upright at a mighty crack from above.

"Whadsit?" she mumbled, throwing her legs over the side of the hammock.

"Sumpin' went," Stubby muttered hoarsely, already moving too.

The bilge door swung open, and the roar of the storm multiplied ten-fold.

"All hands on deck," Plank bellowed down.

They leaped into action. In less than a minute, Ebba was following Stubby up the ladder, Peg-leg and Locks close behind.

"My ship," Stubby bellowed over the wind. His stance was wide, like hers, to combat the violent lurching underfoot.

The starboard tip of the lowest boom hung on by a few splinters. The broken end of the horizontal beam swung wildly in the gale, threatening to splinter off completely at any moment.

Their sails were already furled, but that wasn't the problem.

The problem was where the beam fell when it fell, who it might take with it, if the falling boom would damage the ship good and proper, and most importantly, *what was attached to the boom.*

The rigging and sheets, lacking their usual anchorage on the broken beam, whipped in the powerful wind, lashing out in the air. One of those ropes across the head or throat and the person would be out for the count. Or carried overboard.

"We can't work with those lashin' about," Locks shouted, watching the ropes whip wildly across the deck.

They had to regain safety on deck if they were getting through this storm. If they couldn't move for fear of being lashed or thrown overboard by the sheets or killed by the falling tip of the boom, they were as good as dead.

Ebba wiped her eyes, dislodging the rain that had already soaked her to the bone. She yelled over the wind to her fathers. "I'll go up and break the broken tip o' the boom off. Best if we decide when it happens. And it'll pull all the loose sheets and riggin' down with it to the deck so we can collect it all up."

No one answered, their wet faces grim.

"Ye know it be the only way," she pressed. Ebba was the best rigger here. And there wasn't any way her fathers were going up there.

"I don't like ye up there in this," Peg-leg called, blinking rain out of his eyes. "The swell is near vertical, lass."

Aye, and it wasn't going to get better.

Plank joined them, skirting wide around the flailing sheets and rigging.

Ebba shouted a warning as the rigging swept across the helm. Barrels, at the wheel, barely managed to duck in time.

Someone was going to die if she didn't do something.

"I'm goin' up," she shouted to them, quelling the rioting school of fish in her gut.

Peg-leg looked ready to argue, but he didn't, snapping his mouth closed instead. He jerked his head in a nod.

"Be careful, little nymph," Plank said loudly, squeezing her forearm. "The loose riggin' ye can see comin', but those sheets are whippin' around fierce-like. Protect yer head."

Avoiding lashing ropes and netting on her way to break off the tip of a broken boom? No trouble.

She exhaled shakily and edged closer to the mast. The ropes swung in a chaos of swirls and snaps, and Ebba poised on the tips of her toes, waiting for her window.

The wind surged, throwing the ropes south to the helm and out of her path. Ebba sprinted to the sole intact rigging left on the port side. The wind battered at her as she scurried up to the boom as quickly as possible, knowing a mistake would likely send her overboard.

Ebba straddled the boom, looking back at the mast, and past it to the other side of the boom where the broken tip still swung.

The wind changed, and *Felicity* suddenly heeled from port to starboard. She yelped, pressing herself flat against the boom and hugging it with all her strength. A rope whistled over her head, skimming her dreads.

Ebba stared down at her fathers with wide eyes until *Felicity* stabilized again. As much as she would anyway.

She had to get to the other side. Quickly.

Ebba dared to lift her head to scan the ropes below. Nothing would be gained from waiting for errant changes in wind. She had a dreadful feeling only luck would determine her success. Keeping flat on the boom, she began to shimmy toward the mast in the center. Rain pelted her back as the wind sought to get beneath her body to pry her off and fling her into the black watery abyss.

In her peripheries, the vertical wall of the next swell loomed. Ebba was only halfway to the mast when *Felicity* began to tilt back, back, *back*, traveling up the side of the wave. She choked on a curse, realizing the tilt of the ship didn't bode well for her at all.

Stopping her shimmy, Ebba locked her arms and legs around the boom to wait out the swell.

The ship navigated the slope of the wave, sailing higher and higher until her angle was almost perpendicular to the sea. Before the swell, Ebba was flat on top of the boom. With *Felicity*'s bow now aimed at the sky that was no longer the case. *Now*, Ebba was supporting her entire body weight and clinging onto the beam for dear life. If she fell while the ship was vertical like this, she'd topple directly into the black waters of the Dynami churning below.

Her arms burned from the effort of holding on as *Felicity* continued up to the peak of the swell. Shite, this wasn't good. Ebba was used to climbing, but even with the help of her legs around the boom, the unabated strain on her arms was not something her muscles were used to. And they were certainly letting her know.

Gasping for breath, some morbid curiosity led Ebba to turn her head. Her eyes widened at the sight of the black ocean looming far, far beneath her.

Just as her arms began to shake, *Felicity* crested the top of the swell and began the stomach-lurching plummet down the other side.

But they were in a storm. That meant huge swell after huge swell. Ebba's arms wouldn't be able to hold out indefinitely. Shuffling frantically, she continued on to the slippery mast and pulled herself upright. She hugged the thick beam and took a deep breath.

She glanced to the starboard side at the splintered tip she'd need to snap off.

Halfway there. She lowered flat again, forcing her complaining arms to pull her out toward the tip.

Scalding pain erupted across her back, accompanied by the *crack* on a sheet as it struck her. Ebba shrieked, blinded from the white spots across her vision.

There wasn't time to regain her senses. *Felicity* began to tilt upward again, up the next swell, and Ebba moaned low through the agonizing hurt.

Through the haze, she had the presence of mind to hook her ankles under the boom, like before. Gripping her hands together under the boom, Ebba attempted to breathe through the fiery pain on her back. She panted, squeezing her eyes shut as the ship tilted vertically. White-hot flames licked her back, and this time, her arms began to shake immediately.

Ebba focused on clinging to the beam, certain that if *Felicity* tilted even one degree farther back, they'd capsize anyway, and it would all be over. The pain in her back was sapping her strength. The shaking in her arms became steadily more violent, and soon, as her upper body fatigued to the point of uselessness, the insides of her thighs began to burn and shake also.

When *Felicity* plateaued this time, Ebba remained gasping for breath, lying still to recover. She couldn't hold on through another one of those.

She couldn't move.

A strong hand gripped her calf. "Come on now, Viva. Up with ye afore the next one be upon us."

Ebba braved the screaming protest in her back to peer wearily over her shoulder at Jagger, who was flat against the boom behind her. He lifted his chin in a 'go on' gesture.

She wasn't alone up here, and that made all the difference. Arms feeling as heavy as leaden weights, Ebba dragged herself forward, somehow finding the strength to oblige the flaxen pirate behind.

During the chaos, Ebba had almost made it to the broken tip of the beam. She assessed the damage to the ship. The end wasn't hanging on by much. She should be able to snap it off.

Checking her fathers were well clear of the area, Ebba, still flat, reached forward and pushed down on the base of the broken section. The swinging tip lowered with her pressure but didn't snap off.

Bugger.

She looked at the looming swell and desperately tried again. "It ain't budgin'," she shouted back at Jagger.

"I'm goin' to pull on it from beneath. Ye push as hard as ye can from the top," he yelled.

She was still processing what he meant when Jagger swung underneath the boom. Willingly. She saw immediately what he intended to do.

Head pointing inward, Jagger monkey-climbed out to the splintered tip, directly below her position. Ebba lifted slightly to let him wrap his arms around the beam under her stomach.

She stole another peek at the next swell. "Quick," she called down.

He lifted his legs and looped them halfway along the broken tip. She flinched as a rope belted close to his head, drawing her reaching hand back when the sheet missed him.

"Push," he shouted.

Gripping on with her thighs, Ebba pushed down on the broken part of the beam with all her might, bellowing wordlessly against the agony in her back.

The boom didn't budge. At first. With a cracking groan, the tip began to respond to their pressure, the remaining tendrils splintering.

She doubled her effort, teeth clenched, feeling Jagger doing the same on the underside.

They were rewarded with an almighty crack as the beam gave way. Devoid of the support of the splintered end, Ebba lurched forward, arms flailing in thin air for one soul-dropping moment. She squeezed the beam with her thighs, managing to arch her upper body back and correct her balance.

The broken tip hit the deck below, taking the flailing rigging and sheets with it. Her fathers began drawing in the lashing ropes without delay.

They did it. She sagged against the boom, exhausted, her back throbbing.

Jagger was still suspended below her, only hanging on with his arms. Ebba hurried to shuffle back so he could swing back on top to join her.

There wasn't time. The next enormous swell was upon them. Ebba felt the change of the ship's angle and panic crowded her chest.

Jagger quickly worked backward and then swung his legs up to grip the underside of the beam just as she was gripping the topside.

He crossed his ankles right in front of her face, and she couldn't have cared less.

Ebba pressed her forehead into the wood and drew in large gulps of air, terror filling her at the immediate burning and shaking in her arms as *Felicity* slanted sharply. She squeezed her eyes shut as her thighs joined in.

"Jagger, I won't be able to hold," she panted his way, fear forcing the admission out of her.

His reply carried to her from where his head was located by her feet. "Ye ain't got a choice, Viva."

"It won't be a choice to let go," Ebba snapped. Or she meant to snap. Instead, she just sounded desperate.

Her arms shook violently. Even as she tried to keep her hands clasped together, to put the pain aside, her grip steadily weakened. Her fingers began to slip even as she willed them to keep her alive.

"Jagger, I'm goin' to fall." Doom clawed at her face, her chest, her mind.

Ebba's hands lost contact. With a terrified scream, she slid off the beam, knowing that if she missed colliding with the hull, the odds weren't great for her to survive the impact with the black ocean below. And if she *did* survive that, she certainly wouldn't survive the storm.

Too scared to make a sound, Ebba plummeted through the air. To her death.

With a fierce roar audible over the crashing, howling storm, Jagger lunged. His hand wrapped around her extended wrist, almost ripping her shoulder from its socket.

She came to an abrupt stop and threw back her head, wide-eyed, to look at him. Past him, the angry sky bore down from above.

"Please don't drop me," Ebba begged him, choking on her panic.

"I'll never drop ye, Viva," he said through gritted teeth. "Never." The muscles in his arm strained through his wet tunic. His other arm and legs remained tight around the remaining section of the boom.

Call her a stupid sod, but Ebba believed him, taint, dubious morals, and all. Tears poured down her face as she swung her other hand up to clasp above his wrist.

The storm swirled around them, but she couldn't hear anything, couldn't *see* anything but his determined, high-boned face as he clung to her and her to him. Her body swung freely in the air beneath him and, oddly, though death was a scant whisper away, there was a peace to the moment. An acceptance that her fate was now in Jagger's hands and that clearly, on some buried level, she trusted him.

He tightened his grip on her hand, staring into her eyes.

"Not far now. Ye'll be okay," he said. His calmness was at odds with the shaking of his arm though.

Yet Jagger proved right again.

Felicity peaked and started the plummet down the other side. The dragging downward pull was gone and Jagger circled himself around the boom, towing her with him. She fell into his arms, chest heaving.

"Ye need to get back down to the deck and get yer back looked at," he whispered in her ear.

Mind buzzing, Ebba pulled back, glancing around her. "One o' the sheets is still lashin' about." She had to make the deck safe. She—

"It's done, Viva," Jagger said. "I'll get this last bit, but if ye're up here with that wound when the next swell hits, ye'll kill us both."

Shock had clouded her judgment. She'd become a liability.

Ebba nodded mutely and extracted her limbs from where they'd tangled with Jagger's. Knowing her arms couldn't haul her back to the rigging on the port side, she braved her shaking legs to run across the boom to the mast and then to the far tip.

Half climbing and half falling, she descended the rope squares to land on deck.

Arms enveloped her, and Ebba screamed. The arms immediately let go.

"Shite, she did get hit," Plank called over her head.

"Where are ye injured, lass?" Stubby asked.

She winced at the stinging wounds on her back and choked out, "Nothin' to be losing yer head over. A sheet got me good."

"Locks," Peg-leg bellowed through the bilge door.

"I'm okay," she said, shaking off their hands.

They weren't taking that for an answer, though. Ebba let herself be tugged to the door, past a white-faced Caspian. If the pain was any indication of the wound, she really should get it looked at.

Just before going through the bilge door, she turned and tilted her head back.

Jagger had secured the last flailing sheet and now crouched by the port-side rigging, peering down at her. Another swell fast approached, but he was seemingly unworried as he held her gaze.

Thank ye, she mouthed at the silver-eyed pirate.

Lightning flashed as he dipped his head.

THIRTEEN

She woke flat on her stomach, a throbbing ache covering her back that was sore but bearable.

"The sheet got you bad."

Ebba cracked open an eye, recognizing the deep voice, and spotted Caspian sitting on the opposite hammock. "Feels like it," she said hoarsely.

"You nearly died," he whispered.

Aye, she had. "Naw," she winked at him. "Just a bit of fun."

Wincing, she swung one leg down and sat in the middle of the hammock. A few of her fathers were slumbering lumps on their creaking hammocks in the sleeping quarters.

"How goes the storm?" By the lurching feel of it, they were still in the thick of it.

"Still the same, but nothing else has broken."

Felicity was holding up. Ebba exhaled slowly. "How long was I asleep?"

"Only six hours or so. Locks put something in your drink to help you sleep. We're part way into the last day of the storm."

Thank the seas for that.

She glanced at Caspian and saw that although he stared at her face, it was like he wasn't seeing her at all. "What's the matter?"

A small furrow appeared between his brown brows. "If I'd been up there with you, I wouldn't have been able to save you. If I'd reached to catch you, I would've lost my hold on the boom. I'm trying to believe that I'm still the same as everyone else, capable of the same things, but it's just not true."

"Ye are; ye just need to do it in a di'ferent way. With a rope, ye could've been secured to the boom and reached to catch me. I don't plan to be in that s'tuation often in the future, matey. And if I am, *I'm* plannin' to use a rope. Foolish o' me not to."

A wry smile twisted his mouth. "If you wear a rope in storms, I will too." He shuddered. "I really thought you were going over the side."

Ebba recalled the swirling black water far below as she'd clung to Jagger's hand. She shivered. "Me too."

Caspian stood and sat on the hammock next to her. He wrapped his arm around her shoulders, and she lifted her right arm to hug him back, grimacing at the twinge between her shoulder blades from the motion.

"I never want to lose you, Ebba-Viva," he whispered.

He so rarely used her actual name. It was always Mistress Pirate this, Mistress Pirate that.

She shifted closer to the heat of his body, relaxing in his arms. "The same to ye. No repeats of any taint shite, please."

His shoulders shook. "Well, hopefully they don't take my other arm if that does happen."

Joking had to be a good sign. "Maybe they'll give ye two more. That'd be a sight."

He choked back a laugh and pulled back. She smiled up at him as he lowered his head and pressed his mouth to hers.

The kiss was over before it had begun, but though his mouth wasn't touching hers any longer, she could still feel where he'd been.

She reached up to touch her tingling lips, staring at him in the dim light.

He'd kissed her again. And the kiss still gave her the same thrill as the first time, forbidden and new.

Caspian waited, watching her.

"What did that mean?" She needed to know what was in his head.

His smile was crooked. "It means my heart nearly stopped when I thought I'd lost you, and I thought I might never get another chance to repeat that night on the beach."

"That was practice," she said. "Ye wanted a repeat?"

"Yes, since we first kissed. But I didn't want to scare you off."

That answer didn't fit like a tunic with no sleeves. Ebba enjoyed that she'd shared her first kiss with the prince, but after the second kiss and his comment . . . she had to set matters straight between them. Or at least understand what their stolen touches meant to him.

"Caspian," she began after making sure her fathers weren't moving. "What does the kissin' mean to ye?"

He dropped his arm from her shoulders and reached down for her hand. Bringing it to his mouth, he gently kissed the back. "You needn't be uncomfortable, Mistress Pirate. You've given me no promises, and I'm fully aware of that. But kissing you ignited something within me. What I feel for you is the most real thing in my life."

Her chest tightened. "I ain't sure I can give ye what ye're lookin' for," she admitted. "And I don't want to try for fear I'll hurt ye."

Caspian nodded. "I see. And if I was okay with you trying, knowing you might not return my regard in the end?"

She inhaled, at a loss of what to say.

He smiled wryly. "Waiting is nothing new to me. I'm content to be patient. But if you figure out the answer, you know where I'll be." The prince gestured around the ship.

Ebba drew her hand from his grip and nodded. She sat in the flickering light of the sleeping quarters as he returned to his hammock.

The bilge door opened with a whoosh and Ebba was so focused on what had transpired with Caspian she jumped fully off the hammock in fright.

Barrels, Grubby, and Plank traipsed down the ladder, shutting the door behind them.

"What are ye doin'?" she demanded, rounding her hammock to stand before them. "The storm's still goin'."

"Jagger asked for two minutes alone at the helm as reward for savin' yer life." Plank moved past her.

"But the ship—" she started. One man above deck in a storm like this? That was lunacy.

"Aye, little nymph. But ye know there's naught to be done with the wheel cared for, unless sumpin' bad happens. It's only two minutes, and we honor a life debt. Surprised he didn't ask for more."

Barrels aimed a loaded look over her head at Plank.

It was the 'something bad happening' that she *objected* to. "What if he's washed over the side?" The panic she'd experienced the other day rose up anew. She didn't know why she suddenly cared so much about Jagger's life, but she did. He couldn't die.

Ebba shook her head and moved around Grubby to place her foot on the ladder.

"My dear," Barrels said softly, resting a hand on her shoulder. "Leave it be. It's only another minute anyway."

"It ain't safe. For him or us."

"Nay, it ain't," Plank said. "But ye should ask yerself why a man who did what he did to save yer gullet would want a quick moment alone."

Her next words stilled on her tongue as she frowned back at her father.

A deep roaring sound echoed underneath the howling press of the wind and hissing spray of the monstrous swell. She stilled.

"Did ye hear that?" she asked them, craning her head and fixing her gaze on the underside of the deck.

"He's tainted, my dear," Barrels said, releasing her. "Worse than any of us."

What did he mean?

The guttural sound came again, almost like a hoarse wail . . . like what one might hear at a funeral. Like a child had been ripped from a mother's arms. Like someone had watched their entire family being slaughtered before them. The roaring plea sounded like hopeless pain, endless anguish. And if being tainted had a shanty, Ebba knew that would be it. The raw noise exactly echoed what she'd felt when influenced under the pillars' power.

There was only one person above deck who could be making that terrible sound and shouting his pain into the storm.

The ripping yell came again, and Ebba's heart squeezed.

"Do ye think he always feels that way?" she whispered to her fathers.

Barrels wrapped an arm around her shoulders. "Come away, my dear. Leave him alone for now."

FOURTEEN

Ebba wasn't sure who'd gone above deck after Jagger's time was up, but she hadn't possessed the guts. It wasn't just that he'd saved her life and forced her to admit he wasn't a heartless bastard. . . .

What did she say to someone who made that agonizing sound but strove so hard to hide his pain? Clearly, Jagger didn't want comfort from any of them. For him to ask for time alone and risk alerting them to his anguish meant he must've been desperate—at his wit's end.

Her gut told her Jagger would hate if she mentioned overhearing him.

Everyone on board had experienced the taint's torment. *None* of them had experienced it like Jagger. None of them would be alive if they had. Yet could a person who was alive inside make such a sound? Jagger had always seemed endlessly capable, a person who didn't need anyone else to survive in the world. He bore his burdens alone. Deep down, Ebba had always secretly marveled at that strength.

Jagger had shown he wasn't impervious. She should only feel heartache over his internal suffering.

But she didn't. Knowing that Jagger wasn't impervious shook her. Big time.

Deep down, had part of her relied on his strong demeanor? Ebba didn't know. But as far as she could tell, the panic that swelled when Jagger's life was risked and her newfound discontent in knowing he *could* lose control were both contributing to whatever troubled her so much.

Ebba just couldn't quite figure out what that thing was.

She cracked open an eyelid, rolling onto her back to yawn. *Ouch* —on second thought, that wasn't the best idea. Feeling the throbbing bruises from the lashing of the sheets yesterday just made her feel *sorrier* for Jagger. He'd been lashed one hundred and fifty times. How had he even survived?

"Sal, ye up?" she said, reluctant to shift as the last few days of the storm, and her wound caught up with her.

Hold on a minute. The ship wasn't pitching side to side.

The storm was over.

Ebba swung her legs over the side of her hammock, groaning loud enough to stir the others. She'd missed her next shift by the looks of it. Plank, Grubby, and Barrels were sleeping, Pillage snoozing on her father's chest like usual. Fat lot of help she turned out to be.

Kicking back the lid of her clothing trunk, Ebba selected the only untorn and unbloodied tunic and threw away her old one. Taking care not to loosen the binding that Locks had wrapped around her wounded torso over the lashes, she slipped it on over her head. She decided to forgo a jerkin, certain the pressure on her back would be akin to babysitting Davy Jones' vindictive spawn. She wrapped a green length of material around her head, turban-style, with her midnight dreads encased within.

That'd do.

She heaved herself up the ladder and exited onto the main deck.

Sunlight. The rays were nearly blinding after several days without a speck of light.

Holding an arm to shield her watering eyes, she scanned the deck and beyond. The morning ocean was a far cry from its angry, churning alter ego of the last three days. Ebba released a pent-up breath, letting the belief they'd survived the thunderbird's storm wash over her.

In the much calmer waters, the damage to *Felicity* was blatant.

Overhead, the lowest boom was certainly wrecked beyond functional use. Without it, they could only rely on the foresail, which was a great deal slower and more unstable. The mainsail had been ripped away too. Stubby would want to fix *Felicity* as soon as possible. They carried extra sails, booms, and ropes in the hold, so all they needed was time.

Her gaze sought Stubby, and she caught sight of him running his hands over the deep chips in the bulwark where the falling tip of the beam must've hit. There were gouges in the deck everywhere, but nothing appeared cracked.

Best leave him to mourn alone.

Aside from the lashes on her back, they were all in one piece. She exhaled again, knowing they'd scraped through that mess by the skin of their teeth. Soddin' thunderbird.

Peg-leg stood at the base of the intact rigging, staring out over the sea. Caspian was at the bow, the *veritas* in his hands.

"How's yer back?"

Ebba jumped at Jagger's hoarse voice, spinning to face him and genuinely hurting her wounds in doing so. She winced, squeezing her eyes shut as the lashes panged sharply. "Not too bad till just now."

She kept her eyes closed, remembering Jagger's pained shouting last night. If she looked at him wrong, Ebba didn't want him to guess she'd overheard. Her fathers would certainly be acting the same way. Yet if she didn't look at him, he'd know she knew anyway. Or was she overthinking this?

Ebba opened her eyes. "Have ye been awake all night then?"

"Nay." He joined her under the shade of the bilge, and Ebba watched through her peripherals as he rested against the barrel close beside her. She didn't move away.

"Thank ye," she said belatedly. "For savin' my life."

Jagger's hair hung limp either side of his high-boned, lean face. His gaze was less silver today and more like an unpolished gun. He was exhausted.

"Aye, well," he said. "I had a debt to repay."

About to tell him to go below deck and sleep, instead she replied, "What?"

Ebba scoured her memory but couldn't recall ever saving his life. Or did he refer to one of her fathers?

Jagger shifted on the barrel. "Ye saved my life on *Malice*."

"Oh," Ebba said, eyes widening as she remembered. "Pushing ye off the ship. Aye, well. I was also tryin' to kill ye, if memory serves right."

She snorted, and then smiled because though her time on *Malice* had been the single worst experience of her life, aspects of the haunting memory were finally fading into something she could laugh about. Or maybe she was okay with the thought of killing Jagger. After staring up at him as she dangled in thin air, Ebba knew the latter wasn't true.

His face softened. "That's not what I meant. There was another time." He looked past her, and his face clouded. "Never mind."

She followed his glare to Caspian. Seeing the prince had made Jagger clam up. "Right well, yet another cryptic comment from ye. But I thank ye for what ye did all the same."

Jagger studied her face. "Ye're welcome, Viva."

He stressed the last word like it meant something personal. She shook her head. "Ye should go sleep on a hammock below deck. Can't be good sleepin' crammed in the crow's nest. Ye look like the thunderbird shat on ye."

Chuckling at her own joke, Ebba crossed to the prince. Her steps faltered as she remembered their kiss yesterday and his question to her.

Felicity was becoming far too small. Where were the blissful, relaxed days with a crew of seven?

"Ahoy," she said, opting to hover awkwardly instead of sitting against the ship side next to him.

His amber eyes jerked up to hers. She watched as red crept through his cheeks.

Ebba cleared her throat. "Nice day."

A slow smile spread across Caspian's face. "Yes, Mistress Pirate. A nice day. We have survived the thunderbird's punishment."

"Aye," she answered.

They fell into silence.

"Did you hear Jagger screaming last night?" he asked her in undertones.

Jagger was still on deck—out of hearing distance, but Ebba didn't blame the prince for whispering anyway.

She nodded. "I did. Never heard anythin' like it in my life. And I've heard the *siren*."

He shuddered. "Neither have I. But I've felt it." He tapped a finger on the blade.

Every single person on this ship—except Sally and Pillage—had felt 'it.' *It* being the taint. "I can't imagine what it's like to be him after so long on *Malice*." Or if Jagger would ever regain the person he'd been. She stilled at the thought, her heart pounding hard and fast as the source of her discomfort rose nearly within reach.

"Have you noticed that Jagger likes to hold the *veritas*?"

The remark tore her from the edge of whatever thought she'd been about to understand. Blast it.

"Ye think he likes to hold the sword?" she asked. "Not just when he has to?"

Jagger couldn't hardly hold *purgium*, could he? And she sure as hell wasn't switching with him to hold truth. Unless Caspian wanted to give her the *purgium* and hold truth himself. He seemed okay with either.

Caspian hummed, pushing back his russet curls. The attempt failed; the lazy curls flopped back into place the moment he removed his hand. "He's stolen the sword from me at least twice in the night."

"*What*?" Ebba knelt next to him and sat back on her haunches.

"The sword is always back on top of my trunk by morning," he continued. "But after Sally took the *purgium* at Neos, I've been waking at every creak. I woke the morning before we encountered the thunderbird as Jagger replaced the sword. Then I made sure to stay up the next night and watch him. He takes it each night and keeps the blade until sunrise, I'm certain of it."

"Why didn't ye say sumpin'?"

"I only noticed recently. Then we were battling against the storm. I was going to wait and see what he did with it before alerting everyone. But . . . I think I've figured out why."

"Why does he take it then?" she asked, watching the prince closely.

Light stubble covered his jaw. The neck of his tunic was unlaced, and ink stained his fingertips—he'd been in Barrels' office again. His hair was just slightly too long, the curls in disarray. He sat with one leg straight and the other bent up, draping his right arm over his right knee. In short, Caspian looked nothing like the Cosmo she'd first met.

Ebba had never stopped to look at him as more than a friend. No matter how much she'd pretended otherwise, she'd always noticed how handsome he was—if on the Exosian side of tough—but all those months ago, Ebba had been different. A person who was limiting herself because of fear. She'd never wanted anything except to fill her hair with beads and to become a fearsome pirate. Those things seemed so childish now, in a way, but part of her wished to be that person again; someone without cares and confusing things to think on. Regardless of that wistfulness, Ebba's priorities and her desires had shifted since she first met Cosmo.

Should she take a risk and explore something new with Caspian?

"Where have you gone?" he asked her, closer than before.

Ebba leaned back, shaking herself. "Nowhere. I mean, just here. What were ye sayin'?"

A flirting twinkle entered his amber eyes and Ebba swallowed.

Clearly, his profession last night had uncorked something because she'd never seen *that* in his gaze before.

She inhaled quietly when he didn't tease her further.

"I was saying," he said, casting her another twinkling look, "that I believe Jagger has trouble discerning what is real and not. When the taint had me in its clutches, I had the same trouble."

Ebba cast her mind back, realizing the same was true for her. She'd been convinced that the urge to kill Jagger and leave Verity behind were hers, only realizing it was the pillars' whispering to her via the taint once the *purgium* healed her.

"He holds the *veritas* so he knows the taint's lie from what's really happenin'."

Caspian nodded. "Yes, at least that's my theory."

They'd all felt the taint. If there was a way to help Jagger, they'd do it, simply in empathy's name. Except the look on Caspian's face told her he may not feel the same.

"Will ye give him the sword?" she asked, slightly alarmed at his hesitation.

He lifted his head from staring at the sword again. "It's my family sword—my father's. I don't have anything else from him."

True. But King Montcroix himself had given the sword to Jagger's father to hold in his stead. Though . . . he'd killed him years later, so maybe that wasn't a great point to make. "I can understand that, matey. But is that a good enough reason to not help him?"

Caspian sighed. "It's hard to help someone who has actively attempted to kill your family most of his life. Part of me wonders why I should go out of my way."

Where was this coming from? He'd been darker in recent times but never mean-spirited. Was this to do with the envy and bitterness he'd occasionally voice in regard to the pirate? Jagger had always protected his tribe, and Caspian felt he hadn't. Was that where this had stemmed from?

"I suppose ye don't need to help him," she said slowly. "Seems a good way to show Jagger he's wrong about yer family. Might start mendin' things between ye."

His reply was dry. "I'm not sure things between us will ever be mended, Mistress Pirate. There's a lot in the way of us becoming friends. He begrudges my entire existence."

"But he hasn't killed ye. That's encouragin'," she offered weakly.

He turned the sword over in his hand. "That he hasn't killed me is no indication of what he intends. Jagger is merely biding his time. Should I give the person who means to kill me a sword?"

The question didn't sound like the type that needed an answer. And he had a point, perhaps, though he was acting strange and maudlin.

Ebba changed tactics. "Will ye feel happy to know ye could've helped Jagger but didn't?"

Caspian stared at her. She stared right back.

"If I give him the sword, he *might* be less inclined to kill me," the prince admitted. "His threats worry you, and I don't like it when you worry."

Worry her? Shouldn't they worry *him*?

His eyes burned into hers. "He's threatening *my* life, and I'm going to handle it. You don't have to always protect me. Maybe I should start protecting you for once.

"Thank ye, but I be the sort to protect myself."

"Should I spurn you when you're being protective of me then?" he asked.

She flushed. "That ain't what I meant."

His eyes twinkled again. "I'm merely saying that I'll protect your back as you protect mine."

Her back wounds twitched as though hearing his words for themselves. "Perhaps I could use that," she relented enough to say.

Stubby was stroking the deck on the starboard side.

Ebba blew out a breath. "Better go console Stubby. Good luck with yer choice."

The prince made no answer, and Ebba beelined for her father, ignoring Jagger who still stood in the bilge shadows.

Closer to the helm, Ebba listened to Stubby whisper to the ship.

"We didn't leave ye, girl. We were as nice as we could be durin' the storm. I'm fierce sorry for the scratching to ye—"

She scrunched her nose at his ramblings. They all loved *Felicity*, but Stubby took things a scant step beyond love.

"We better start with the repairs," she said loudly.

Stubby glared at her and returned to his whisperings. Finishing his apology to the ship, her father stood.

"Jagger spotted an island through the spyglass. The current be takin' us there," he said. "We'll anchor there for hope there's sumpin' suitable to replace the boom with."

Sally pushed open the bilge door, nearly catching Jagger. Not noticing him, the sprite floated sleepily toward Ebba.

"Why do we need to gather materials? We have a spare boom in the hold," Ebba said, eyes on Sally.

"We *had* a spare boom," Stubby growled.

The sprite heard him and wrenched to a halt in midair. She quickly began reversing back to the bilge.

Ebba braced herself for Sally's latest antic. "What happened to it?"

"It has chunks taken out o' it is what," he snapped. "Yer recoverin' sprite exchanged her grog habit for a wood chewin' habit."

She caught Sally's eye just as the immortal reached the bilge. The sprite shrugged and disappeared from sight, away from Stubby's wrath.

"Sal's been chewin' on wood to stop herself drinkin'?" Ebba asked, her mouth bobbing open.

The sprite was a bloody animal!

"She's your pet," her father accused.

Aye, but Sally's title as queen of the wind sprites was a smidgen more concerning, considering what she'd taken to doing to stop a drinking relapse.

Ebba blew out a breath. "But we can lash bits and pieces together to form a boom."

"Ye think *Felicity* deserves bits and pieces?" He withered.

She should answer that with a no. Peg-leg's moods over the lack of fruit and veggies were more frequent, but Stubby could definitely match his sulkiness when the situation arose.

"It'll take a while to get to the island." Ebba changed the subject, jerking her head at the missing mainsail.

Stubby's face darkened. "Aye, we'll be havin' roast thunderbird for dinner if I'm ever seein' him again. Hurt my ship, he did. Not just phys'cally. Em'tionally too."

That sounded a wee bit like hysteria in his voice, but she left him to vent, peering about while listening with half an ear.

"What's Peg-leg starin' at?" she asked when he paused to suck in a breath.

"Who cares?" Stubby snapped again, selecting a tool from his belt, sniffing mournfully.

Ebba edged away, striding past the mast to the rigging on the opposite side. She leaned against the bulwark alongside Peg-leg who was gazing out to sea, eyes unfocused.

Sally appeared out the bilge door again and checked both directions. She zipped straight for Ebba when Stubby's back was turned, squeezing beneath her turban.

"Couldn't ye have chewed on an empty barrel, Sal?" Ebba muttered.

Her answer was a series of highly defensive squeaks before the sprite fell into a mulish silence.

"Stubby's lost it," she whispered to Peg-leg.

"Ye're only learnin' that now?" he asked, deadpan.

Fair point. She studied her father; like all of them, his face was drawn and pale. Hopefully when they got to the island, there would be time for rest. But though the storm was over, they were still in the Dynami with no idea when or where the next danger might come from. "Ye all right, Peg-leg?"

He sighed and leaned onto his arms, bending his left knee up to take weight off his peg-bearing joint. "I'm okay, lass. I'm just angry that ye were hurt."

"We're on a pirate ship, matey. That's goin' to be part of the job sometimes. Ye know I can handle it."

"I know," he said, smiling slightly at her. "It's not that I'm doubtin'. But no parent likes to see their child hurt, no matter how old they be gettin'. My bad mood is more me than you anyhow; there was a time I'd've been up that riggin' in the middle of a storm, no problem."

Sally whirred sadly, and Ebba wanted to do the same. "Do ye miss it much, Peg-leg?"

"Aye, lass. Every day. Ye have the rigger's blood in ye. Ye know what it is to be up there. I have my memories to go off, and I'm glad to have those. But they're sad and lifeless compared to the real thing."

She shrugged. "Why don't ye climb the riggin'? Ye climb the ladder."

Peg-leg glanced at his peg without shifting his body.

"Ye're always sayin' Caspian can do anythin'," she countered. "Why don't ye take yer own advice?"

He set his peg down and turned to gaze up to the shrouds. He frowned.

"Well?" she pressed.

Peg-leg's hand closest to the rigging shook before he curled his fingers into a white-knuckled fist. "There ain't no good reason, I s'pose."

Ebba stared at her father, at the way he stared up at the rigging, his eyes filled with memories and pain. Did she look the same when staring at her beads tucked away out of sight?

"Yer strong enough to climb the riggin'," she told him.

His mouth was ajar as he faced her. Peg-leg searched her face. "I'd hope so. I still do a fair bit around here."

"Nay." Ebba cut him off, resting a hand over her heart. "Ye're strong enough here, m'hearty."

Would her words be enough to fix him? That's all that Ebba felt she needed to put her beads in again, after all—permission and reassurance. But maybe that wasn't the case. Her father's throat worked, and she waited on tenterhooks.

"I ap'reciate ye sayin' so," Peg-leg said, eyes misty. ". . . I'll think on it. How about that?"

Forcing her disappointment down, Ebba nodded. "I'd like that."

There was his answer. A big, whopping no. A part of her had expected as much, really; she'd just hoped for an easy solution to his problems, seeing as she was experiencing a similar thing with the beads. Yet only Peg-leg could climb the rigging, and maybe only Ebba could decide what the worst moment of her life would make her.

She leaned against the bulwark, shoulders sagging as her mind worried at the bead predicament. Stupid flax pouch. Stupid *Jagger* for giving them back to her.

Her attention was caught by Caspian crossing the deck to Jagger, *veritas* in hand. Peg-leg turned around and followed her gaze. Together they watched as the prince passed the sword to the pirate.

"Why's he doin' that?" Peg-leg asked. "Jagger wants to kill him."

"He thinks the sword helps Jagger put the tainted thoughts in one pile and the normal thoughts in another."

Peg-leg grunted. "That's why Jagger's been stealin' the sword each night?"

"Ye knew?"

"No one farts on this ship without me knowin," Peg-leg answered.

Ebba laughed and shoved him.

Caspian looked her way and smiled as Jagger disappeared through the bilge door, the *veritas* in hand. She'd only seen him enter the hold two or three times on their journey so far. If the truth sword made it easier for him to bear darkness, did it also help him cope below deck? Ebba recalled how cagey he'd been when she encountered him down there. On *Malice*, Pockmark had put disobedient pirates into a locked room in the deepest part of the hull where the pillars were at their strongest. That's where he'd chucked her, too.

She knew Jagger had avoided going below deck on *Malice* because fresh air helped him keep a clearer head, but was he genuinely afraid of the lower levels now? Maybe there was more to his rare visits below deck than she'd thought.

She watched the prince return to the bow. "Hey, Peg-leg? I need some advice."

"Aye?"

How to put the predicament with Caspian? "I've had a shift of prior'ties," she said. Probably best to keep the conversation businesslike. "I be wantin' things I didn't want afore, and I'm unsure what to do about that."

"Yer readin?" he asked, a crease between his brows.

She pondered that. "Aye, readin'. If I want to know whether I like readin' or not, should I throw myself into lessons so that I might know how I feel a little sooner? Or should I wait and not rush the process, knowin' I'll figure out whether I like readin' or not at the right time?" Ebba finished, happy with where she'd gotten.

Peg-leg's brows arched. "No question about it. Practice all ye can, lass. It be the only way I know o' to get better at things in life."

Ebba scrunched her nose. "Do ye miss Sherry then?" Sherry was Peg-leg's tea-drinking buddy on Maltu.

"Huh?" His eyes narrowed. "What're we speakin' o'?"

"Readin'," she blurted.

He watched her and shook his head. "Well then. Aye, never wait for things to happen. No one's goin' to raise the sails for ye; ye raise them yerself."

Hmm. "With every single thing in life?" she pressed.

Peg-leg slapped the bulwark. "Aye, lass. Everythin'."

Peg-leg was telling her to take the stingray by the barb, in reference to reading perhaps, but *still*, his logic made sense when applied to her dilemma over Caspian too.

She smiled at him. "Thank ye."

He kissed her forehead. "Anytime, lass. Never let it be said that I don't give great advice to my daughter."

FIFTEEN

"There are certainly trees on the island," Barrels said as all eleven of them, including Sally and Pillage, stared at the land mass ahead.

"Yeeeoow!" the ship cat whined, butting Barrels hand for attention.

Ebba hummed. The island was an odd kind of. . . .

"Have ye even seen land shaped like that?" Plank beat her to asking.

"Nay," Ebba chorused with the others.

Spray flew upward as sea met rock, giving their crew a general sense of the island. The land mass appeared to have a large core and all manner of rocky protrusions wriggling outward from the beach.

Sally floated in front of them, waving her arms. She held her hands splayed out atop her head.

"Moose?" Caspian guessed. To the others, he said, "I saw one once but couldn't stand to shoot it. Magnificent creature."

Jagger scoffed. "Moose. She's bein' an octopus."

Sally drifted closer to the pirate, blushing slightly, but shook her head.

"Tree?" Grubby asked next.

They all turned to the wind sprite. Ebba tilted her head. She could see a tree. Kind of.

The sprite groaned, high-pitched and faint, and then pointed at the island and then dragged a finger across her throat.

Stubby coughed. "That's pretty clear-like."

"How do ye know sumpin' be wrong with the place?" Plank asked her.

The sprite weaved her hand up and down in a horizontal line.

"Ocean," Ebba guessed.

"Wind," Barrels said.

Sally pointed at him, grinning broadly.

Stubby glanced at him. "How did ye guess that?"

"She's a wind sprite."

That made sense. But also didn't. Ebba screwed up her face. "Ye're sayin' ye know things because o' the wind? How far does that work?"

Sally placed her forefingers either side of her head to indicate a crown and then inspected her tiny nails casually.

"We can take that to mean pretty far, I'm supposin'," Locks said drily.

Jagger glanced back. "It don't matter, does it? We're missin' a boom, the spare be damaged, and we have no notion where more land be. But there ain't any birds flyin' around here. I ain't liking that."

Such a mysterious tribesperson thing to say, Ebba thought, rolling her eyes. She conveniently ignored all the times they'd spotted land because of seagulls.

"There are other islands on the Dynami map," Caspian said.

"Was this one on there?" Ebba asked.

He and Barrels hesitated. "Well, no," the prince admitted.

Barrels added, "And the closest island is about a week from here, if we've managed to correctly pinpoint where we ended up after the storm."

Grubby looked between them, and Ebba patted his hand absently, saying, "Looks like we be needin' to anchor and head in."

Sally shouted in each of their faces before disappearing to the bilge.

"That queen has a temper. I'd hate to be one o' her underlings," Stubby said. "And what the flamin' eels is she doin' with us if she's supposed to rule her own people?"

A papaya bounced off his head. Stubby rubbed the spot and scowled over his shoulder at Sally, who—judging by her own scowl—had heard every word.

They hadn't had time to talk about her royal majesty. After the thunderbird, they'd been thrown into chaos that wasn't exactly slowing down. Ebba didn't just want to know more about Sally, she wanted to know more about Jagger being 'the immune'. And what the god of souls said about Caspian and Jagger picking her. And all that other mumbo jumbo.

But survival came first.

"Well, we can't row back to Zol," Caspian said. "It appears we only have one choice."

Peg-leg tapped Ebba's hand. "Up to the shrouds with ye," he said. "We'll take the ship in as far as is safe. Bringin' the beam back out on naught but a rowboat won't be easy. We'll have to make a raft."

Plank eyed the spray. "I'd say we worry about reachin' shore at all."

Aye, so much spray was a bad sign.

"I shall see if I can get anything more from Sally about what's on the island," Barrels said, hurrying away.

Ebba turned for the mast to climb the sole intact rigging and spotted Jagger already on his way there, *veritas* swinging from his belt.

What was he. . . ? The pirate grabbed the rigging, swung up and began to climb.

Sodding. Cur.

That was her job!

Ebba sprinted for the rigging and began to climb after him, several paces behind and much slower because of her back. How dare he? Two weeks on their ship, and he thought he owned the place? She gritted her teeth at the thud above as he landed in the crow's nest.

Ten seconds later, her back aching, she swung over the side and landed.

Jagger doubled over. Her knee in his stomach might've had something to do with it. . . .

Ebba ripped the spyglass from his hand as he wheezed for air and set it to her eye, adjusting the end to bring the glass into focus. Using the spyglass, she scoured from the outer rocks all the way to the shore and then along the shoreline, assessing the island for the best way in.

"Ye're angry I'm faster than ye, I take," Jagger said. She felt him straightening behind her.

She snorted and didn't answer. They were more than even—when her back wasn't injured.

"We could share the job, ye know."

"I don't share—I'm spoilt" she replied, throwing his words back at him.

She studied the water between the ship and the shore again. The long strands of rocks were uniformly spaced where they protruded from the center, except for two, which appeared much farther apart. The island was shaped kind of like a sun.

Jagger said, "Exactly what I'd expect from a girl with six parents."

"Aye," she answered, only half listening. "I'm a fierce woman-pirate. And I take what I want." The words left a bitter taste in her mouth. If Ebba was being honest, she felt nothing close to fierce.

"Do ye now?"

Ebba lowered the spyglass and jerked at how close he was. "Why are ye so close?"

Unshifting, he arched a brow. "Not much room in here."

"Nay," she agreed. Though the cramped nest was definitely more his fault than hers. "So ye're much better to stay on the deck where ye belong, Jagger."

"Maybe I don't mind bein' cramped next to ye."

She narrowed her gaze. He was laughing at her. His eyes were silver again, and he was teasing her about something. "Well ye should," Ebba said, placing a hand on his chest and pushing gently. "Keep out o' my nest."

"That ain't what ye were sayin' when I helped ye on the boom."

"I didn't say anythin' when ye helped me," she retorted.

Jagger pitched his voice higher, batting his lashes. "Thank ye for savin' my life, Jagger."

Despite herself, Ebba laughed. "What are ye actin' like a codfish?" Or was he acting this way because of where they were on the ship and because *veritas* was swinging from his belt?

He smiled, glancing out to sea.

Ebba leaned over the side, shouting down. "Oi, head west to anchor. There's a larger gap to be gettin' through there."

Peg-leg called back to acknowledge her order, and soon the ship lurched as he adjusted their course.

She turned. "Why ain't ye gone yet? Get out o' my nest."

"Ye said ye take the things ye want, so I'm waitin' for ye to do so," he said low.

His tone made her shiver. Were they still speaking of the nest?

He continued, "Is that what ye were doin' kissing the Exosian on Zol? Takin' what ye wanted?"

Ebba's cheeks warmed. "Why do ye keep bringin' that up? Why does it bother ye so? I asked him to kiss me because I wanted to know what kissin' was like."

Jagger moved closer, until only a hand width separated them. Not enough distance to stop her feeling the warmth of his body. Not even close.

"If I were you, I wouldn't push me." Ebba crossed her arms, tilting her chin.

His lips trembled.

"Why are ye laughin' at me?" she exploded. He never acted like this. Though she'd never spent time with him up here before.

"Ye're bluffin' and not even well. It's funny." His smile transformed his face, and she eyed the change warily.

Since he'd saved her life during the storm, Ebba had stood on the precipice of deciding to finally trust Jagger. If he was loyal enough to keep her alive in dire odds, the mean comments had to be from the taint. She'd been just about to relax more in his company and accept him as a friend and crewmember. Then he had to go and change on her again. There was just so much she still didn't know about Jagger. And that made her feel like he'd never be a friend.

Clearly, the pirate was uncomfortable opening up. Or maybe just since being on *Malice*.

Actually. . . .

Against his size, Ebba didn't stand too much of a chance. But just like Ladon, Jagger did have a weakness. Ebba couldn't believe she hadn't thought of it prior.

"What do ye think the thunderbird meant by callin' ye the immune?" she asked him.

He blinked. "I don't know."

"How did ye stay on *Malice* for so long?" she asked next. "What kind o' things do they teach ye in the rainforest? Do ye have siblings? How many? Who do ye like the most? Tell me a secret. Anythin'."

Jagger fidgeted on the spot, and she held in a snicker, continuing, "What's yer favorite color, Jagger? What were ye and Caspian talkin' of when he gave ye the sword?"

The pirate slung a leg over the side, and she followed close behind.

"Where are ye goin'?" she called as he rapidly descended. "I wanted to talk!"

He didn't look up, and Ebba laughed so hard her stomach ached.

She shouted down again. "Aye, Jagger, ye shroud-stealin' heap o' fish guts. Don't mess with the queen o' the crow's nest." She leaned over farther. "*Queen* o' the crow's nest. Don't forget it."

EBBA PICKED her way up the rocky shore as her fathers tethered the boat. She perched on a boulder to dust the sand off her feet. The rock was cold; it'd make her butt numb in no time.

Pulling her boots on and peering around, she said, "It ain't exactly the kind o' beach for sunbathin'."

"Aye," Stubby said. He stared at her booted feet. "Hold on, did ye just wil'ingly put on yer shoes?"

She arched a brow. "It's rocky. Why wouldn't I?"

Stubby blinked at her. "Aye?" He tore his eyes away and exchanged a long look with her other fathers. "Aye," he repeated.

Whenever they told her to wear shoes because of glass and what-not, they were usually right. Ebba had just thought to spare them the trouble of sneaking the boots onto the rowboat.

Caspian pointed directly up the beach. "There are trees right there. Are we looking for any particular kind of wood to replace the boom?"

Locks stood next to him, peering up and down the beach. What they'd seen from the ship had proved accurate. After navigating through two strands of the rocky outcrops in the rowboat, they were now on the core of the island. The rocks had grown in size as they rowed farther into shore, and now, either side of them, huge black boulders—at least three times Jagger's height—took up most of the pebbly beach.

"We want a straight tree," Locks said. "But beggars can't be choosers. We'll go with the best we can find and hope it holds true until we can fix *Felicity* properly."

Stubby sniffed. "As she *deserves*."

Plank rubbed his temples.

"Guess we head inland then," Ebba said. At the back of her neck, Sally held on tight, shaking her head and rustling Ebba's dreads.

She pushed her brown bandana back into place. "Sal, don't be a wimp. We know yer afraid of sumpin'. We'll walk on tiptoes, all right? And if ye want to try and mime out what ye're worried about again, ye be most welcome."

Ebba yelped at the answering sharp pinch at her nape as the sprite bit her. "Ye can't be a queen, Sal. Queens don't bite, and they surely ain't recoverin' alcoholics who replace their ad'iction with chewin' on wood."

"Maybe she got sick of ruling," Caspian said as their party set off toward the middle of the island, picking their way through the boulders and scattered stones.

"Chh, who gets sick o' tellin' people what to do?"

He cracked a smile. "Not that part. The responsibility part. The restrictions on what you can do with your life. The lack of freedom."

Jagger lifted his head, and Ebba watched as he studied the prince intently.

"Ye just need to manage the burden right," she answered when the pirate didn't utter whatever he so clearly wanted to. "When I'm captain o' the month, it's all about delegatin' the tasks."

She steadied Peg-leg as he stepped over a rock, his peg sinking down a few inches in the charcoal sand.

"Ye can't compare bein' 'captain o' the month' to years of respon-sib'lity," Jagger said to her.

. . . so he'd respond to her, just not the prince.

Caspian replied, but also looked at her as he spoke. "And when you haven't chosen that life, such a burden is harder to . . . come to grips with."

When did she become a messenger pigeon?

"Especially when failure means the death of everyone ye love," Jagger added gruffly.

Ebba slid a look his way. He'd never once shown that he begrudged the burden of caring for his tribe, but she supposed that was a terrible burden to carry. She certainly wouldn't want to carry her fathers' lives in her hands. Ebba felt rather sad for Jagger right now.

Probably wouldn't last.

The silence grew heavy. Apparently they were done talking to each other through her.

Ebba chh'd again, saying in a teasing tone, "What? Ye think people can't die if a captain makes the wrong call? Ye think just anyone can be captain o' the month?"

He and Caspian glanced over the present company. They both nodded. Was the two men agreeing a good 'I might not kill you' thing or a bad 'Jagger plots for future murder' thing?

"Nay." She answered her own question. "Ye still need the respect o' the people ye're leadin' or nothin' will work right. Ye still need to know yer ship and what needs doin'."

The prince grinned, his eyes twinkling. "A good point as ever, Mistress Pirate."

"I'm full o' them."

"I'm aware."

Jagger muttered, "I ain't standin' here while the two o' ye flirt."

Ebba tripped over her own feet, quickly recovering to gasp, "That ain't what's happenin'."

The pirate smirked at her. "Are ye sure, Viva?"

She threw a glare at him and strode away from the pair.

Her. *Flirting*? Honestly. Did he even have eyes in his head? Ebba's cheeks burned fiercely, and she was glad neither of the young men could see.

The ground underfoot evened out into smooth and slightly sloped black rock as they neared the tree line. Patches of shrubs, an odd milky spearmint color, increased in number until eventually they stopped before a sparse forest.

Plank's raven curls fell back as he craned to study the trees. "I ain't seen this wood afore, but I reckon the grain be straight enough."

Stubby turned from the tree, folding his arms. "Just pick the best one."

Grubby wrapped an arm around his shoulders. "Don't be sad, Stubs. *Felicity* will be just fine."

He sniffed. "I'll believe that when I'm seein' it."

"This one be the straightest," Jagger said from where he was weaving through the trees.

Peg-leg snorted. "We'll be the judge o' that, lad." He limped to the tree and slowly moved his gaze upward.

Stepping back, he rubbed his nose, muttering, "It's pretty straight-like."

"Aye, looks like it could be a boom to me," Ebba said, hardly looking at the brown trunk.

Something blurred in the trees to her left. She blinked and looked again, but the blur was gone. A cool breeze swept inward from the ocean and shook the leaves. "Sal, ye've put me on edge, ye flamin' stirrer. I'm seein' things."

"What are you seeing?" Barrels asked, squinting into the trees.

What had she seen? Ebba couldn't be certain. "Just the leaves catchin' the light, perhaps," she replied.

Locks adjusted his grip on the ax and studied the tree.

"Stand clear," he called.

"Hold on," Ebba said. Stepping to him, she extracted the *dynami* from her sash. She tucked the tarnished silver tube into the back of Locks' belt.

The rest of them returned to the shore, safely out of the way of the soon-to-be toppling tree.

Ebba strolled around the rest of the group as Stubby and Plank returned to the rowboat to collect the other tools they'd need to form the beam. It'd take days to get it attached to *Felicity* and then to fasten the ropes and mainsail again.

A high-pitched clatter came from the boulders. To the left again. Ebba whipped her head to face the noise and saw nothing. It had sounded like small, falling rocks.

"Stop stressin' yerself," Jagger said. "It's botherin' me."

She placed her hands on her hips. "I ain't. And I don't care."

"There ain't nothin' there."

Someone thought just because they were a tribesman that they were always connected to nature, in her pirate opinion.

"Timber," Locks shouted.

They turned to watch as the tree tipped toward the right of them, slower and then faster until it careened to the flat, rocky ground with a rustling crunch of branches and leaves.

Stubby and Plank returned from the rowboat. Plank dropped his load of axes and saws on the beach while Stubby placed his on the rocks one by one, a uniform distance between them.

Ebba smiled, but the curve of her lips fell away as something else blurred in her periphery to the left. Except this time. . . .

"Ebba? Get workin' on cutting off the branches, lass."

She took the ax from Stubby, her mouth dry.

Jagger snorted. "She's too busy staring into nothin'."

Ebba jerked and glared at him. "What I just saw wasn't nothin'."

She strode to the thick bottom of the trunk and began hacking off the limbs alongside Plank. Licking her lips, she asked, "Plank?"

He wiped at the perspiration on his brow. Normally, they'd be dripping with sweat just standing here, but the climate in the Dynami was much cooler. "Little nymph?"

She glanced back at the rocks, not really sure how to phrase her question, only certain she didn't want Jagger to hear her asking. "What do ye know o' a man with wings and a hawk head?"

"And ye'd be askin' that because. . . ?"

Ebba hacked at the tree and whispered, "I just saw one."

"Where? Which way?"

"The boulders at my back, sixty feet."

"Ye're sure?"

"Nope," she answered. "But I'm hardly likely to think up such a thing myself, am I?"

Still bent over the tree, Plank scanned the boulders behind her. "I can't see anythin', but we best alert the crew to be on guard."

Ebba paused in hacking. "Aye, but what are they?"

He paused. "Daedalions, if I'm right."

Plank sauntered to the others and Ebba watched the tiny ripple of tension flutter through them.

Stubby came down to join her, chipping away. "We get this done as quick as possible and leave."

She nodded.

"What's a daedalion?" Ebba asked, trying to act normal as they worked to clean the trunk.

Usually a prompt to Plank for a story would be met by heartfelt groans, but while her other fathers might groan in the safety of the ship, they wouldn't when danger might be looming close by. At least, not anymore.

Plank opened his mouth, and Ebba knew that when he spoke, it'd be in his ominous voice.

"Thousands o' years ago, on a land no longer above the sea . . ." He paused, and when none of her other fathers made sarcastic remarks, his brows shot up into his raven curls, and he continued. ". . . There existed a blacksmith and a builder who hated one another after the tragic death o' a woman they'd both loved. Their lives were a constant struggle to best and undermine each other to the other island dwellers; to hurt the other's business and family however possible. That is until, quite by chance, the blacksmith's daughter and the builder's son found themselves injured and alone with only each other to depend on."

Plank stumbled to a halt as they continued to listen. "What's wrong with ye?" he demanded. "Ye've norma'ly interrupted five times by now."

Locks shushed him. "Hurry on with yer tale."

Pink spread across Plank's cheeks. Maybe praise from this quarter had been few and far between.

"The young woman and young man fell in love, continuing their secret tryst long after they were saved. But their luck soon run out; they were seen and heard by the island dwellers, who'd always found amusement in the rift between the blacksmith and builder. The lovers were caught by the blacksmith, who locked his daughter away and flayed the young man within an inch o' his life afore sending him back to his father. Yet nothin' could diminish what lay within the young lovers. An endless, soul-deep love such as theirs could never die. In fact, their love was so strong that a powerful goddess felt their connection from afar and settled in to watch. The young woman had listened to her lover's screams from her confinement. She'd cried at the window as he was thrown into a wagon and carted away. And as the young woman sobbed for her lover, the goddess sobbed for the young woman's suffering. Unable to bear such pain, the goddess twitched her finger and unlocked the door holding the blacksmith's daughter prisoner."

"Did the young woman save him then?" Ebba whispered, her job forgotten.

Plank smiled sadly. "She stole into the house o' her enemy and found her barely healed lover. Together, they made for a boat stacked with provisions, but the way was cut off, their plan come upon by both fathers. It was then, in the fevered hours of early morning, torch-lights blazing and tempers high, that the fathers declared death for the young lovers, urgin' the other members o' their families to the battle. *Death first before family shame*—such was the blind extent of their hatred for each other. The two families chased the lovers from opposite ends o' the island, converging as one on the highest cliff, trapping them against the crumbling edge." Plank's voice dropped to a hoarse whisper. "The lovers looked at each other, knowing what they'd seen in their fathers' eyes. This was the end for them, but neither could bear to watch the other suffer. As much as such things were beyond them, love such as theirs transcended logic, and both of them knew what they felt would survive death. They would be together in the next life. Such was their connection."

Plank rubbed his watering eyes, and no one made a sound. Ebba didn't feel so far away from crying herself.

When he began again, his voice was thick. "Hand in hand, the lovers ran for the ledge and launched themselves off the cliff, relinquishin' their fate to the jagged rocks below. But the powerful goddess sat bolt upright, face tear-streaked, furious at such an end to the lovers' tale. Casting her powers forth, the goddess transformed the couple, giving each of them the wings o' a hawk so that they might survive the fall, and sharp eyes so they might always see each other and their attackers, and finally, a sharp beak with which to protect themselves from harm. With a second burst, she killed every single person upon the clifftop, turning both fathers to stone, and ending the age-old feud in one fell swoop." Plank looked at their faces, holding the tension calmly. "So it was for one happy second the two lovers were flyin' into the sunset together, human but for their hawk additions. Yet an emptiness filled the goddess at the sight of them leaving. For once, long ago, she'd known pure love, and had it torn away. She could not be parted from them, so tethering the lovers to herself and her immortality, she instead took the lovers for servants so that she might look upon their love forevermore."

Caspian broke the leaden quiet. "Did the goddess treat them well?"

Ebba hoped so. To go through so much to be together only to become slaves would be horrible.

"To begin, or so sources tell us," Plank said, swallowing hard. "But to look upon pure love while never finding it again yourself will decay even the strongest resolve. Slowly but surely, the goddess was twisted inside, the cracks in her yearning heart turning to rotted crevices, tresses turning to snakes, goodwill turning to jealousy and loathing. Forever witness to the undying love of matched souls, she transitioned from goodness to gorgon over centuries and was afterward known as Medusa."

SIXTEEN

"Medusa?" Stubby repeated as Plank trailed off. "Ye think she's here?"

Plank shrugged, wiping his eyes again. "No idea. But if her servants are, I think we'd be foolish to assume she ain't."

"Human-sized hawks and a lady with snake hair," Peg-leg mused. "How do we get ourselves into this shite?"

Barrels cleared his throat. "Perhaps we should leave immediately. We can make do with pieces of wood until we find another island."

"*If* there's another island," Ebba said, kicking at another limb to snap it off the trunk.

Locks handed her back the *dynami*, and she tucked it into her belt. She reached for a thick branch with her hands, and it snapped like a twig.

"Let's get this log done smart-like and make back for the ship," Stubby said. "If we get the branches off, we can do the rest on *Felicity*."

There was a general murmur of ayes.

Their crew, Caspian, and Jagger bent back to the task, working double-time; Sally even deigned to help, breaking off the thickest branches. When only the long, straight tree trunk remained, they set driftwood horizontally underneath and began rolling the future boom down to the boat.

Once there, Locks hacked the log in half as they watched on.

"Shake a leg," Peg-leg called from the back.

She turned just as he extracted his pistol.

A screech split the air, and Ebba ducked as a huge mass dive-bombed them. Hands over her head, she stared at the creature tucking its five-foot wings in to land up by the tree line on very human feet.

The daedalion had the streamlined head of a hawk. This one was male, his body entirely muscle, a brown length of material tied about his hips. Tawny wings bent in at his back, extending from the crown of his bird head to the ground.

"Are ye all seein' that too?" Grubby breathed.

Ebba replied, "Aye, matey. There be a hawk-man there."

"That be a daedalion, all right," Plank said.

Jagger crouched. "He dropped this." The pirate held up a bottle. Inside was a curled piece of parchment.

Stubby waved at him. "Go on then, what does it say?"

"Maybe Ebba could have a turn?" Barrels edged in.

Ebba shook her head quickly, shooting a look at Jagger.

Peg-leg sighed. "Not the time for a readin' lesson, methinks."

Reaching into the jar, Jagger extracted the parchment and unfurled it, reading aloud.

The pleasure of your company is cordially requested for dinner.
In exchange, you are welcome to leave with one of my beloved trees.
Yours truly,
Medusa

The daedalion didn't budge from the tree line as Jagger finished. *No one* budged as each of the crew stared at the note.

"What do I say about things bein' too good to be true, Ebba-Viva?" Locks asked her.

"That they are."

Her other fathers hummed in agreement.

"Keep an eye on the hawk-man while we get one o' the logs latched to the boat. We'll have to leave the other," Peg-leg said.

Ebba turned away from the ocean to watch the hawk-man, hand resting on the hilt of her cutlass. Jagger came to stand on her right, the sword clutched in his hands, and Caspian stood on the left, *purgium* tucked in his belt, just as the *dynami* was tucked in hers.

"Uh," she mumbled as dark blotches appeared far beyond the trees. "More o' the hawk-men are comin'," she whispered back, uncertain how well the creatures could hear. "I thought there were only two of the things in the story."

"And I'm guessin' they've had ample time to make children," Plank grunted.

Ebba's eyes rounded as she glanced back at the flock of male daedalions currently landing. That *was* a lot of tea drinking. Impressive.

Jagger stepped closer to her. "There's a lot o' them. More than us."

"They might just be watchin'. We shouldn't use our weapons unless they attack," the prince answered him, speaking to her.

Not this again. Why didn't they just speak to each other?

Ebba hummed darkly, eyeing the creatures' beaks as more of them landed, boosting their total number to ten. "They have weapons too. I ain't liking the curve o' their beaks." She glanced back. The log was nearly attached to the rowboat.

"Everyone in," Grubby called cheerfully.

Caspian placed a hand at her elbow to lead Ebba to the rowboat. "Come on, we need to move."

"Nay," Jagger said. "They have wings. What do ye think happens when we're out on the water?"

Valid point that they'd have to figure out on the go. She took another step, and Jagger placed a hand on her stomach to halt her.

White light exploded from their bodies, just for a second, until Caspian and Jagger, seeing what they'd accidentally caused, ripped their hands away from her to break the connection.

But it was enough.

"Shite," Ebba said, her eyes tracking the straight line where a glowing beam of light appeared a blink ago. The light had pointed into the trees.

The other two stared at the same spot through the gathered daedalions.

More of the creatures landed, and in a row, the hawk-men began to advance to the shore.

Caspian echoed. "Shite."

Her fathers assembled behind them, but Peg-leg pushed between Ebba and Jagger, the bottle in his hands.

"We'd love to come to dinner, mateys" he said with a broad smile, stopping the daedalions in their tracks. "Tell Medusa we'll be *right* along."

A PIECE of the weapon was on the island.

Unfortunately, the hawk-men hadn't left Ebba and the crew to pick their way through the forest, searching for the part at their leisure.

Ebba trudged behind Grubby, a daedalion on either side of her. The first ten minutes of their tramp through the forest had been ample time to stare her fill at the hybrid creatures and realize their powerful frames and hawk features probably made them a smidgen more difficult to fight than she initially expected. They towered over all of them.

"Where does Medusa live?" Plank asked one of his two escorts at the front.

The daedalion screeched in reply.

"Do you happen to know the thunderbird?" Barrels asked the one to his left. "He's a good friend of ours."

The creature ignored him, and when Peg-leg sniggered, Barrels shrugged. "Maybe they know other birds. Worth a try."

Stubby snorted. "Anything else we should be knowin' about Medusa, Plank? Beyond her army o' hawk-men and the snakes on her head?"

"She can hypn'tize ye with her snake eyes," he called back.

"Oh great," Locks said sarcastically. "When were ye goin' to mention that? I was worried they'd just *bite* us. But she can take over our minds? Not a worry!"

His short fuse was fraying. Ebba glanced back where he walked at the end of their single-file line. "Easy, matey, just don't look at them."

Plank's voice trailed back. "Of course, there *are* conflictin' reports. Some say the snakes'll hypn'tize a person, and others say ye'll turn to stone. Best be avoidin' them, I say."

"Aye," she murmured with the others.

Caspian murmured from directly behind her. "Ebba, you don't suppose Medusa has the next part?"

"Probably, aye." Why didn't people hide these magical tubes under a rock in the middle of nowhere? If she really wanted to hide something, that was where she'd put it—somewhere no one would ever look.

"That's my thought," he replied grimly.

Jagger was behind Caspian and said, "We would've had to eventua'ly meet her then, Viva. This is workin' out fine. We're bein' taken right to her."

"Ye would say that." She withered over her shoulder

"My apologies, queen o' the crow's nest," he drawled.

Ebba scowled back at him and stumbled. Caspian gripped her elbow, releasing her quickly to wrap an arm about her middle when she overcorrected into him.

The heat of his arm reached her skin through the thin tunic she wore. Ebba could feel him pressed against her back. His lips were by her ear.

A daedalion screeched in her face, one of his wings extending to flap her forward.

"I'm goin', I'm goin'," she said to him. "Don't get yer feathers in a tangle."

Ebba started forward again, feeling Caspian's arm slide away. She hurried to catch up with Grubby, now very aware of the prince at her back and the way his arm had felt around her waist.

The trees were thinning up ahead.

They were led between steaming rock baths filled with cerulean water. The rocks where the water touched had been bleached white, giving the entire area a marbled appearance. It was simultaneously beautiful and—Ebba could guess—extremely painful should any of them fall in the water. The stone hadn't managed to keep its color, and Ebba certainly wasn't as hard as rock. She did like the sweet smell the pools gave off, however; almost as nice as sea salt.

They picked their way through the pools between the two rows of daedalions escorting them. The hawk-men at the front stopped either side of white-rock steps which disappeared underground.

"Medusa doesn't feel like an open-air dinner, does she?" Stubby asked weakly, whispering to them, "Nothin' good happens underground."

Ebba agreed, but the daedalions didn't seem to share that opinion. They screeched in his face, flapping their wings in a thumping flurry.

Plank led the way down the white-washed stairs, and the rest of them followed suit.

They entered a tunnel that sloped gently downward. Ebba glanced behind, seeing that only one daedalion remained with them now, his head just clearing the top of the passage. The other hawkmen had stayed outside. That evened things up a bit—except that the creatures remained at the exit. But maybe there were other ways to get out.

The floor was rock and dirt. The walls, marbled white and black as though washed over and over with the sweet water outside to streak them. The tunnel was well lit by periodic torches, and as Plank led them farther into the tunnel, Ebba kept a careful eye on the walls, but no other passages appeared to branch off.

Sally gripped the back of her neck, and Ebba hushed her under her breath. "Quiet, Sal."

The wind sprite shook her head frantically and began squeaking. She burst out from Ebba's hair in a glowing explosion and hovered in front of her long enough for Ebba to glimpse pure panic on the sprite's face.

Like a lightning bolt, the glowing ball of light that was Sally zipped past their line and the daedalion, disappearing back up the tunnel.

Ebba watched her go, her heart sinking. "Abandoned by Sally *again*," she said angrily. At least Ebba was used to it by now.

She was surprised the coward hadn't bolted back at the rowboat.

The immortal screeched at the back, turning between them and the escaping glowing sprite. He seemed torn between chasing Sally and escorting them onward.

He chose them.

"She doesn't like places without wind," Jagger called softly.

"She manages the hold on the ship just fine," Ebba shot back.

Caspian whispered, "Yes, but she was terrified of Medusa even before we came."

Yeah, yeah. Weren't they all. If the sprite loved their crew properly, she would've never left. She and Ebba got on so well between times, enough to make her feel that next time the sprite would be there for her, only to be constantly disappointed. They were all scared of Medusa, but no one else was ditching the others to save their own gullet.

Ebba's anger occupied her until the tunnel widened into an expansive room with a low ceiling.

Ornate chaise lounges were scattered about, dividing the chamber into loose sections. Lengths of fabric fell from the ceiling to the floor at intervals, obscuring the entirety of the room. Their group weaved farther into the space, and Ebba took in the statues of naked men and women bordering the walls. Pottery sat stacked in teetering towers, coins tossed haphazardly around; paintings were propped against the rocks pushing out of the otherwise smooth floor.

If Ebba had to describe the chamber, she'd say it was a collection. All of a person's favorite objects strewn around so she might always look upon them.

The daedalion took the lead from Plank, guiding them to the opposite end, past a fountain of wings carved out of the white bleached rock from above ground.

A short flight of white-washed stairs led upward, bright cushions scattered over them at random.

Ebba counted fifteen steps as they ascended.

The space at the top was flat, with a ceremonial feel—like a prism with the top cut off. A large white table sat in the middle of the platform, and more of the gauzy material fell down from the ceiling, cloaking the area with an intimate feel.

At the far end hung the largest painting Ebba had ever seen, a tragic depiction of two lovers staring into each other's eyes.

At the base of it stood a woman, gazing upon the painting as though nothing else existed.

She also had snakes for hair.

"Don't look," Ebba muttered to the others.

The hawk-man screeched, and Ebba quickly focused on the tabletop.

"Is that so?" Medusa asked her servant, turning.

Ebba could feel the pinpricks of one hundred eyes on her. A subtle hissing washed toward them, like the warning growl of a predator. Unable to stop herself, Ebba shifted her eyes to watch the woman's feet as she glided to them.

Her feet were the same milky spearmint of the shrubs lacing the forest floor outside. Each toe had one or more rings upon it, easy to spot through the translucent onyx material of her gown. Medusa's jewelry chimed with each step, turning her approach into some semblance of music. A deadlier version of a rattlesnake.

Risking a higher peek, Ebba followed the dress upward; through it most of Medusa's skin was visible. She took in the stacks of bracelets covering the gorgon's arms from elbow to wrist before tearing her gaze away.

She peered sideways to make sure the crew was looking down. All of their eyes were fixed on the white-washed rock floor as Medusa glided around them.

"My servant tells me your ship sustained damage during the thunderbird's latest tantrum."

"Aye, Lady Medusa," Plank said, clearing his throat.

Her feet halted before him. "You know my name, pirate?"

"Aye, milady. Ye're well known outside o' the Dynami Sea."

That was laying it on a bit strong.

"Indeed," she said, resuming her inspection of them. "And you have come to join me for dinner of your own accord."

No one spoke; Ebba couldn't be alone in recognizing the tense undercurrent to her statement, nor the way the hissing of her snakes swelled. Why did the really bad immortals always have snakes? Ladon had worn serpents like a bloody scarf. It was as though these magical folks *wanted* people to dislike them.

Countless candles cast light downward from the low ceiling, and the snakes' writhing shadows were a moving picture on the ground.

Then the shadows stopped moving. The snakes went limp and Ebba had to stop herself from reaching out to hold the closest hand.

"But you are not dressed for dinner," Medusa said, her purring voice washing over them anew. "It is not often I have guests. You must dress for the occasion. *I insist*."

Peg-leg bowed. "We apologize. Yer servants barred us from returnin' to the ship to change."

The snakes lifted high. "You are sure of the truth of your words, pirate? Did you not seek to return to your ship with a tree stolen from my lands? And if not for the beam of light my servants tell me shot directly for my home, would you ever have accepted my invitation? Do not lie to me, mortals. I am a goddess."

"Ye're a gorgon," Grubby said happily.

The hissing cut off.

"Gorgeous," Caspian said, bowing. "He meant gorgeous, my lady. Just pirate talk."

Medusa was standing in front of the prince before Ebba could blink.

The goddess dipped her head to his level, but Caspian closed his eyes.

"Gorgeous, you say?" she asked. "But how can you be sure when you have not looked upon my face?" The delicate tone of her question was a thin covering for the dripping venom beneath.

"I can see your body," he replied. "And your hands. I can hear your voice, and your floral scent reached me as you walked by. I doubt a goddess could disappoint anyone."

Medusa gave a throaty laugh, circling him. "Your words are silken. A charmer. I always did like a charmer." She walked to the table, calling back, "But you have nothing to fear from me, mortal male. My snakes do not have the power to harm you."

"I hear truth in your words, my lady," Caspian replied. "However, the risk is great if I should look upon your fair face only to be turned to stone."

"Would not it be worth it?" she answered.

The prince bowed again. "If I might suggest an alternative?"

The goddess gestured for him to continue, her bracelets jangling.

"You wish for our company, which would surely be more pleasant for you should we not be staring at the table for the meal. We have with us something that will show us if you speak truth. If you consent, we can confirm the truth for ourselves—enough for us to relax in your company. I'm sure it must get tiresome without a companion."

The snakes went limp again, and Medusa half-turned to the painting of the lovers behind her.

Ebba held her breath.

"You will do this and go change for dinner," the goddess ordered.

"Aye," Ebba murmured with the others, watching a few of the daedalions appear at each side. Not all of them were male this time; two females stood among the others, wearing gauzy, gold togas tied at the base of their necks.

Which were the original two lovers? That was assuming Plank's story was correct. The painting behind the table did seem to confirm his prior tale.

"Bring forth the *veritas*," Medusa said, bored.

Jagger jolted and she stared at him. He stared right back. Medusa knew what the sword was called?

"I am aware of the objects you hold," she continued. "Do not tarry; I desire to eat. You have no idea how ravenous I am."

Stubby gulped audibly.

Jagger glanced away from Ebba and approached with the sword. Without preamble, he touched the flat of the blade to the goddess's upper arm, his eyes averted. "Do yer snakes have the power to harm us in any way? By turnin' us to stone or hypnotizin' us?"

"No," Medusa said. "Though I've always enjoyed that particular myth when tormenting mortals. And you know, it is a gorgon's *face*, not their snakes' eyes, that can turn you to stone anyway."

The sword flared white. Truth.

No one moved.

"Excuse me, Medusa," Plank said hesitantly, still staring at the ground. "The stories tell us that you *are* a gorgon."

After a beat, she murmured softly as though to herself, "I long for darkness to take my heart at last, to crush the useless thing into non-existence. But I float somewhere between goddess and gorgon for now. Such changes take millennia." Bitterness filled her voice. "As I am still transitioning, I do not possess the full powers of a gorgon. Neither do I possess the powers of my previous goddess form."

Medusa jerked and glared at the glowing sword. "Remove it," she hissed at Jagger, who obliged.

"Well, I ain't lookin' first," Locks whispered.

Barrels sighed and lifted his head. Ebba tensed, her chest tightening until a few breaths passed and Barrels didn't turn to stone or lose his marbles.

"I'm quite all right," he said mildly.

One by one, they did the same. Ebba raised her chin and looked upon Medusa's face.

She'd expected that someone with venomous reptiles wiggling out of her head would be as ugly as her pets, but that wasn't true. Her mouth was full, her lips painted with a deep orange that complemented her milky-green skin. Her body was lithe and draped with the black dress in the same way cloth was draped over some of the statues and artwork in the chamber.

The snakes forming her hair were black, and a thin strand of the milky-green was wrapped around them in rings to match Medusa's skin. Her eyes were sharp, normal-shaped but with the vertical irises of a serpent.

Ebba hadn't been turned to stone yet. Things were looking up.

The candlelight from above snagged on the centerpiece of Medusa's onyx dress. The material hanging from her shoulders was gathered into a short cylinder which also held up the material covering her from waist to ankle.

The cylinder was short and situated vertically between her breasts. Through the black gauzy material wrapped around the object, tarnished silver glinted.

Ebba would recognize a tarnished silver tube like that *anywhere.*

They'd found the next part of the weapon.

SEVENTEEN

Ebba couldn't see the others from where she stood obscured by gauzy curtains, but she could hear her fathers complaining from the far side of the chamber.

Two female daedalions had whisked Ebba off down the stairs.

They'd separated her dreadlocks into sections and the layers overlapped into some bun arrangement at the nape of her neck. A white dress had been flung over her head, unfortunately of the same gauzy make as Medusa's, but the immortals had wrapped solid lengths of fabric around her chest and hips, so at least everything wasn't hanging out for dinner. They'd then crisscrossed golden twine up her arms to just above her elbow, and from ankle to knee, careful not to scratch her with their scaled talons. And *more* of the gold thread wound just above her hairline in layers.

Rings were shoved on her fingers and toes, but Ebba managed to fend off the hawk-women from removing her golden hoop earring.

"How do I look?" she asked the two daedalions.

They tilted their heads to an unnatural angle only birds could achieve and nodded.

Ebba wouldn't mind taking the golden thread and rings with her when she left, but the dress could go to Davy Jones. The ladies at the Maltu brothel had shoved her in some fairly uncomfortable dresses during her stay, but they'd been uncomfortable because of the boning in the corsets. The white dress she wore showed no more skin than when Ebba changed in the sleeping quarters each day or went for a swim, she *supposed*, but the barely-there fabric, plunging cut, and leg slits appeared designed to entice and seduce.

The dress she'd worn back at Zol had reflected who she was. Ebba didn't feel the same about this dress. In fact, she'd spent the last twenty minutes reconciling with herself the fact that Caspian and Jagger would see her in this garb.

She brought her hands to her narrow waist, saying quietly, "I ain't sure I want to be seen in this."

That Ebba was confessing her fears to two hawk-women she'd just met didn't escape her.

One of them watched, not reacting, but the older of the pair stepped closer and leaned in to embrace her, careful not to touch the scabbing wounds on her back.

The unexpected hug had Ebba blinking back a burning behind her eyes. She had to be tired or something.

"Are ye the woman who loved the man from the enemy family all those years ago?" Ebba asked her.

The woman held a finger to her beak.

"Sorry," Ebba whispered. Would that comment make Medusa mad? She'd thought the creatures were mindless servants to the immortal's will, but they clearly had minds and thoughts of their own.

The younger daedalion drew the curtain aside, and Ebba took a huge breath that threatened to upset the feeble parameters of her white dress.

Have dinner with Medusa, steal the middle of her dress, escape the army of daedalions, and row the log back to their ship while fighting off the hawks as they attached the new boom and the various sheets and sails. No problem.

Feet bare, Ebba padded back to the table, the two hawk-women at her back. From the voices at the top of the steps, she gleaned the others had beat her there. Sink her. She'd hoped to get seated before them to conceal as much of the dress as possible.

Holding up the hem of her dress, Ebba reached the top of the steps and hurried to the table, eyes on the ground as though the whole lot of them had snakes for hair.

"That ain't a dress." Locks pounded his fist on the table. "Surely there's something more decent for our daughter to wear."

Ebba took the only empty seat as Medusa laughed. "Your daughter is a young woman. It is her nature to think of reproduction and to dress for a potential mate."

She what now? "There ain't no lookin' for mates or brats here, Lady Medusa," Ebba told her. "Not by a long shot. And I'd be preferrin' a dress that covered more."

"You will wear the dress," the goddess boomed, her snakes winding into a tangled chaos. She took a deep breath and the snakes slid free of each other, hanging limply once more.

Ebba *was* wearing the dress. What she wanted was for the subject to change.

Gathering her courage, she glanced up at her fathers. They all wore togas made of solid white material. Thank the fishes for small mercies; she couldn't have handled it if they were dressed in gauzy stuff.

And that was as far as she was letting her eyes roam.

She was seated between Jagger and Caspian. The prince sat next to Medusa. Despite Ebba's intent not to look, she stole a look from her peripheries. They were showing a fair amount more skin than her crew—only wearing loose white pants, their torsos bare.

Ebba took another steadying breath.

"But, my dark beauty," Medusa purred, "won't you take a proper look at the younger males? I dressed them especially for you."

She had? Why? To mess with Ebba's skull? She scrunched her nose. "I'd rather not. Ye can look, though."

Medusa's orange lips spread wide. "Oh, I will. You have no idea how long it's been since a mortal man came to this place. There is something so enticing about mortals. Their emotions, their fragility." She glanced at Caspian. "I must admit, I have always found them intoxicating."

He smiled at her and peered about the table. "I'm starved," he announced.

Medusa's eyes tightened, but she recovered from his unsubtle change of subject, clicking her fingers. The daedalions surged forward at her command, and Ebba tensed before realizing they were just removing the covers from the food.

"Stop yer stressin'," Jagger whispered.

She turned to him and frowned at his gleaming, muscular arms. "Jagger, are ye wearin' oil on yer body?"

He quirked a brow, his eyes glinting. "I am."

Her eyes flicking across to where his tribal tattoo covered the top of his chest and out to each shoulder tip, she traced the leaping animals and the waves and swirls of the piece.

"You prefer the flaxen one then," Medusa said, making Ebba jump. "I am glad," the goddess continued. "For I find myself enamored with your one-armed companion."

Ebba glanced at Caspian and found him watching her, jaw clenched.

"I ain't enamored with anyone," she said, very aware of her fathers at the table.

"Don't say that, Viva." Jagger wrapped an arm about her shoulders, and Ebba slapped his hand until he removed the offending limb. She ignored his quiet chuckle in her ear.

"You were staring at his body, my beauty, even when you didn't want to. That is the first sign of deep attraction. Just ask my two lovers." Medusa pointed at the woman who'd hugged Ebba and then the male daedalion standing directly opposite.

The immortals stared at each other as though no one else was in the room.

"Disgusting, aren't they?" Medusa hissed, her snakes spitting at the two lovers.

Ebba didn't think it was disgusting; she felt profoundly sorry for all of these creatures, despite the fact they'd been the ones to put them in Medusa's lair.

"There ain't nothin' deep-like goin' on here. I was only lookin' at Jagger because I like his tribal tattoos," she said, cheeks heating.

Medusa leaned forward over the table. "I know. Aren't they *delectable*?"

Ebba shrugged. "They're beautiful; I ain't sure about de-lickable."

"Keep telling yourself that, my dark beauty. One day, you will care enough to admit your feelings."

Her words shouldn't have affected Ebba, but they did. Her stomach churned with a heavy discontent.

"Is that roast beef?" Peg-leg exclaimed.

"Carrots," Stubby said.

Never more relieved for her fathers' overprotectiveness, Ebba loaded her plate with the succulent beef and array of roasted vegetables. Her fathers were doing the same, and it wasn't until Grubby made to pop a carrot in his mouth that everyone paused.

Ebba peered at the food she'd selected . . . from Medusa's table.

Medusa smiled, tapping a curved nail against her orange mouth. "You believe I would poison you, do you? You are my guests."

Caspian popped his loaded fork of roast beef into his mouth and chewed. Ebba made a sound of alarm and reached for him. He placed his fork down, and took her hand under the table, bringing her fingers to the *purgium* at his waist.

Her shoulders relaxed. Right, he'd be healed if he ate it.

Did a part of her still wonder if Caspian would give himself over to melancholy again if she let her guard down? Or was it that she'd had to watch over him for so long that Ebba had trouble accepting he could protect himself now? He was darker than he'd been, perhaps, but he wanted to *live*. She could see it.

They all watched as he swallowed.

How long would it take to poison him? Should they wait? Or. . . .

He shrugged after a full minute. "Seems okay?"

"Well . . . I'm hungry," Peg-leg said, shoveling carrots into his mouth. "Nice to see a balanced meal on the table."

Stubby groaned. "We still have fresh produce on the ship."

"Not for long," Peg-leg snipped.

They tucked into their food with varying states of mistrust.

The tender meat fell apart in her mouth, and Ebba groaned, only slowing her chewing as a group of the daedalions came in with buckets of the sweet, steaming water they'd passed above ground.

Without prompt, the creatures began to wash the outer walls of the chamber with the water.

"Why do ye bleach the rock with that stuff?" she asked Medusa, who'd cut a dainty morsel of beef to consume.

If the goddess had time to eat that slow, she had too much time. Clearly, she hadn't grown up with food-stealing pirates.

Meanwhile, Jagger was appropriately stuffing food into his gob.

"Light," the goddess replied, setting her fork and knife down to answer. "My snakes prefer to be underground, but it is too dark for my liking. So we bleach the stone."

"Ye should hurry it along and get it all done," Ebba replied. "All streaked like that, it just looks like scratch marks in the stone."

Medusa smiled and said nothing. She picked up her fork and ate her plankton-sized portion of beef.

A shiver worked up Ebba's spine.

She scooped up the last loaded fork of carrots and leaned back as she chewed. Ebba placed her hands over her gut and groaned. How long since she'd eaten so much? And actual meat instead of fish? She eyed the gravy and potatoes with longing.

Maybe if she waited a bit, she would be able to fit more in.

She glanced across the table at her fathers and discovered Plank and Stubby were having a furious silent conversation. It ended when Stubby folded his arms, and Plank straightened.

"Medusa," Plank started. "We've come to ye because we're on a dire quest to save the realm."

Her snakes quieted, and for a heartbeat the only sound in the chamber was the splaying bristles of the daedalions' brooms as they washed the walls.

"I know what it is you seek, mortal." She drew a ringed forefinger between the valley of her chest to the bottom of her breast bone. "You wish to take the *scio*."

The *scio*.

Ebba stared at the tube that formed the centerpiece of her dress. The fourth part. So very close.

"Come and get it," Medusa purred at Plank, her eyes flickering over his raven curls and upright bearing. Apparently, age wasn't a factor for the goddess when considering whom to fall in love with.

Grubby squinted at the woman's writhing snakes. "Give her a haircut first, Plank."

Jagger choked on a laugh, and Locks shushed Grubby as the goddess froze. The light in the chamber seemed to snuff out before resuming normal levels. The change made Ebba realize just how little they knew about the woman's powers. Was Medusa humoring them? Could she have killed them at any point? Obviously, she could turn people into hawk hybrids at whim. Or was that only back when she still had her goddess powers? The immortal had confessed she didn't have the full powers of either a gorgon or a goddess at the moment.

"You threaten my snakes?" Medusa hissed at her father. The question, a clear threat, hung heavy in the air.

The scrubbing hawks were moving closer, now working on the stairs below the raised area where they sat.

The goddess stroked the snake closest to her face, and the reptile leaned into her touch. "Only my snakes have been loyal," she murmured, watching the creature. "Only my snakes love me. Only they understand and stay true as eons go by."

They were part of her body, so the snakes didn't really have a choice. This wench seemed high maintenance. The goddess couldn't expect to find a true love who would jump at the click of her fingers or to the hiss of her snakes. Medusa seemed to be going about love the wrong way. Not that Ebba was one hundred percent certain what the right way should be. But if a thousand years had passed without success, that surely had to be an indication to switch tactics.

Ebba blinked slowly, inhaling as much air as her stuffed gut would allow. Caspian was resting back too. Jagger still ate. Oversized sod.

Water exploded from the cup Grubby held as he jumped.

Ebba jolted upright and stared down the table to where Medusa had blurred to her father's side. Locks was half raised from his chair, hand on his cutlass as he watched the goddess.

She leaned into Grubby's side, and a snake slid over his cheek; a menacing caress.

"Would you like to harm my snakes, selkie?" she asked him. "Answer wisely."

If wisdom was required, Grubby was going to die.

"I don't like to hurt any creature, if I can be avoidin' it," he replied. "But I'll kill anythin' to save Ebba."

Medusa's eyes slid to her, and the goddess left Grubby to walk to her side, hips swaying. "Anything to save Ebba, you say?"

Ebba wanted to speak, but she also wanted to keep the food inside her. She'd really eaten far too much.

"You inspire such loyalty from your males," the goddess murmured. "How?"

Sink her, a direct question. Ebba lifted her eyes to look at Medusa. The effort it took was colossal. The immortal's snakes danced before her, their motion almost hypnotic.

"They're my parents," she answered, pressing her lips firmly together and swallowing hard.

"And these two?" the woman said, gesturing to Jagger and Caspian. "Where does their loyalty come from?"

Ebba snorted, immediately regretting it. She closed her eyes and breathed deeply, willing the masticated mess of beef and vegetables to remain within.

"Ebba saved my life," the prince said.

His voice was slurring and she wanted to look at him, but now that she'd closed her eyes, she couldn't seem to open them again. Her chair had felt hard and rough when she first sat, but appearances were deceiving because not even *Felicity*'s hammocks could compare to such comfort.

"Ebba saved my life too," Jagger said, chewing.

His voice wasn't slurring. Ebba's eyebrow twitched at his remark. That was the second time he'd mentioned her saving his life. She wished her fathers would reply to the pirate and ask why. But they were silent.

The scrubbing of the daedalions was soothing, like listening to a gentle tide on a pebbled beach. The sound was growing louder. They'd reached the top of the steps and were working around the table. Close as the hawk-people were, Ebba could smell the heady aroma of the water from the pools above emanating from their buckets. *So sweet.*

"How did she save your life?" Medusa demanded.

The clang of a fork alerted Ebba that the immortal was back in her chair.

"She was full of life. I hadn't seen joy in so long; it was like starin' at the sun for the first time. The workings of her crew offered ha'piness too. I was jealous o' their life to start, but then I just wanted it. When I went back to *Malice* after Pleo, all I could recall was the look in her green eyes as I left. She'd be sad if I died. I wanted to preserve her *viva*. When I could barely see straight through the dark, that's what I clung to. Then I focused on findin' her beads. I couldn't recall my own name sometimes, but I had the memory of her face and her joy."

Ebba listened. Her shock palpable even through her near slumbering state.

Medusa didn't speak for a long time. "And did you collect all of these beads?"

"All but four. Two were lost to the sea. Swindles destroyed the other two when he caught wind of what I was doin'."

"I see . . . and did you give her these beads?"

". . . I did. I hurt her though. Didn't mean to do that. Just wanted to make things right. Wanted her to be joyful again and know her time on *Malice* hadn't changed who she was."

He had? Why hadn't he told her all that at the time? Actually, why was he saying all this now? The thought reached her with all the urgency of a soothing tendril of a soft, white cloud. She gripped at the wisp in her mind with both hands, holding to it. Jagger gave her the beads, and she'd shoved them in the bottom of her trunk. If he'd told her that story, however, she would've at least accepted them with good grace.

Jagger didn't think she'd changed after *Malice*?

Ebba tried to turn to him and her head flopped onto his shoulder.

"What have you done to them?" he demanded. "Why are they sleeping?" Jagger's voice was too loud.

"No, mortal. The question is: Why aren't you sleeping?"

Under her head, Ebba felt the shift in Jagger's posture as he glanced around. "It's the water, isn't it? That's why your daedalions are scrubbin' the floor."

Ebba frowned. They were being drugged? Through her drifting state, panic swelled, yet still she remained as limp as wet seaweed.

"It is," the goddess hissed from directly behind them again. "But you have not succumbed to its sleep-inducing qualities? It affects you; you have spilled your deepest truths to me. Yet you are resisting, though I sense you have no magic."

Jagger shrugged. "So what?"

"Immune," Medusa breathed. "You are the immune. I wondered which one of you it would be."

Immune? That rang a distant bell, but Ebba couldn't access the thought.

The woman shoved her aside and, unable to control her fall from the chair, she ended up sprawled over Caspian's lap like a naughty child.

Medusa rushed. "I have not seen your like in seven hundred and sixty-eight years. An *immune*," she whispered to him. "In my clutches."

There was something about that time frame, but Ebba couldn't recall what it was. Regardless, she didn't like the goddess' tone, slightly reverent and definitely possessive. The immortal had moved from Caspian to Plank and now to Jagger in the blink of an eye, but now she seemed decided.

"What is an immune?" Jagger asked her.

Water was being poured and a spark of anger lit within Ebba. Was Jagger pouring himself a drink right now? They were all immobile, and he was just concerned about washing down the meal?

"An immune, my male, is a mortal who possesses immunity to magic. Only one line has ever and will ever exist."

"Then that ain't me," he answered. "I've been possessed by magic plenty. The taint."

"I said immunity, not that you are impervious. If you are exposed to enough magic over a long period of time, you will feel the effects, but as soon as you are removed from the source, you will begin to press it back."

He inhaled sharply, and Ebba was glad he was as shocked as her. For once.

She could guess that all the others were too. Was that how he'd resisted the taint on *Malice* for so long? He had something that helped him—this immunity.

"Though," Medusa mused, "if you've experienced the taint, you have resisted the darkest and most powerful magic of all." Amusement seeped into her voice. "I see you've already met my masters, mortal? You have met the pillars six."

EIGHTEEN

Medusa was a lackey of the six pillars. The enemy they were trying to defeat. The woman must've guessed they were working against them as soon as she saw the two magical cylinders and *veritas*. Old as she was, she'd surely guessed their reason for wanting to collect the pieces.

"I have met the pillars," Jagger said. Was the heady aroma still making him speak truth? "Their taint, anyway—for two years."

"And yet you stand before me, cognizant," Medusa answered him. "In that, you are stronger than even I. For though I embrace the power their darkness gives me to help me become a gorgon, even I am their minion. But you, what you could *be* if you were at my side."

Would their kids have snakes coming out of their heads?

"How am I immune?" he asked after a beat.

Medusa stood. "The role of immune is passed from parent to child. Your mother or father was also an immune."

"I didn't know my parents," he confessed. There was another pause.

It was a great thing that Jagger wasn't rushing to save them. This was the best possible time to have a lengthy conversation, with her sprawled over Caspian's lap. Just perfect.

Could the prince feel her here? He had to, if he was still conscious like her.

Medusa's knee knocked Ebba's head as she resumed her seat once more.

"Why is my family immune? Why aren't others?" Jagger's voice shook as he asked.

"Because there is only one family of immunes. The eldest of the line is always one of the three."

"The three what?" Jagger leaned forward, his calf brushing Ebba's bare foot.

Ebba was all ears as well. That's all she could be at the moment. And even listening was becoming steadily harder.

The goddess sighed. "I hope you will not always ask so many questions. But I plan to keep you, mortal, and so I shall suffer your ignorance. And in truth, when immortality was ripped from this world, it disappeared in all forms, so your ignorance can be forgiven. The immortal leaders of this realm through the ages were always regulated by mortals who had the ability to assemble and dissemble the root of magic. Though the complete and intact root could not be held by a mortal, no immortal could reassemble it. In this way, immortal and mortal kind were balanced."

Codfish. There were only so many times the number three could crop up before Ebba was forced to align things in her head. The Earth Mother had mentioned the three watchers who eventually locked the six pillars away. The thunderbird mentioned that Ebba was chosen by her two counterparts. And now Medusa was yammering on about a trio who could assemble the root of magic. A beam of light shot out when she, Caspian, and Jagger touched, leading them to the next part of the root. Adding to the mix that only their crew could assemble the weapon to defeat the pillars, and Ebba had a sick feeling the three watchers might be in this very room. And worse, that she *was* one.

Shite. This was bad. Being one of the three heroes was a whole new level of commitment to merely saving the realm.

"What are you going to do with them?" Jagger asked, voice low.

Medusa tapped a long nail on the table. "My masters are on their way to collect them. If I present the three watchers to the pillars, they might gift me with the immune, coveted though you are."

The pillars were coming here? In her terror, Ebba managed to twitch her foot against Jagger's leg.

"They will take your friends and enslave them as they are already enslaving the realm. Delicious darkness once more," the goddess purred. "I will finally become a gorgon. But you, my immune, my treasure. You will remain here by my side, exalted amongst men. All I ask in return is that you fall in love with me."

Jagger's leg shifted against Ebba's foot.

"Mortal, I ask you as I have asked countless others under the power of my special water: Could you love me?"

The temperature plummeted too fast for magic to not be involved.

The scrubbing was right next to Ebba's head, and feathers brushed her arm.

"Nope," Jagger said, standing. "I'd rather go to hell itself. Whatever ye once were, ye're twisted inside now. I want no part of ye, except to see yer heart out of ye and yer body burn."

Ebba sighed inwardly.

"As so many have said before you, though none so graphically," Medusa said. The sound was tight, as though made through clenched teeth. "Yet you are the only one of your kind. I cannot give you up."

"Then release Viva—and the others. Return them to their ship with the log. Let them go on their way, and I'll remain. Do this, and I'll stay willingly. I'll even try to like ye."

"This I cannot do, lover. For my duty to my masters is greater than any love I can have."

"And that be why ye can't find love, Medusa. For duty and love belong together."

A breeze fluttered against Ebba's shoulder. It teased the loose parts of her dress and cooled her skin.

Medusa's chair scraped back. "What was that?"

The breeze strengthened, pushing away the heady aroma and bringing the sea air in with it. Medusa's cries filled the chamber as the breeze heightened, rising, streaming until wind flooded the cavern.

Ebba groaned as the air pushed away the heady smell filling her senses. She tried to move her fingers and toes, hearing the groans of her fathers and Caspian above her.

Strong arms pulled her up and cradled her. Then they began running.

The wind strengthened, whistling as the person carrying her jolted down the stairs, and clearing away some of the clouds in her mind.

Ebba cracked open her eyelids, squinting back over the person's shoulder just as a brilliant glow erupted in the cavern. White light filled every space, converging around Medusa at the head of the table. The light was moving, and as Ebba's eyes came into focus, she discerned the large light was made of many tiny floating lights.

One zipped right by her face.

"It's the wind sprites," she slurred. Sally had come to save them. And she'd brought friends.

Ebba scanned for her crew and jerked, seeing they were cradled in the daedalions' arms. Half were behind, and she assumed the rest were in front.

She looked up, shrieking when the older hawk-woman who'd helped her dress peered down at her. Heart leaping in her throat, Ebba searched for the rest of her crew and caught sight of the rest of her fathers and Caspian in front. Jagger was directly in front of her, running without aid, the *veritas* in hand.

The air grew lighter and lighter as they were carted out of the tunnel and up the stairs to the surface.

The line of daedalion didn't stop until they were beyond the pools filled with the same water that had almost seen the crew of *Felicity* incapacitated and carted off to the six pillars. Why were the daedalions helping them anyway? They were Medusa's servants. Not that Ebba was in a position to argue.

The immortal placed Ebba on her feet and stumbled to her lover, holding him close. Ebba weaved to her fathers and clung to each of them in turn before hugging Caspian. Hesitating briefly, she strode to Jagger and hugged him too. He grunted, not returning the gesture, and she pulled back, staring up at him. Everything he'd said down in the cavern hung heavy in the air. The sweet water had made him speak truth, and what he'd confessed was enough to force Ebba off the precipice she'd balanced on since they first met.

She was going to trust Jagger, for better or for worse.

"Lass, get back here with ye," Peg-leg instructed, his eyes on the tunnel exit.

Ebba strode to his side and watched as the daedalions converged outside. Their ranks swelled, more and more exiting the underground tunnel to gather behind Ebba and her crew.

Eventually, what she assumed was the last one joined the ranks, and silence descended over the pools in the forest clearing. Eyes turned to the tunnel entrance as a glowing light blazed. Wind sprites zipped out to float above their heads like lanterns, enclosing the tree line where they stood around the perimeter of the pools.

A very naked Medusa was forced into the open, still surrounded by the glowing light. Eyes watering, Ebba squinted to see. The goddess was wrapped in a white chain, an iron ball dragging along the ground behind her, attached to a manacle about her ankle. Sally, the source of the glow, led the prisoner.

In her tiny hands was the part they'd come to the Dynami for. The next part of the weapon.

"Ye got it, Sal," Ebba said, stepping forward.

Not only that, Sally came *for them*. After all the times she hadn't been there, the sprite had finally pulled through.

Sally nodded over her shoulder at her sprite minions.

"You'll regret this, Saliha," Medusa screamed, bucking wildly, her eyes bulging with an insane edge.

The sprite queen flipped the goddess off.

"You'll destroy the sprites," the goddess hissed. "You're too weak to rule."

Sally tossed the cylinder to her minion sprites, who scrambled to catch it, and slowly rounded on the goddess.

Medusa smirked, but the curve of her lips disappeared as the sprite raised two fisted hands out by her sides. A swirling funnel of air encased the goddess, and her piercing shrieks were barely heard over the howling wind.

Smiling, Sally opened one hand, a wrinkle between her tiny brows. Ebba jumped as a hurtling procession of daggers whipped out of the tunnels, a blur to her eyes. The daggers entered the wind funnel around Medusa, and her shrieks turned to screams for an instant before the goddess-sized hurricane was gone, the daggers clattering on the stone ground.

The sprite queen crossed her arms, and Ebba stared past her pet sprite, blanching.

"Blimey," Peg-leg hushed.

Sally had given Medusa a haircut. Not a single one of her writhing snakes remained.

The sprite queen waved her hand, and the resultant gust shoved the goddess into a large pool of the bleaching water.

The gathered mixture of daedalions, sprites, pirates, and royalty watched in silence as Medusa sank to the bottom. *Ouch.*

"Is she dead?" Barrels whispered.

Sally shook her head. She gestured to her minions, who scrambled to return the cylinder to their leaders. The sprite waved the tube in Ebba's face.

Hastily, Ebba passed the *dynami* over to Peg-leg so she could take the new part.

The *dynami* was rounded on one end, the *veritas* was a sword, the *purgium* two flat, circular ends, and this part was different again. Though made of the tarnished silver with the pearly sheen swimming beneath the surface, the shape was new. On one end, the tube tapered into a sharp point; the opposite end was a flat circle. The letters S-C-I-O were engraved up the side.

The six parts had to make one weird weapon.

"Medusa won't die," Sally said, her voice rich and velvety. "She will stay there until she's freed. And if the pillars have already sent their lackeys, that will be sooner rather than later. We should leave as soon as possible."

"She said the six pillars are on their way," Ebba replied, glancing up.

Wait.

"Ye just spoke to me." Ebba rushed forward to the hovering sprite.

Locks grabbed her arm. "She's just squeakin' like normal, lass."

She shook her head. "Nay, I just heard her. Her voice is kind of deep, actua'ly. Masculine-like."

"Stately," Sally countered, her tone smooth and full.

One by one, they all glanced down at the pointy tube in Ebba's hands.

"Guess we know what the *scio* be doin' then," Plank said, echoing her thoughts.

Stubby stepped forward. "What did she say to ye?"

Ebba broke her stare with the sprite, who was smirking. She could hear Sally. "Sh-she said that Medusa won't die, but she'll stay there until she's freed. The pillars' lackeys will be comin', and we should leave as soon as we can."

"Hopefully they'll take long enough for us to get out o' here without another fight," Peg-leg said.

They were interrupted when the two oldest daedalions—the ones Ebba had identified as the original lovers—approached and dropped to one knee before her and the crew.

"What're ye kneelin for?" Ebba scolded. "Up with ye." They shot to their feet, making her feel bad.

"You'd make a terrible queen," Sally said, inspecting her nails.

Flamin' pet.

"My lady." The male spoke.

Ebba jolted before realizing the *scio* didn't just work on sprites. Did the cylinder work for all magical people who couldn't talk in the mortal language? Sink her, there needed to be a book on all the different creatures and who could do what. She'd make Barrels start one—if he hadn't already.

"Just Ebba, please," she told them. "And I thank ye and the rest of yer . . . flock for helpin' us out o' Medusa's lair." *Even if ye were the ones to bring the sleeping water in.*

"When we saw that one among you could resist, and that you had magical beings on your side, how could we not? All immortals know of the three watchers. We know what objects you hold and the burden you bear for all. For thousands of years, we have been tied to Medusa, her servants for eternity, though we did not ask it of her. It was time to do our part to help this realm, regardless of the consequences."

"But she saved ye from death," Ebba said. A quick glance at her crew's confused faces reminded Ebba this conversation was entirely one-sided to them. "Why wouldn't ye wish her to save ye from that?"

"We had chosen death. We wanted the freedom to be together in the way we wished, without restraint."

"And Medusa took yer ability to love freely from ye," Ebba said slowly, her head tilted.

The female daedalion at the male's side dripped her beaked head. "Yes, lady. She did."

"Can ye be free now she's in the pool?" Ebba asked.

The lovers shook their heads.

"No, but there is another way," the male said. He turned to look at Jagger, to what was clutched in his hands—the *veritas*. And then to the *purgium* Caspian held before returning to look at her. "The beam of light the three of you create can dissolve dark magic."

She stared at him. "I-it can?"

He nodded.

Ebba stared into the creature's eyes and shifted to face Jagger and

Caspian. "They be sayin' that we can sever their tie to Medusa with the beam o' light. They want to be free."

"What will happen to them if we do?" Locks asked.

She cocked her head to the daedalions.

The lovers shared a glance, and the air between them seemed to pulse with their connection. So much so that *Ebba's* chest ached. That was love?

That was . . . *otherworldly*.

"We will pass from this realm," the woman admitted. "Once our tether to Medusa is broken, we will be forced to follow our original path to death. We will be together at last as vessels, and our children will live on, free to roam and love as they please."

Ebba scanned the rest of the flock. "And they'd be on their best behavior?" she asked. "I don't want to unleash anything bad on the realm; it's already in a sorry state."

"Despite Medusa's best attempts, we have raised our children to be kind. No, they will not harm others when they are free. Syrion," he called.

Every time Ebba thought she might be done with magic, she found joy and heart and happiness within the immortals. Grubby, Sally, these daedalions—nothing had worked out for the lovers, and yet they still knew right from wrong.

One of their sons strode forward.

His father nodded and the creature nodded, dropping to one knee. "Lady, my name is Syrion, and I swear on behalf of my siblings that we shall harm none except those who deign to hurt or cage us. I would also like to offer you our friendship. If you find yourself in need, please call upon us. We will do whatever we can to aid you."

That seemed fair enough. If someone hurt or caged her or her crew, she'd harm the person too. She relayed it to the others and waited until they'd voted.

"Aye," she said, conveying the crew's decision. "We believe ye." She would've done it without their offer of aid, but Ebba wasn't about to tell them that.

"So how do we do this?" Caspian asked.

"Watch and learn," the sprite queen said, cracking her knuckles.

Sally floated forward and—as far as Ebba could make out—ripped off some of her glow and held it to her mouth. The sprite blew her light, and it drifted down to the space between the original daedalions and Medusa.

Twin cords, previously invisible, were illuminated by the sprite glow.

"Wait," Stubby said, resting a hand on Jagger's and Caspian's shoulders as they started forward. "Let them say goodbye to their children."

Their crew stood aside as the lovers embraced their family.

Ebba hadn't ever thought to see a bird cry, but the sight of it nearly drew tears to her own eyes. Her fathers felt the scene before them stronger than she, tears marking each of their faces as the lovers untangled themselves from their children.

"I'll never kill a bird again," Jagger said.

The crew turned to look at him, and Jagger lifted a shoulder.

Ebba asked, "And what about Caspian? Will ye kill him?"

The pirate tightened his grip on the *veritas*. "He saved my life, and now I've saved his. We be even, in my eyes." Darkness filled his gaze. "So I can go back to killin' him."

That was pirate logic if she'd ever seen it. But the words lacked the venom they'd once possessed? Jagger looked about as murderous as ever, so maybe that was highly wishful thinking. In fact, maybe Ebba would bottle some of Medusa's water to dose him with. She'd learned more about him over Medusa's dinner than in months of having his acquaintance.

Ebba peeked at the prince, who widened his eyes dramatically. She grinned, hurrying to tuck her amusement away as the daedalion lovers came to stand before her again.

"Fare ye well." Ebba spoke for her fathers, who were still blubbering. "I hope ye get what ye've wished for. If ye see the thunderbird, could ye tell him Jagger has said he won't be killin' any more birds?" They'd probably have to sail past the god of souls again soon.

The female smiled, bobbing her head.

"Let's get to it then," she said, looking at the other two. Her two counterparts. Ebba shivered, still not entirely happy about the three watchers development.

She walked to join Jagger and Caspian. "Ready?"

Jagger gripped her upper arm and Caspian held her hand.

White blazed outward, coating them in mystical light that transformed them. Having done this a few times now, the otherworldly bronze glow of her skin didn't leave her quite so breathless. Ebba studied the beam of light shooting out from them.

Directly north. Bugger. The next part was still in the Dynami.

The three of them maintained contact as they rounded the two lovers, so the beam of light would come into contact with the couple's tether to Medusa. The other daedalions screeched and, far above, the sprites' glow flared. Sal's powers still illuminated the twin cords. And as the three of them took a final step, Ebba watched their shooting beam connect with the bond enslaving the daedalion.

The two lovers fell to their knees, bodies pressed close, one of their hands against the other's cheek.

Jagger's hand slid away, breaking the connection, but Ebba hardly noticed. She swallowed thickly as the lovers' feathers began to disappear to golden dust, faster and faster, taking away the firm edges of their form, eroding deeper until soon their bodies were gone.

Their tender gazes were the last thing Ebba saw before the gold dust was caught by a breeze and lifted high into the sky to where all deserving souls were taken. Peace filled her for knowing the pair would pass their judgment.

She hadn't had many chances to see lovers together, but even Ebba knew love of that measure was rare. To find a partner of your soul like that made death appear almost feeble.

The son who had spoken to them approached once more, wiping the tears from his eyes. He bowed. "Thank you for granting my parents' wish. You have no idea how long they have endured, fighting against Medusa's attempts to break their love. My siblings and I will leave you now; we go to mourn our loss. But remember my promise." He looked directly at Ebba.

"I will," she said hoarsely, blinking furiously to keep her tears at bay.

Without another word, the daedalions took off into the sky, chasing the golden dust. The beating of their wings grew fainter until quiet reigned once more.

NINETEEN

"I can't believe ye saved us, Sal," Ebba said, voice muffled as she changed out of the stupid white dress and into a fresh tunic and slops. Reasonably fresh, anyway.

Ducking under her hammock, she knelt and threw back the lid of her trunk, adding, "Ye came back for us—and after all the horrible things I thought o' ye after ye ditched."

Sally squeaked from her mini-hammock.

"Hold on," Ebba interrupted. She grabbed a belt and pulled it tight, then reached for the *scio* on her hammock.

'Scio' apparently meant 'know,' or so *Saliha* said.

Ebba tucked the new tube into her belt. "Go on then."

Sally's rich voice filled the sleeping quarters, the sound only punctured by the yells and clunking above deck where her fathers and the sprite minions worked to attach the new boom.

"I was *saying*," the sprite queen said, eyes narrowed, "that you've been laying on the guilt for weeks. You forced me into helping." She crossed her arms. "But for the record, I helped you in Syraness. I stole the key that Caspian dropped to you on Exosia to free you all from the cages. I went to search for the parts when everything went belly-up, and *then* held the pirates in the castle off with my powers so you could escape. I couldn't save you from *Malice* for fear they'd take my magic and rise to power. And perhaps I should have left the pink champagne fountain," she said, clearing her throat. "Honestly, I'm on a kind of. . .holiday, and it was a *champagne fountain.* I've seen your crew in enough scraps to know you could handle the rest."

Ebba's mouth was ajar.

"Oh," Sally added, holding up a tiny finger. "I saved all of you from the thunderbird's storm."

"Ye can't claim everythin'." Ebba rolled her eyes.

"Wind," the sprite said with a pointed look. "I combated the wind. He would've crushed you, even if not intending to. Once he starts a storm, it's hard for him to control the urge to annihilate anything and anyone. You didn't think you got through that on skill, did you?"

Perhaps that was true, and Sally had helped that much. Though it hadn't felt that way at the time.

"You have no idea how much heat incurring Medusa's wrath puts on my people," Sally added. "Which, if we're being honest, is why I couldn't interfere too much with King Montcroix. If he hadn't been killed, I would've had to work with him in the future."

"Now who's layin' it on thick?" Ebba asked, snorting and rummaging in her trunk for a bandana.

Sally cracked a grin. "Can't have you complaining I didn't do enough."

Ebba grinned back. "Nay, don't s'pose so."

The bilge door opened with a bang, and two glowing sprites floated down, bowing before their queen.

"Queen Saliha," one said.

Saliha, Sally. Ebba was pretty proud she'd managed to name her pet something so similar to her queen name. She pulled up a bandana and squinted at it. Brown. Where was her orange one?

Sal grunted. "What?"

"Your subjects wish to know if you will return to your rightful place on our throne," the same sprite said.

Ebba's heart sunk even though five of her fathers had already pulled her aside and warned her this could happen. Grubby had pulled her aside, too, and then stared at her with a frown that Ebba took to mean he'd been sent by her other fathers and couldn't recall why.

When she'd found Sal in the grog barrel at Kentro so long ago, having her around never felt like a permanent thing. But somewhere along the line, her presence aboard *Felicity* had started to feel necessary.

Sally licked her lips, and Ebba arched a brow, pulling out another not-orange bandana.

"Should I get ye some wood to chew on?" she offered the queen sprite. Chewing wood was better than relapsing with the grog, after all, but it was better if Sal gnawed on the scrap stuff. Stubby couldn't take more damage to the spare booms already loaded in the hold.

Sally's cheeks pinkened, and she swung off the bed, flying to her minions. "Gather the present sprites together. I shall address them forthwith."

As the sprites flew off, Ebba said loudly, "Should I get ye some wood *now*?"

Sally glared at her, white glow blazing, and whizzed out after her messengers.

Under her hammock, Ebba snickered, wiping at her eyes that, unfortunately, weren't just moist with laughter. She looked at the bandana in her hand. Black. Ebba groaned. If Plank had taken her stuff again, she'd cut a slit in his hammock. Or take something of his, like that pretty length of white braided leather he had stashed there.

Her lingering smile slid away as her fingers touched the flax pouch containing her beads.

Squeezing her eyes shut, Ebba drew the pouch out. Sitting back on her heels, she opened her eyes and unwound the fastening.

There they were. Nearly all of them. Certainly enough for her to look as she once had. But would she *feel* as she once had?

The answer to that was a resounding no, and expecting that to happen didn't seem reasonable. Caspian wasn't the same after losing his arm, and her fathers weren't the same after sailing with Mutinous Cannon. Jagger . . . well, who knew with that man. Why would *she* be the same after her time on *Malice*? Ebba craved the connection with her memories again. A part of her wanted to wear the beads as a badge, a *sign* to everyone that what happened hadn't broken her . . . a way of flipping off the pillars, Pockmark, and the other pirates aboard *Malice*.

Except it had broken her.

Such a simple thing—to put beads back in her hair. To climb the rigging. To return to Exosia. To shake off despair. And yet none of them were.

She was still waiting for permission of some sort. From herself or another. Permission that might not ever come. Was that idiocy? Ebba told Peg-leg he could climb the rigging, and that hadn't seemed to do anything.

Ebba exhaled heavily and refastened the pouch, running her thumbs over the braided material that Jagger must have made himself.

"*Then release Viva—and the others. Return them to their ship with the log, and I'll remain. Do this, and I'll stay willingly. I'll even try to like ye,*" he'd said.

Whatever her hang-ups with the flaxen-haired pirate were, an odd warmth filled her chest when recalling his words to Medusa. He hadn't given Ebba the beads for malicious reasons. He'd pleaded for her life, willing to trade his own, and he'd been under the influence of the truth water.

. . . Why had he clung to the thought of her and the crew while aboard *Malice*? Had she really saved him just by not being miserable? For all his derisive comments about her being foolish and spoiled, he'd confessed that those very things helped him fight the taint.

The crow's nest was hers for good.

She jerked violently as the bilge door was wrenched open.

"Ebba-Viva," Peg-leg called. "All hands on deck, lass. We're puttin' up the boom."

Ebba exhaled shakily. "Aye, comin'." With another glance at the flax pouch, she tucked it back in the far corner of her trunk and swiped up the black bandana.

She shoved the material over her hairline, feeling her bead-less dreads spilling down her back, and climbed up the ladder.

Months prior, if Ebba had exited the bilge to the current sight, she would've thought she'd lost her bloody mind. Sprites whizzed overhead, glowing white balls carrying ropes. The majority of them were lifting the new boom off the deck and floating it higher. Her fathers, utterly unfazed by what had to be near-on one hundred tiny creatures with wings, were waving their hands to direct the beam into place.

"Help us with this, will ye?" Peg-leg called to her.

Ebba crossed to where he was untangling the rigging they'd salvaged after the storm. She took an end and began pulling on a knot.

"Ye okay, lass?" Peg-leg asked, the other corner in his hands. "We've gone through a fair lot recent-like."

Her mouth dried. "I'm okay. I ain't sure what to think about a lot o' things is all."

"Like?"

The beads. Caspian's deeper regard. The things Jagger had said on the island. The ongoing struggle of her fathers. "We know Jagger be the immune and what it means. But I guess I don't know what I am and what that means—or what Caspian is and what *that* means. Jagger's only one part of the three watchers. I don't know what we're meant to do with the weapon. I don't know how we'll ever be ready to battle the pillars." *Or how we'll all survive.*

Ebba needed her fathers to get through this alive. More than that —she wanted them to heal enough to live for themselves. She—

That was it.

She stared at the rope squares in her hands, glancing across the deck to where Jagger lurked at the bow. *That* was why he couldn't be thrown overboard or die. That was why she'd felt such panic at the thought. And such consternation over whether or not to trust him.

If Jagger could be rid of the taint, so could her fathers. And then they'd be okay. Yes, Jagger was an immune, but if he could throw off the taint entirely, surely her fathers could find joy and happiness again.

Ebba had to know they could fight against the darkness within. That they wouldn't crumble without her. That was why Jagger unsettled her so much. In some ways, he was an acute representation of her fathers' pain.

"That be a lot of things to be in one head," Peg-leg said, breaking through her shock.

What? What were they talking about?

Throat working, Ebba returned to untangling the rigging, scrambling to collect her thoughts.

"I be thinkin' that when we're ready to know more, we'll know," Peg-leg mused.

That's the way they'd always worked—on a need-to-know basis. "I ain't sure I want to wait."

"The world doesn't just hand ye things on a platter all nice-like, lass." He held up the rigging. "Ye can't force things to happen. Things have a way o' leadin' ye places, just like the thunderbird's storm led us to this here island. When the time be right, ye just know."

She watched the way he looked at the rigging—as though it was a great puzzle. "Like ye climbin' the riggin'?" Ebba whispered.

He cast her a curious look. "Aye, like climbin' the riggin'," he said, busying himself again. "I wanted to thank ye for puttin' the notion in my head. Ye're right, havin' a go is a good idea. In truth, it be an idea I've had myself many-a-time; I just could never seem to. . . ."

"Give yerself permis'ion," she finished in a soft voice.

"Aye, lass. It was just that." He put down the rigging and with a *tap, tap, tap* was at her side.

She fell into her father's arms, inhaling his familiar sea salt and sweat smell.

He rested his bald head atop her dreads. "The way ye say these things makes me feel there be more on yer mind. And ye don't need to say anythin' if ye don't wish. But I hope *ye* know how special ye are, lass. How others look at ye and see someone who's right fierce and capable. Ye say things how they are, and that swine Jagger was right about one thing when he poured his innards out. Ye're pure joy. Not just to yer biased fathers."

Tears slipped from her eyes, and she hugged Peg-leg back tightly, unable to speak.

"Ye're a fierce pirate," he whispered in her ear. "And ye don't take no for an answer."

Ebba's shoulders shook as she cried in her father's arms. She choked out, "Ye don't think I'm fakin' strength and I'm weak under it all?"

"Is that what ye think o' me? Or my co-parents?" he asked plainly.

"Nay," she said with a loud sniff. "Never. Nothin' could take ye down."

Peg-leg pulled back and kissed her forehead. "Then ye can believe me when I say there be no doubt in my mind that no matter who or what knocks ye down, ye'll always pick yerself up again. Because ye're our daughter and I be knowin' just who ye are."

Raising her chin, Ebba looked at his face. The twisted knot began to slowly loosen until she was able to take a fuller breath than she had in weeks.

"Better?" he asked her.

More tears spilled across her cheeks, but she nodded, a tremulous smile forming on her lips. "Aye, bit better," Ebba whispered. She sniffed. "I just wonder why these things keep happenin' to us, is all."

Out of everyone in the realm, they were meant to shoulder these burdens. Right now, *real* heroes could be on this quest while she drank coconut milk and swung in a hammock on Zol, blissfully ignorant of any strife.

"It ain't all bad," Peg-leg said, pulling back to peer down at her.

She wiped her nose. "Feels like it sometimes."

He glanced up and his face firmed. "Nay, I can't agree with ye, lass. But . . . perhaps ye need remindin'."

Peg-leg took hold of her hand and drew her with him to the port side, leaving the tangled rigging behind.

They reached the opposite bulwark, and he let her go, reaching up to grip the rigging.

Her mouth dried as she realized what he was doing.

Her father glanced back at her, a nervous edge to his words. "What do ye say, lass? I've always been more o' a starboard rigger, but I'll go up if ye stop cryin'."

Ebba dashed an arm across her eyes as Peg-leg swung up onto the ship's side and studied the intact rope lattice extending to the crow's nest.

"Ye can do it," she whispered to him.

He peered down, nodding. "I can."

The work on *Felicity* stuttered to a halt as Peg-leg began to climb, relying on both arms and his sole leg. None of the sprites but Sally could know how monumental this moment was, and yet even they detected the change of atmosphere on deck.

Ebba's heart rose into her mouth as her father pulled himself higher and higher up the squares of rope.

She knew exactly what he was feeling, the lurch of the rigging, the small cut and roughness of the ropes. A lump filled her throat, and Ebba didn't feel any embarrassment as hot tears spilled over her cheeks.

"Go Peg-leg," she called to him, clapping her hands as she cried.

Her other fathers joined her, Locks looping an arm about her shoulders.

They watched in silence, aside from the sounds of her happy

tears as Peg-leg reached the first boom and shook out his arms. A sheen of sweat covered his brow. His tunic stuck to his back. But none of that compared to the *joy* on his face. A broad smile was there. His shoulders were drawn back to his full height.

Her father was *happy*.

An answering smile curved her lips as he continued to the next boom.

The entire crew, mortal and immortal, royal and pirate watched Peg-leg; watched as he passed the second boom, climbing to the shrouds for the first time since he'd been crushed and left in ruins. Their crewmate, a member of their family, was opening a door he'd slammed shut on himself in his lowest, darkest time.

By the time he reached the crow's nest, by the sounds of it, not a dry face remained.

Her father swung himself into the nest and waved down at them, shouting wordlessly. He was on top of the world. And Ebba would move the realm itself to get her other fathers to the same place.

Peg-leg was right. Life wasn't all bad. Not at all.

"Guess what?" she said to the others as Peg-leg continued hollering in the crow's nest. "I'm goin' to get my nose pierced once we're finished savin' the realm from evil."

"No, ye ain't," Stubby immediately replied. The rest of her fathers had stilled.

Ebba turned to them, hands on hips. "I'm fierce, and I don't take no for an answer."

TWENTY

The rest of the crew were attaching the ropes and sails, and Ebba sat against the bulwark in the bow. Sally had settled cross-legged on the tops of her bent knees.

Caspian sat beside Ebba. He'd placed the *purgium* to the side so he could also touch the *scio* and talk to the sprite queen.

"Sal? Were ye really on holiday? Is that why ye snuck onto our ship all those months ago?" Ebba asked, watching Pillage roll around on the deck in the sun by Caspian's feet.

The sprite sighed and glanced away. "I've only recently come into my rule. My mother died just before you entered Syraness."

Caspian and Ebba shared a look.

"Sal, I'm so sorry," she whispered.

"Don't be. I'm not. She never would've saved your crew in Syraness. She was a horrible, horrible person. Alas, while she ruled, I did not have to. When the time came, I'm afraid I decided running away was a better choice."

"I can relate to that," the prince said, rubbing the back of his head and disrupting the russet curls there. "Though I ran before my father died, I suppose. Then I just failed to keep the throne."

"Leadership is no easy choice," the queen said, shaking her head. "More so when there is no choice in it to begin with."

Caspian hummed in agreement.

Ebba wasn't entirely sure Sal was as uncaring about her mother's death as she professed. Even if your parents were cruel brutes, it'd be hard not to care a smidgen over their death. Maybe that was why Sally had turned to the grog.

She poked Sally in the stomach. "So ye went on a massive bender and ditched yer minions for months on end?" She snorted again.

"Some of them are really irritating," the sprite confessed. "I wasn't ever allowed to have the friends I wanted. Only the most elite were accepted by my mother." She turned to Ebba. "You were the first true friend I ever had."

"Ye were my second friend," Ebba said, thinking of Cosmo, a.k.a. Caspian.

Sally bent forward and bit her.

"Ouch, ye glowin' excuse for a queen," she roared.

The sprite threw her head back in laughter and waved several shocked sprites away.

Ebba joined her. "I'll sure miss ye, Sal. It doesn't feel right that ye're goin'. Ye're part o' our crew."

Sally nodded. "I believed my place was here, helping to search for the pieces. But I was wrong. I must do what I can to protect my people and ensure your return with the weapon is possible."

"I hadn't thought that far ahead," Ebba confessed.

"Not unusual for you."

She glared. "If I want to stop hearin' ye, I just stop touchin' the *scio*, aye?"

Caspian's brows were lowered. "We wouldn't have gotten away from Medusa without you, Queen Saliha. I worry about our success without your help."

"He thinks ye're stupid to go. He only wants you here for yer magic," Ebba translated.

The prince sighed and she swatted his thigh, grinning.

The wind fluttered at the sprite's hair, appearing to toy with the loose white strands affectionately. "I'm not really going," she said when the breeze ebbed. "Do you remember what the Earth Mother said, Ebba?"

She thought about that. "Not really. Just that she killed bunnies when she was angry."

The queen of sprites blew out a breath. "You recall far more than that, and I know it. *Bloody pirates*. She said eight were needed in the end. Not including Pillage, we had ten. The root of magic has a role for each of us, but I don't believe mine is here."

"We'll still have nine when you leave though," Caspian said, straightening. "What does that mean?"

"Nine and a little with Pillage." Ebba corrected, glancing at the cat again, whose ears were twitching in response to hearing his name. "And I don't think ye should listen to the Earth lady. She was a whole heap of unhelpful. Though she didn't outright try to kill us like the thunderbird."

Sally pursed her lips. "Papatuanuku is probably considered unhelpful by mortal standards, I agree. Most immortals are slaves to their nature. But when it comes to foretelling what beholds the realm, she has never erred. She's just useless at doing anything about it."

"So you're really going?" the prince asked her.

Ebba blinked rapidly as moisture filled her eyes. "I'll *really* miss ye." Sally was part of their crew, and though some part of her had always understood the sprite would leave one day, Ebba hated that their group was about to split.

"I'll miss you, too, Ebba-Viva Fairisles," Sally said with a smile. "You'll always have a friend in me."

"Aye, and the same goes for you." Ebba sniffed, adding, "Ye may not've been my first friend, but ye'll always be my first pet."

This time she was ready for Sally's bite and batted her away, snickering.

The sprite resumed her seat. Ebba was certain that if they

weren't saying goodbye, Sally would be hanging her over the side of the ship.

"Will you be okay once you go back to your queendom? The pillars are close to Syraness," Caspian said, amber eyes regarding the sprite intensely.

Sally sighed. "There will be a huge change, and I suppose we've got to fight off the six pillars before any of that can happen. Suffice to say, I've got work to do." She rolled her shoulders back. "I'm just not afraid of it now."

That was how Ebba felt, in a way. That she had so many problems to sort out, it was overwhelming. Except Ebba didn't see herself fixing everything *after* the pillars were defeated. Instead, the constant feeling that time was running out reminded her their problems had to be solved *before* they could save the realm.

The prince replied, "Your subjects may not realize it to begin with—change is not comfortable for most—but they'll thank you in time."

"And you, Prince? Do you know what you'll do with your kingdom?"

Caspian shrugged his shoulder. "I'm not sure I even have a kingdom. If I have any subjects left to rule at the end, then I suppose I must. Though, like you, I worry that the changes I want to make are too large for Exosia."

The sprite echoed his previous words. "They'll thank you in time."

The two shared a glance and a smile. Ebba felt left out of this royal conversation.

"What changed yer mind to return?" Ebba asked.

Sally watched as the final rope was attached to the new boom, answering, "Jagger changed my mind."

"Jagger? How? Because ye're smitten by him?"

"She is?" Caspian asked, brows raised.

"I'm not smitten," Sally scowled.

"Aye, ye are," Ebba retorted. She raised her voice, fluttering her hands either side of her body like wings. "'Oh, ye want to destroy Ladon? Sure, I'll come with ye. Ye tunic be off, Jagger, I'm goin' to stare at yer muscles and blush. Ye're so rugged and handsome."

A shadow fell over her and Sally smirked widely.

"Viva, ye can stare whenever ye like," Jagger said, his eyes dark as he looked down at her.

"I was being Sal," she muttered to him, wiping at her face.

He sat and placed the *veritas* by his side before extending a finger to touch the *scio*. His arm rested on her thigh and she stared at the touch before deciding not to make an issue of it. The weather here was cooler, and it was nice to be wedged between two warm bodies, even if one of those warm bodies had spouted off a whole reel of truths involving herself not too long ago.

"You're blushing," Sally said to her.

Sodding. Pet.

"What about Jagger?" Caspian interrupted loudly.

"Aye," Jagger rumbled beside Ebba. "What about me?"

Sally flushed.

"Well," the sprite queen said, "when I went with you to defeat Ladon, I realized even if I hadn't been born into rule, I would still choose this life—about the same time I flew us off the collapsing mountain."

What was Jagger's deal? How did he inspire such change within people without effort—or even caring? Ebba was going to understand him if it was the last thing she did.

Caspian mused, "Speaking of being born into things. You heard Medusa, right? She said there were three mortals to regulate the immortal leaders. We have to be the three watchers."

"Aye," Ebba and Jagger said together. She glared at him. "Get yer own aye."

The pirate ignored her. "If I'm an immune, what does that make the pair o' ye?"

They all turned to the sprite queen for the answer, who shrugged.

"I don't know. That happened before my time. I'm only one hundred and fifty years old."

"One hundred and fifty?" Ebba said. "Shite, ye old bugger. Ye know Jagger only be fifteen, right?"

He corrected her. "Nearly twenty."

"Fifteen going on twelve," she haggled.

"You've never heard of the three watchers who locked away the six pillars?" Caspian asked, shifting closer to Ebba.

The sprite queen nodded. "All of magical kind have. I suspected there was more to your crew after hearing the Earth Mother on Pleo. And when the three of you touched, I knew there was far more to the three of *you* than I'd guessed. Everyone knows of the three heroes. You're meant to keep this realm safe from darkness and maintain balance between mortal and immortal kinds. Beyond that, I don't know anything of use, I'm afraid."

"Were we all born into our roles, do ye think?" Ebba asked. If it was by birth, then Aroha, her birth mother, might know more.

The queen shook her head helplessly. "I'll have my scholars check our records when I get back to my throne. I'm sure there will be more there that I'm unaware of. As I said, the last three watchers that immortal kind had contact with existed long before my birth."

"You heard Medusa," Caspian said. "Only we can assemble the weapon and take it apart. That's something to go on."

"We have almost nothing to go on," Jagger said calmly.

Ebba shot him an exasperated look. "We know more than we knew a week ago—as much as I ain't sure I want to be one o' the three watchers at all."

The pirate hummed. "Aye, I be guessin' that's true. And ye ain't got a choice."

"I know that," she withered. Jagger was so infuriating sometimes.

Her fathers traipsed wearily toward them and fell to the deck with hearty groans.

"The boom be up," Stubby said, sighing. "*Felicity* feels nearly right again."

"I'm right glad to be here on *Felicity* instead o' in that tunnel," Grubby said, smiling his toothy grin.

"Ye can say that again," Peg-leg said, rubbing his knee.

They listened dutifully as Grubby repeated the comment.

Jagger shifted his arm on her thigh, and Ebba saw Plank staring at the touch. Her father narrowed his gaze and nudged Stubby on his right and then Grubby on his left.

. . . Ebba wondered if Jagger was immune to being thrown overboard.

"Where to next then?" Jagger asked, watching her fathers and not removing his arm.

That was the question, wasn't it? They had to keep going to save the realm. North, if they continued following the beam of light. Continuing on this path put that all at risk. Yet if she did nothing, their demise was *assured.* More and more, Ebba saw that without her people, the realm was nothing to her.

Stubby held up a hand. "Nay. Stop. I need one day o' normal afore I talk about any more motherfishin' magic. *One day*," he begged. "My body ain't young-like."

"Aye," Locks said. "I'm agreein'. We'll sing shanties, drink grog, and tell stories tonight, and I'll hear no plans to the otherwise."

Grubby stood. "I'll grab my flute."

"Be a good fellow and grab my fiddle, too?" Barrels called after him.

"Sure, Barrels."

Barrels looked back at them. "If I go down the bilge ladder, I'll never make it back up."

"I feel ye, m'hearty. I feel ye," Locks said, adjusting his eye patch.

Ebba watched her groaning fathers, sharing an amused glance with Caspian. She leaned into the prince as the temperature dropped with the sun's descent.

Jagger muttered, "I'm headin' up to the crow's nest."

"With my permi'sion, ye may," she replied. She glanced to where he'd been sitting. "Wait."

He turned back, hooking his thumbs in his belt. The dying rays of the sun illuminated him from behind. She'd always wondered at how the twilight turned his hair silver to match his ever-gleaming eyes.

"What did ye want, Viva?"

She was gaping at him like a flamin' fish. "Uh, the sword. Ye need to take the *veritas* with ye, don't ye?"

Surprise flickered across his high-boned features. He walked back and bent to pick up the sword. "I guess so."

He was too close for comfort, but this was important. Ebba fixed her gaze on his and said firmly, "Well, I *do* know ye won't always be needin' it, even if ye do right now."

Jagger blinked and wrenched back. He opened his mouth but lifted his eyes to peer past her at Caspian. His mouth snapped shut, and he spun away without a word, disappearing to the rigging with the *veritas*.

. . . Not entirely how she expected him to react. Then again, that pirate was as unpredictable as the thunderbird's wings, so maybe that was him responding well.

Her fathers spoke among themselves, mainly complaints by the sounds of things. She kept quiet, chuckling as Stubby became steadily more horizontal on the deck. He'd never get up again without help.

Caspian whispered low in her ear. "Are you all right, Mistress Pirate? Truly? You have no idea how much I wanted to help you down in that lair."

"Aye." She laughed to hide her lingering embarrassment. "I was flopped all over ye. Sorry about that."

His voice deepened. "I didn't mind."

No, he probably hadn't. She inhaled deeply. "Ye know, Caspian. This mornin' I was thinkin' about what ye said. About how if I wanted to explore things with ye to let ye know."

"I remember," he said, mouth twitching.

Ebba scowled to cover her answering smile. "I'm mostly a pirate, but I'm also a few other things, too, and I guess what I'm tryin' to say is, before ye said what ye did on Exosia, I'd never thought about ye as more than a friend."

Caspian winced.

"*Anyone* as more than a friend." She quickly amended. "But . . . I ain't averse to explorin' the concept. With ye."

She'd seen love for herself with Locks and Verity; she'd now felt the pulsing connection between the two original daedalions. Even Medusa, a *goddess*, had been obsessed with finding another to share her life with. Ebba remembered the ache in her chest just before the original lovers passed.

Love was . . . powerful.

Perhaps the pursuit of love was another adventure. A pirate should *want* to embark on adventures. Ebba shouldn't limit herself by being closed-minded about finding love, in the same way she'd limited herself to being one thing for so long. Verity had said she'd constantly change, after all, and that appealed to Ebba—that she'd never become stagnant.

The sea was ever-flowing. Ebba would be like that.

"You return my feelings?" Caspian asked her. He darted his amber eyes to her fathers, but they weren't paying attention, sprawled and whining about old people things.

Ebba chose her words carefully—which was starting to become a really bad habit. "I'm open to the idea of thinkin' o' ye in that way. I ain't sayin' I return yer feelings now or that I ever will. I'm saying there be sumpin' excitin' between us, and I want to explore it. I don't want to say words that'll give ye false promise or lead ye on. And ye can be certain that if I do end up returnin' yer regard, it won't be because ye want it. It'll be because it just . . . *happened*." Ebba trailed off with an awkward shrug. Everyone should love freely. Just like the daedalion lovers. They'd inspired her.

Caspian picked up her hand, and conversation drew to an abrupt halt as the gesture stole her fathers' rapt attention.

The prince kissed the back of her hand as he'd done in the past, yet now—knowing what she knew of his deeper regard, and with her last declaration ringing in her ears—the kiss felt as forbidden as his lips against hers.

Plank got up and lowered himself between them, forcing Ebba and Caspian to shift apart.

But the prince leaned forward, a secret smile on his lips, and said, "Mistress Pirate, I understand you completely."

ACKNOWLEDGMENTS

Getting Ebba to willingly put on a dress wasn't easy. Between you and me, I was surprised it only took her three books.

But I digress.

To my friends and family. I love ye, m'hearties! Thank you for your support over the years.

To my husband, Scott, who helps me in all kinds of ways; from input on covers and the business side of authoring to being an unwavering and loving presence in my life.

My beta readers for this series are so in tune with the small details. A massive thank you to these ladies for their early input during the manuscript process.

Next, to my swashbuckling manuscript team:

Editor One
Melissa Scott

Editor Two
Robin Schroffel

Proofreaders
Patti Geesey and Dawn Yacovetta

Map Illustrator
Laura Diehl

Cover Designer & Illustrator
Amalia Chitulescu

I must give thanks to my pirate crew—my readers. If you don't finish each of these books thinking and speaking in pirate, then I'm not doing my job right ;) Thank ye kindly for bein' here, Mateys!

Lastly, I'd like to take a moment to speak about A.J. - to whom this book is dedicated. Suicide is one of the greatest tragedies I can think of for any family to go through. Simply because there is choice involved. So, please, if you ever feel the urge to harm yourself, *choose* to seek help. Because when you're at rock bottom, the only direction is up. It's just hard to recall an up exists.

But it is there, my friend. I promise you that.

Global suicide hotline list: *http://www.suicidestop.com/call_a_hotline.html*

Happy Reading,

Kelly

ABOUT KELLY ST. CLARE

When Kelly is not reading or writing, she is lost in her latest reverie. Books have always been magical and mysterious to her. One day she decided to unravel this mystery and began writing.

The Tainted Accords was her debut series. Her other works include *The After Trilogy*, *The Darkest Drae*, and *Pirates of Felicity*.

A New Zealander in origin and in heart, Kelly currently resides in Australia with her ginger-haired husband, a great group of friends, and some huntsman spiders who love to come inside when it rains. Their love is not returned.

ALSO BY KELLY ST CLARE

The Tainted Accords:

Fantasy of Frost
Fantasy of Flight
Fantasy of Fire
Fantasy of Freedom

The Tainted Accords Novellas:

Sin
Olandon
Rhone
Shard

The After Trilogy:

The Retreat
The Return
The Reprisal

The Darkest Drae (Trilogy) Co-written with Raye Wagner

Blood Oath
Shadow Wings
Black Crown

Pirates of Felicity:
Immortal Plunder
Stolen Princess
Pillars of Six
Dynami's Wrath
Veritas

BONUS CHAPTER

VERITAS

"Just keep her away from grog," Ebba-Viva Fairisles hollered, hanging over the port bulwark. "And if she ain't drinkin', keep her away from wood. She chews it sumpin' fierce."

The queen of the wind sprites had switched one bad habit for another when the *purgium* cured her of alcoholism.

Sally, or queen Saliha as she was actually called, waved from the middle of her minions. Or flipped Ebba off. That was very possible.

Stubby rested a hand of her arm. "They'll be takin' care o' her, lass. And ye know she can hold her own."

After her mother died, Sal decided to take a holiday. That holiday turned into an alcohol-filled bender. But she was finally listening to the call of duty to her people. The sprites would go back to their kingdom by Charibdys, the great whirlpool.

"Aye, don't worry over her, little nymph," Plank said. "She has fierce sharp teeth." He rubbed his forearm where the queen bit him just that morning.

Ebba sniffed and dashed a stained sleeve over her eyes.

She cast another look at her tiny flying friend, now a speck in the distance, and then glanced behind at her six fathers, Jagger, and Prince Caspian.

"Why are ye all loungin' about," she snapped. "We've got sails to furl and. . .and. . .lots o' other stuff. Get to it."

Edging closer, Peg-leg patted her shoulder. "Aye, lass. We'll get to work." He hobbled away with the signature *tap-tap-tap* of his wooden peg.

Her lower lip trembled.

Barrels adjusted his cravat and reached forward to squeeze her hand. "I'll see to the sheets with Plank."

"Good," she replied hoarsely. "They ain't tight enough."

Considering the sails weren't raised, that was a given. Stubby and Plank glanced at the bare mast but, very wisely, didn't voice their thoughts.

Locks disappeared after her other fathers, shooting a small smile her way.

Grubby stepped forward. He twisted his Monmouth cap in white-knuckled hands. The cap had frayed along the edges from the regular abuse, and probably wouldn't last until they were back in the Caspian Sea.

If they got back. That was a real concern—especially as the only immortal being in their company just flew away.

Grubby inched closer and Ebba blinked furiously to keep her tears at bay. The youngest of her fathers, just forty-six, quit his cap twisting and wrapped both arms around her. He rested his head atop hers.

"It's okay to be sad about yer friend leavin'," he said. "I was sad to leave my selkie kin behind."

Ebba swallowed several times, panic rising in her throat as she began to lose the battle not to cry. She whispered, "But ye can talk to them when ye're in the water."

"Not now we be in the Dynami Sea," he said, rubbing her back. "Too far away. Or maybe it be because the water here is full o' magic creatures."

Or maybe the taint had spread through the sea in the Exosian Realm and Grubby's kin no longer possessed their will. Though Grubby's Octopi still traveled between Zol and *Felicity* to bring messages, so Ebba's home seas couldn't be completely taken over.

She buried her face in Grubby's chest, using it to wipe away the few tears that had escaped her iron grip.

He pulled back. "Ye'll see her again."

Grubby made for the bow, and Ebba turned to face the sea, her face wet. Jagger and Caspian still lingered, and out of the whole crew, they were the people she *least* wanted to see her cry.

"Someone will need to. . . ." she trailed off.

Sod it, Ebba couldn't think of a single thing to order them about with.

A large warm hand rested between her shoulder blades. She took a shaking breath, knowing if she lifted a hand to dry her tears, the game would be up.

. . . Though maybe she'd already failed at that.

Caspian stood close, just behind her. "Mistress Pirate, it's okay to cry."

Ebba sighed. "Caspian, ye ain't supposed to say someone be cryin' if they're tryin' to hide it."

He paused and she could practically hear the rum in his skull sloshing about as he pondered that comment.

"That's a pirate truth, I gather?" the prince said.

Well, he was less a prince and more of a king shoved out of his kingdom by the most powerful evil force of all time. The pillars of six ruled and resided on *his* throne, enslaving *his* people, but Ebba wasn't about to point that out. Everyone knew not to point out such things. Apart from him, obviously.

"Aye, pirate truths are the only truths worth knowin'," she answered flippantly.

His teeth clicked as he snapped his mouth shut.

Granted, pirates pretended not to see the truth an awful lot. But that was the essence of a pirate truth—only seeing the truths needed for survival. Of course, Ebba now believed *some* truth might be a necessary evil. The question was: How much truth was enough? And how much was too much?

Those answers were as yet unclear, and she wanted to make an informed choice about this whole truth business.

Caspian's hand still rested on her back. Warm. "What do you need me to do?" he asked.

Ebba quickly dried her face. "Nothin'. Just go and see if the ship be ready."

He dropped his hand but hovered for several more seconds. Enough to make her feel bad because she badgered the prince not to shut her out. After losing his left arm, he sank into himself for a good, long time.

"You're sure?" he murmured in a low voice that made her shiver.

Ebba would be lying—to herself, which she was trying not to do anymore—if she didn't confess their recent conversation about deeper regard had made the prince even more caring and bright-eyed than usual. Since telling him she wanted to explore the waters between them, Caspian stood closer and touched her in small ways—like the hand on her upper back thing.

Ebba didn't mind it.

She often found those small touches exciting. But not right this moment.

Not with Jagger standing there.

His silver eyes scorched into the back of her skull as he most likely judged her. If he wasn't there, Ebba might have leaned back against the prince and talked of how sad she was that the only other female on *Felicity* had left. She might have spoken about how people leaving her never felt right. Her fathers leaving tore her apart inside, but even when friends left, their absence played constantly in the back of her skull. She *might* have said all that if the flaxen-haired pirate wasn't lingering—likely for nefarious reasons—to eavesdrop on their conversation.

After the Medusa run in, Ebba decided to trust Jagger, but he'd always put her on edge and that hadn't changed; that puzzle remained unsolved.

"I be sure," she replied.

Caspian moved away, leaving her back cold.

Ebba shivered again. The Dynami Sea was a far cry from the cerulean tropical sea they'd left—black water, frigid air, dark skies, and a constant rolling swell that would only be experienced during the start of a storm back home. This sea was every bit as dreary as Plank had recited in his tales of old magic. She couldn't wait to be back in the Caspian Sea, safely anchored at their sacred haven at Zol. But for that to happen, Zol had to *be* a safe haven. So first they needed to form the root of magic by finding the remaining two parts. And somehow defeat the six pillars to save everyone in the realm.

No problem.

She shook her head. Luck had to be a big part of winning because Davy Jones knew there was no planning of any sort happening on their end. All their crew knew was that Ebba, Caspian, and Jagger were the three watchers—mortals who brought balance to the presence of immortalkind in the realm by regulating the root of magic. And that Jagger was an immune—resistant to magical influence. As for Ebba's and Caspian's role? Nothing. No notion.

"I'm goin' to climb to the crow's nest," Jagger said.

Ebba wrenched her thoughts back to the present. She whirled from the bulwark as Jagger strode past her.

"What did ye say?" she called.

The oversized pirate didn't stop but glanced over his shoulder. "I'm goin' to climb the shrouds."

Ebba dashed a sleeve over her face and scowled at him. "Nay. That be my job."

She ran across the deck after him and grabbed his arm. He slowly turned, and Ebba tipped her head back, and back some more. *Definitely* oversized for a pirate.

"Ye seem content to be gazin' out at water and orderin' others about, so I'll be takin' it upon myself to do the job," he said.

He didn't even bother to sneer anymore. Not like before when he was part of *Malice*'s crew. Now, he looked at her without expression, as though he couldn't be bothered with the effort to arrange his facial features into disdain. Only very occasionally could she glean his true thoughts. Was the impassive mask a step up or a step down?

He pulled free of her grip and continued striding toward the rigging.

"Nay," Ebba said, walking quickly to catch up.

His hip bumped hers. *On purpose.* She bumped him right back.

They lunged for the rigging at the same time.

"Aye," he told her.

"*Nay*," she hissed, flinging an arm out to whack his thieving hands away from the ropes.

Her fingers touched his bare skin and she hurriedly wiped them off against her slops. His scraggly flaxen hair swung forward as he watched her, jaw clenched.

Jagger had a natural resistance to magic however he'd sailed aboard *Malice* for two years. In time, he'd throw off any remaining taint, but having been victim to the taint herself, Ebba wasn't about to risk catching it again. His eyes weren't flooded black. That meant he wasn't contagious. But none of the crew were taking any chances. She'd keep wiping her hands just in case.

His eyes bore into hers. "Ye only want to go to the crow's nest because I said I'm goin'. Or is that it, Viva? If ye want to spend time with me in close quarters, ye just have to say the word."

What word? Her mind stuttered. How did they get onto this subject? She narrowed her eyes, realizing Jagger was attempting to unsettle her.

Heat crept up her neck, and Ebba leaned in, opening her mouth.

Peg-leg's wooden peg tapped in rapid staccato, interrupting her thoughts. Ebba blinked. Sink her, when had she and Jagger drawn so close?

She leaned back slightly, but Jagger crowded her, so they

remained nose-to-nose. A twinge of alarm coursed through her as his mouth drew within a finger-width of hers—not quite touching.

"Ye're still a spoilt princess," Jagger declared.

Ebba *was* a princess. Not that being tribal royalty meant a whole bunch to her. She objected to the first part. "I ain't so spoilt." *Anymore.*

It was mostly true.

"Aye, yer fathers cater to yer moods."

Her moods were Peg-leg's fault. He taught her that. And anyway, there were some perks to having six fathers that she wasn't willing to part with.

Jagger was a bloody pain in her hull.

Heat crept from her neck into her jaw. The moods she could blame on Peg-leg. Her temper was all Locks.

"Has anyone ever told ye that ye're an annoyin' shite?" she shot at him, fists clenching.

"One coin for the swear jar, my dear," Barrels sang, ambling over with the rest of her fathers.

Ebba waved a hand, not breaking the stare-off with Jagger. She hated paying the coin jar. Which was Barrels' fault. He was tight with his coin and had instilled such principles in her. "I only said it because it be true. And. . .I was upset about Sal leavin'."

Locks clucked sympathetically. "Aye, true enough. We'll let her off this once, lads."

"Only cause yer heart be hurtin'," Plank agreed.

Jagger whispered low, "See? Spoilt."

The heat flooded her face. Ebba shoved him away and whirled for the rigging.

He was back beside her in a flash.

"Get off my riggin'," she hissed at it.

"That be enough o' that, children," Stubby said, joining them from the helm.

Jagger stilled and drew himself tall as he turned.

Stubby lifted his gray brows. "That's right. Ye're actin' like a child, too, Jagger."

"Ha!" Ebba shot him a triumphant look through her thick, black lashes. Then frowned. "Hey."

She wasn't acting like child. *Much.*

Surprisingly, Jagger didn't seem angered by her father's comment. A small smile curved his lips and Ebba studied him with no small amount of suspicion.

What was he playing at?

"Now, ye both need to. . ." Stubby's voice took on a droning quality.

Babies with shark's teeth, he was settling into a lecture.

Ebba stopped listening and let her eyes drift out over the ship's side again. She sighed. The sprites were completely gone from sight, as though they'd never been here. Deep down, a part of her had held hope Sally would change her mind and come back.

Jagger dug his elbow into her gut.

"Ouch," she exclaimed, more from shock than actual pain. "Why'd'ye do that, ye flaxen bastard?"

"Ebba-Viva Fairisles," Stubby said in a quelling tone. "Mind yer tongue. Are ye even listenin' to a word I be sayin'?"

Her spine snapped straight, and her face dropped. "He dug his elbow in my gut."

"How old are ye, Ebba-Viva?" her father demanded.

"Eighteen and a bit," she muttered.

Stubby shifted his firm gaze to Jagger.

"Twenty," the pirate supplied without prompt. His eyes slid to her and he added, "And a bit."

"Ye had a birthday?" she turned to him, cutting off her father. "When?"

Jagger folded his arms, glancing away "A week ago. Not long after yers."

They'd missed it. Not that she should feel bad when he'd kept it a secret like he did everything. "Well, Stubby be right. Ye should act yer age. Ye're in yer twenties and should know better than me."

"Ye *both* need to act yer age," Stubby boomed.

Where was this coming from? She never had to act her age. Ebba cast a woeful look at her father and Stubby's expression faltered. She watched as Plank grabbed the back of Grubby's belt to stop him approaching.

"Ebba's sad," Grubby whined.

Plank grunted, visibly digging his heels in. "She ain't sad, matey. We be tellin' her off. This be disc'pline."

Stubby's tone had softened when he spoke again. "What I was *sayin'* is that we need the three o' ye to focus and find out where we be headed next."

She was still attuned to Jagger's buzzing presence next to her and snuck a look up at the crow's nest. There was no way Jagger was reaching the shrouds before her. He'd become too comfortable in her territory and it had to stop.

Ebba prepared to jump onto the bulwak. "I'll just—,"

"Nay, ye won't. Neither o' ye will," Stubby snarled.

She scanned the faces of her fathers, searching for the weak link. Grubby was restrained. Barrels, avoiding her eyes. Yet one of them held a particular softness for the heights of the nest.

Her eyes sought out Peg-leg.

He wasn't avoiding her, and he stared for a long beat before saying, "I know why ye want to go up there, lass."

Ebba's eyes began to burn again. His comment stole her voice for a scant second; long enough she couldn't come up with a quip in return. His assumption was correct. There were few places aboard a ship to have a good cry. Below deck echoed. There was the tip of the bowsprit, but Ebba wasn't sure she wanted to perch over the black Dynami Sea as she tended to do in the safer waters of the Caspian. According to Grubby, there were a whole heap of things under the surface that gave him the willies. Then there was the crow's nest.

Sally had left and Ebba wanted to leak a tear or two in private.

"I'll go up again," Peg-leg announced.

He would?

Her father used to be a rigger until the depraved captain of *Eternal* ordered his leg amputated in petty revenge. Minus a leg, carrying a past filled with horrific abuse, and with the taint still in him driving his thoughts to black places, her father only recently regained the confidence to climb the shrouds.

He'd gone up once, and Ebba knew the more he climbed to the nest, the more he'd heal.

Mouth drying, she rushed to say, "That be a great idea, Peg-leg."

"What's going on?" Caspian said, exiting the bilge door.

"I'm goin' to climb the shrouds," Peg-leg told him. "Locks, did ye get a chance to make me that foot?"

Locks nodded. "Aye, it be below deck. I'll grab it."

The ship carpenter disappeared to the hold, and everyone's gaze dropped to Peg-leg's fake leg.

"Thought a wider surface would be makin' it easier to climb," he said defensively.

Caspian's breath hitched in his throat. "A missing limb doesn't change a thing, Sir Pirate?"

Peg-leg winked at him. "Nay, lad. A missin' limb doesn't stop ye from a thing."

Locks returned and knelt to fit the end of Peg-leg's peg into a deep groove on an otherwise flat strip of wood about the length of a foot.

Stubby clapped the cook on the back. "Up ye get then, matey. We'll ready the ship and figure out where to go."

Testing his new foot a few times, Peg-leg then ambled to the rigging. Ebba scowled at Jagger, waiting until he released the ropes before doing so herself.

The oversized pirate walked to the mast, and she trailed after him toward Caspian.

She stood on the prince's right, patting her belt. "Hold on, I put the *scio* down somewhere."

"You tied it to Pillage again, my dear," Barrels reminded her.

Oh, aye. She'd wanted to re-test the ship cat as a hiding place. She'd used the *scio* so he didn't gouge holes in the deck again.

Blast. Pillage could be anywhere. Whenever she didn't want to find him, he was around. As soon as she did, he tucked himself into some obscure corner of the hold. The ship cat did it on purpose, she was certain.

"Where be the *dynami*? I'll use that instead," she said. The could use any three parts of the root to find the way to the next piece.

Barrels blew out a breath. "I'll go find the *scio*." No one answered, and he exhaled loudly again, leaving through the bilge door.

"Anyone have the *dynami*?" she called across deck.

"Here, have the *purgium*. I'll go search for Pillage as well," Caspian replied.

From the starboard bulwark, Plank called, "Aye." He reached under the sash holding his pistols to his chest. He drew out the *dynami*. "Here ye go."

Caspian handed her the *purgium* as Plank tossed her the *dynami*. Flustered, Ebba dropped the healing tube to catch the *dynami*, but managed to miss that too.

Both parts rolled across the deck and everyone immediately started after them–though the tubes were too big to be lost out the scuppers.

The bilge door crashed open.

Ebba jumped and whirled about, clutching her chest.

"She stole my bloody cat," Barrels shouted.

Plank asked, "What?"

"That *sprite* stole Pillage. I found the *scio* on my desk with a note saying the queen has 'borrowed Pillage to act as her noble stead'."

No one on the ship really liked Pillage aside from Barrels, but Ebba pushed down her bubbling laughter. "That be terrible."

Plank snorted. "Ye need to put a mite more effort into that, little nymph."

"That be terrible!" she cried.

Plank nodded. "Better."

Caspian threw her an amused look, the corners of his lips quirking, and she flashed a grin back.

"Laugh if you will, but I consider this a gross misdemeanor after the hospitality we afforded her," Barrels snapped, some of his peppered hair escaping its throng.

Fancy words. Ebba took them to mean her father was greatly peeved.

"She was *your* pet, Ebba-Viva Fairisles," he continued. "I expect you to put things to rights."

They were in the Dynami, so she felt pretty safe agreeing to do so. "Sure thing. Wait, has Sal been able to write this whole time?"

"I wrote the note for her," Jagger told them, drawing everything to a screeching halt. "She dictated usin' the *scio*."

"You *knew*?" Barrels screeched, rounding on the pirate.

Jagger shrugged a shoulder. "Aye."

Ebba snickered, taking a large step away from him.

"Oopsie," Grubby exclaimed from directly behind her. "Look what ye dropped."

She peered over her shoulder to where he stood across deck. Ebba whipped fully around as Grubby bent down, his fingers stretching to the *purgium* and *dynami*.

"No matter," he said happily.

"Nay, Grubby," Ebba choked out. "Don't touch them."

Too late.

White light exploded.

www.ingramcontent.com/pod-product-compliance
Lightning Source LLC
Chambersburg PA
CBHW020934310726
48980CB00007B/765/J

9780648334484